LONG LIVE ROCK
A Grown-Up Romance

LONG LIVE ROCK

A Grown-Up Romance

by Leslie Baldacci

Cover art by Mason Rosati
Author photo by Ashlee Rezin Garcia © Chicago Sun-Times (2018)
Interior design, formatting, cover design by Sunacumen Press

Library of Congress Control Number: 1-8879830341
ISBN 978-1-7355705-0-1
Printed in the United States of America

For Jeanne Ellen Wright

Chapter 1

Lisette watched the intermediates in the mirror as she led the students in *reverence.*

"Stretch into the music," she intoned in her clear, low voice, demonstrating the timing that perfectly synched each movement with the adagio, smoothly achieving the ultimate pose at the last beat of the measure.

"Lovely, Shannon," she murmured to a girl in the front row, turning to face the group and circulate, lifting an elbow here, correcting a turnout, tilting a chin.

Students this age were like colts, she thought, with their long limbs and flat chests, their strength and giddy energy. At school, they wore baggy t-shirts to conceal their gangly, changing bodies. In the ballet studio, the uniformity of black leotards, pink tights, pink shoes, hair pinned into tight buns, provided a sense of camouflage, even though every bone, muscle, and lingering bit of baby fat is as visible as in a science lab model of the human body. Lisette, with her dark hair and dramatic white streak, wore the same traditional leotard and tights as her students, with a short black wraparound skirt that just covered her compact derriere. She had no clue that her coltish students called her "Skunky" behind her back. It would have made her laugh out loud, though, payback for the nuns she had tagged "Crypt Keeper" and "Skeletor."

How many thousands of times had she performed this traditional end-of-class ritual of curtsies and *ports de bras,* from childhood to middle age? She regarded the girls as they strained to perfect their technique and gracefully acknowledge the applause of future audiences.

"Just hope your boobs don't get too big," she thought, remembering the development that ultimately tanked her short-lived professional career. At 22, her bra size went from B to D and that was that. She'd never rise above the corps. It was another era, before Misty Copeland and women's sports changed the notion of what strong, athletic female bodies look like. And then there was Carl…

"Very nice," she complimented the class as the music ended, clapping her hands softly. "Thank you, Madame," the girls responded with quiet applause before scattering to collect their things and heading for the door.

"Goodnight, Jules, thank you" she said, passing by the piano. The great part about teaching dance at a conservatory was the never-ending supply of student pianists eager to earn a few dollars as accompanist for beautiful, practically naked girls. Men far outnumbered women at auditions for this gig and tended to stay more than one year.

Lisette straightened the rosin box in the corner with her toe and plucked her bag from the hook near the door. She reached deep inside the huge black shoulder bag, a cornucopia of helpful items for various emergencies: Band-Aids, granola bars, deodorant, an extra pair of ballet slippers, a pale pink sweater, now vintage, that she had thrown over her shoulders since she was a student. She foraged for her cellphone.

Five messages from Maria during the intermediate class! Her maternal alarm went straight to red. Her 17-year-old daughter and several friends had tickets to a concert that night by a rock band that had risen to fame during Lisette's own youth. With shaking hands she jabbed at the screen to access the messages, which were about 10 minutes apart. The first was a man's voice, and the message crackled and broke up as if it had been placed from the International Space Station.

"Miss Du ---, this is ---geant Hoskins, Lake Cou--- Sheriff's De--------. We have your daughter ---ia in the first-aid tent here at the Pa------. --- --- - minor mishap. Please call back."

Minor mishap? Her mother's intuition raced through the possibilities, starting with the worst, shooting, and quickly moving through the roll call of dread: car accident, sexual assault, drugs, defenestration, concussion . . . Maria was a good kid, but anything can happen at a rock concert – crowd stampede, fall from the balcony onto the main floor seats (wait, the Pavilion was outdoors, there was no balcony, praise God) fall from high scaffolding then, after an impetuous climb for a better view (wait, Maria would never do that), hit by a car driven by a drunken driver, kidnapped into white slavery by bikers, beaten up by drunk biker girlfriends who pick fights with pretty young girls their man looks at, what's that date rape drug, roofies? Her mind raced on. The band was notorious for its drug use back in the day. They were big with the motorcycle and metalhead crowds.

The second call was Maria's voice. "Mom, I ---- ------ ankle and I'm -- --- -----aid tent. -- -- --- -- really hurts. Call -- ----ack!"

Lisette was out the door and jogging to her black Volkswagen Jetta SportWagen as she listened to the other three messages, all hang-ups. Her callback went straight to Maria's voicemail.

"I'm on my way, sweetie," she said, trying for a calm, reassuring voice that still came out unnaturally high and tight. She turned the ignition and roared out of the conservatory parking lot, blind to the waves of her students waiting at curbside for their own parents, her face a pale moon behind the wheel, heart pounding.

The drive to the outdoor Pavilion was nerve-wracking at the tail end of Chicago rush hour. Nearly an hour elapsed before she finally saw the entrance. Cars inched forward as the bass and drums of the warm-up band drifted across the parking lots.

"Hey! Emergency! Can you help me?" she shouted to a kid checking parking passes. "My daughter is in the first-aid tent, I got a call from a policeman..."

She must have appeared unhinged. The parking attendant flagged her right through, directing her to the "limo lot." He wondered if that streak in the crazy lady's hair had turned white on the way. She's got a surprise coming when she looks in the mirror, he speculated.

She repeated her story at the limo lot and once more at the gate, where a beefy guy with a security tag took her arm and escorted her to the first-aid tent.

"Wait," she said, before going in, holding up a finger. She closed her eyes and drew a couple of deep breaths, blowing the air out through her mouth. She shook out her arms, collected herself. straightened. "Ok."

"Mom!" Maria's voice came from a corner of the tent. She was on a cot with her foot elevated on a pillow, encased in numerous ice packs.

Lisette crossed the space in four leaps, assessing the situation while still in motion.

"Oh honey what happened does it hurt?" she asked in a rush, encircling Maria's head with her arms and nearly buckling with relief. All limbs were accounted for, Maria's eyes and speech were clear – no roofies. Lisette perched on the side of the cot searching first her daughter's face, then taking in her swollen ankle.

"We parked in the far lot on the grass so we could get out easier after the show. We were walking across the field to the Pavilion and I stepped in a hole and twisted my ankle," Maria explained. "The paramedics said it's probably a sprain because I can wiggle it, but they said a sprain can hurt worse than a break."

"Where are the other girls?" Lisette asked.

"When I got your voicemail I sent them inside so they wouldn't miss the show," Maria explained. Ah, Maria. Never a diva. How Lisette got so lucky with her only child, she could only wonder. She had her mother's dark hair and gray eyes and her father's height. Lisette, at 5-foot-5, was at maximum height for a classical dancer – ballerinas can't be taller than their male partners when *en pointe*. Maria was 5-foot-9. Named after Maria Tallchief, Lisette's idol, she had been her mother's student for years, but as a high school senior was taking a break from dance to play volleyball.

A tent flap snapped open behind Lisette with a sudden gust and a loud male voice demanded: "Where is the goddamned seamstress? I've split my pants. Does anyone in here have a needle and thread?"

Maria's eyes bugged as she looked beyond her mother to the source of the outburst.

"Shane Stewart?" she croaked.

Lisette turned and looked up into the weathered face of a tallish man she recognized as instantly as she would have known a close family member. Shane Stewart indeed. Ubiquitous fixture of pop culture. Singer for the multi-platinum Disgracefuls, pitchman, perennial talk show guest. His wavy hair was longer than Lisette's, with cowry shells and feathers strategically woven in by a stylist. His hazel eyes were rimmed with black eyeliner. His classic features did not require further adornment. While he had to be over 60, his fine bone structure still showcased his striking beauty. He was wearing a long Indian print duster over a tight black t-shirt and the troublesome pants.

"Ouch, love," he said, looking from Lisette to Maria's ice-encased ankle. "You OK?"

"I think it's just a sprain," Maria said in a gulping kind of voice.

"I fell off a stage and broke mine a couple of years back," he replied.

His eyes actually twinkled, the practiced move of someone accustomed to charming on cue. "Had to wear a damned boot for half a tour. What's your name?"

"Maria."

"Does it hurt?"

"Not as bad as before."

He whipped around and repeated to no one in particular, "Does anyone have a needle and thread, then? I have a wardrobe emergency!"

"I do." Lisette was already rummaging in her giant black bag. She took out a granola bar, the extra pair of slippers, and a make-up bag, from which she retrieved a sewing kit. No *maitresse de ballet* left home without one. Someone's ribbons were always tearing off their pointe shoes, costumes at recitals inevitably needed quick repairs – more than once she had sewn a ballerina into her costume for a performance and cut her out afterward.

"Well look at you," said Shane, in fact looking at her with amusement and relief. He turned his back, kicked off his shoes, and wriggled out of his pants, using the long duster as curtain. He handed his pants to Lisette and, wrapping the duster around his lower half, sat down on a nearby cot.

"If you'd be so kind," he said. Again with the practiced eye twinkle. Two EMTs across the room were staring, star-struck. One pulled out a cell phone and started snapping pictures.

Lisette's needle was already threaded and knotted. She set to work, rapidly and neatly pulling each stitch into a solid seam that bit by bit closed the gaping tear. Watching her progress, Shane was surprised by a welling-up feeling of intimacy in the moment. He was used to having "people" who took care of just about all his needs, but this stranger's help struck chords of gratitude and relief, mixed with a feeling of homesickness, a longing he couldn't explain.

"Here you are!" A tall blond woman in a very tight, very short, strapless black leather dress with pointed metal spikes along the bodice swept into the tent, demanding in a shrill voice "What are you doing? You're on in five minutes!"

"I split my pants and couldn't find the damned seamstress," Shane explained to the woman, who might have been his daughter.

"I'm almost done," Lisette said. "Just going over it one more time to make sure it holds."

"Well do hurry!" said the woman.

"Calm down, darling," Shane told her.

As Lisette's fingers skillfully plunged the needle in and out, Shane studied her intently, taking in the white lightning in the dark night of her hair, the intensity of her furrowed brow as she bent over the chore, the tiny ballet skirt, her long legs folded beneath, and the now mud-stained pink ballet slippers on her feet.

"And people think I dress funny," he said, cracking a smile. "I really appreciate this. You are an angel of mercy."

The tent flapped again and a man in denim burst in.

"Jesus Christ," he bellowed in an English accent, "we're about to go on!"

"Wardrobe malfunction," Shane calmly explained. "Under control."

Lisette tied a final double knot, bit the thread with her teeth, and handed him the repaired garment. He turned his back once again and slipped into his pants, then his shoes.

"Capezios," Lisette observed. She knew well the black leather jazz shoes that fit like gloves, with rubber soles that both cushioned impact and offered spring.

"Only the finest," he replied, wiggling a foot at her. "Thanks again," he said, turning to leave. He paused at the exit, then turned to Maria. "It would be a shame for you to miss the show. How's the ankle?"

"Not so bad now," Maria replied.

"Someone get her a wheelchair. Derek, take them to stage right and set them up with the VIPs. Put her on the far end where no one will bump her."

"Oh, we couldn't," Lisette said. "She needs to go for X-rays."

"Mom!" Maria protested. She wiggled her ankle around. "See? It's probably not even broken. I'll keep the ice on it. Please? It's only an hour or so."

She locked her mother's eyes in a teenage laser beam and exaggeratedly mouthed the letters V-I-P.

"I'm not dressed," Lisette said, indicating her outfit with outswept arms.

"Who cares," Maria said. "Mom. Come on. Where's your sense of adventure?"

"You'll see plenty of people dressed stranger than that," Shane assured her, his eyes sweeping her head to toe. "Stay for a couple of songs. If Maria is uncomfortable, let Derek know and he'll make sure you get out safely."

"Pleeeeeease," Maria begged.

"All right, I guess we could stay for a song or two," Lisette decided. "Um, thank you."

"I didn't get your name," Shane said.

"Lisette. Lisette DuPre."

"Well, Lisette DuPre, are you ready to rock?"

"I guess so?" Lisette replied, still looking doubtfully at Maria, who responded with "Yesssssss!" and a high five.

"Derek, take care of these ladies. Ladies, I will see you onstage. Come along, darling." With that, Shane Stewart swept aside the tent flap and waited for the young woman in the dangerous dress to follow.

"Thanks *mom*," the blonde said pointedly to Lisette. As she exited the tent Shane looked over her head at Maria and Lisette and rolled his eyes.

"Let's not stand near her – we might get impaled," Lisette advised.

Derek barked orders, quickly securing a wheelchair and extra ice packs for Maria. With Lisette following, wondering what kind of mother could be so permissive and careless, Derek ably wheeled Maria through a nondescript metal door and into a long cinderblock corridor cluttered with large black flight cases emblazoned with silver gothic letters that spelled out "Disgracefuls."

"Don't worry, Mum, I'm quite good at this," Derek said over his shoulder. "I was on the Jethro Tull Tour when Ian Anderson blew out his ACL."

"Mom, this is *so cool*," Maria's voice floated back.

Lisette was surprised at the waves of nostalgia and excitement that welled up in her as they made their way through the backstage labyrinth. As a young woman, she had been quite the music fan. She had walked many similar hallways. Dancers, musicians, and artists tend to flock together, and at a conservatory, there is no escaping each other, only intermingling. Dancers and musicians especially are yin and yang to each other. Music is air to a dancer, a life-giving necessity. In turn, music's purpose is to stimulate activity, in the brain, in the body, ideally both. As George Clinton put it: Free your mind and your ass will follow. Emotion is the knot that ties music and dance together.

Back then, friends in bands were captivated by Lisette's uninhibited moves on the dance floor and counted on her to be their starter switch. Once she hit the floor, the crowd was close behind. She was music in motion, a Pied Piper who incited others to let the music literally move them.

Lisette's concerns about being a responsible mother were unexpectedly giving way to an effervescent bubbling up of joy and excitement as the chants of the crowd – "Disgracefuls! Disgracefuls" – grew closer and louder.

She had been a fan, bought their records and seen them live a number of times. She had been one of the chanting voices in the audience clamoring for the band to start.

"Here we go," shouted Derek, wheeling Maria around a black curtain with Lisette close behind. Once around the curtain, she saw they were on the actual stage, just feet from the drum riser! About a dozen chosen ones, mostly women who looked like lingerie models, were clustered together in the shadows of the stage. Lisette was mortified anew by what she was wearing. Derek parked Maria's wheelchair at the farthest edge of the VIPs.

"I'll be back to check on you after two songs," he promised, the "ngs" swallowed by the roar of the crowd as five dark silhouettes took the stage from the other side. She gave him a "thumbs-up" in acknowledgment.

Screaming, whistling and foot stomping built to a frenzy as the bass line from a Disgracefuls' hit introduced their first song, joined by drums, finally exploding into bright colors as the stage lights flashed to life and Shane Stewart spit out the first words. The VIP section screamed as one, moved as one, a writhing, shimmying cheer squad on the sideline. Lisette watched Maria's face in the lights, a mask of wonder and delight. She couldn't help but match her wide smile. Yes. This was cool. Very cool.

She also couldn't help but start to sway to the music. Her hips had a mind of their own. Positioned behind the wheelchair, Lisette managed to conceal herself from the chest down. Her face and neck stood out against the black curtain, her black leotard and hair blended into the darkness. Shane Stewart's eyes sought out her ghostly floating presence. Their eyes met and he nodded an acknowledgment. The exhange did not go unnoticed by the woman in the dangerous dress, who appeared to be the cheer squad captain, and she intensified her own dance, squirming and performing tiny jumps, clapping her hands. She seemed determined to shed her leather dress like a snake sheds its skin.

The band burned through three of their signature numbers with barely a breath between songs.

"He is on fire tonight," observed Derek, who had quietly materialized at Lisette's side. "Everything all right?"

Lisette bent down to Maria's ear. "You OK? Need to go?"

Maria stopped singing along to "Thunder Thighs" to bark an emphatic "No way!"

"What a trouper," Derek said. "I'll check back in a bit."

Maria snapped pictures with her phone from her once-in-a-lifetime vantage point. She knew from organizing the ticket purchase for her friends that to be up front cost 10 times more than the seats they had procured. The VIP onstage experience had no price tag.

Shane jogged across the stage gripping his microphone by the stand to briefly mug into Maria's camera shot before ricocheting back in the other direction. Lisette was surprised by his athleticism and grace. How many thousands of times had he done this, she wondered, echoing her own thoughts earlier. Lisette closed her eyes and melted into the moment to imprint it on her memory. She had never expected to be backstage at a rock concert again in her lifetime. She thought these days were done and gone. She felt like her 17-year-old self, that pure, unfiltered joy. The lyrics were still in her head from the first time she heard them 40 years before.

The tune ended and Shane took a breather to greet the crowd – "Hello, Chicago!" – and banter a bit. Lisette checked again on Maria, noting she was looking a bit strained, probably coming down from the initial excitement and feeling her ankle throb along with every pounding beat.

"We're gonna slow it down for a minute," Shane was saying, "This next song is one we've been playing since we were teenagers, but we haven't played it live since we graduated high school. This is for Lisette, emergency seamstress – thank you. Boys?"

Maria turned around and looked at her mother with awe and disbelief. Then her face split into a comic "Mommy's got a boyfriend" look and she squeezed her hand. An uninvited thrill shot through Lisette's very core while daggers shot from the eyes of the woman in black leather and spikes.

The blues were where Shane Stewart could showcase his vocal range. Warmed by three ear-splitting songs that galloped from the gate, his voice now easily slid across octaves, from a growl to a lustful howl, dripping with sexual innuendo.

Lisette willed herself to slip deeply into the moment. She had taught herself to withdraw and focus, to savor moments that she could conjure later and replay. Her eyes closed and she was unaware she was singing along. Back in the days of vinyl, Lisette had worn through the grooves of Led Zeppelin's cover of "You Shook Me." She knew every version, Muddy Waters and Jeff Beck, the songwriter himself, each note of every instrument, every nuance of every honey-dripping word. Her memories of the song stretched across decades. Her favorite was sneaking into a smoke-filled blues bar with a fake ID to hear Muddy himself on Chicago's South Side. Until now.

Shane's quick side glance registered surprise to see Lisette singing along, eyes closed, her lips forming the words "baby, baby please come home." Ballet girl knows Willie Dixon, he observed, damn. He felt the unspoken recognition between people who shared an era, a generation, history, context. A song can do that, ignite spontaneous, intense connections. He was used to the reverse striptease of women dirty dancing in front of the stage as he performed, and the younger fans had apparently been twerking since they were toddlers. But he was seriously turned on seeing somebody older, comfortable in her own body, grooving to the music.

As the song ended, Lisette realized her thank you from the band was actually a gift. She applauded wildly and called out "Thank you!" Glancing down at Maria, Lisette could see strain through her daughter's determination. Hopefully Urgent Care would still be open for an X-ray.

Derek again materialized to check on Maria. The band was tearing through another hit, with Shane shedding his duster and stripping down to the black t-shirt, striding out to meet the lead guitar player at the end of a catwalk into the audience. His pants were still holding together, Lisette noted with relief.

"Thank you so much," Lisette told Derek. "It's time we got going."

Maria did not protest as Derek again took charge of the wheelchair and capably maneuvered her behind the curtain and through the tunnel. He waited with Maria while Lisette brought the car around, and helped her up and into the passenger seat.

"Lovely to meet you, ladies," he said. "Hope everything works out."

"Thank you, and please thank Shane for us," Lisette said. "It was an unexpected pleasure in spite of everything."

"Will do," Derek replied, shutting the car door waving them off.

"Wow. Just wow," Maria said, propping her foot on the dashboard.

"Amen," Lisette said. The surprising turn of this day would become lore between mother and daughter. They would tell this story forever.

The two chattered nonstop, replaying the evening as they drove quickly through the night. Traffic was light and the parking lot was empty at Urgent Care. They were quickly processed ("Thank god for Carl's premium health care," Lisette thought) and the X-rays were done in minutes. A doctor confirmed that it was a nasty sprain, but no broken bones. Maria would be able to practice with the volleyball team within two weeks. Until then she was in a walking boot and on crutches.

Shane noticed immediately as he returned to the main stage from the catwalk the empty spot where Lisette and Maria had been. He approached Derek at the side of the stage.

"X-rays," Derek said.

"Did you get her number?" Shane asked, adding "uh, in case we need to check on them… "

Derek shook his head, a knowing smile of amusement crinkling his eyes.

"She shouldn't be too hard to track down," he said.

Black leather girl watched the exchange with a sad, knowing realization that her days were numbered. This was how a lot of songs ended.

Chapter 2

Lisette was surprised to see lights on at the house.

"Carl?" she called, holding the door open wide for Maria to hop through on her crutches.

Carl came from the kitchen, a drink in hand. His expression switched from relaxed to alarmed as he took in the crutches and clunky walking boot.

"Hi, Dad," Maria greeted him. "Don't worry, it's just a sprain."

The three moved to the living room and settled Maria comfortably onto a couch as she chattered a mile a minute about the concert experience. Carl and Lisette crowded near as Maria chronicled the night with pictures from her phone. The close-ups of Shane on stage stirred in Lisette an even greater excitement now that Maria was safe and sound. It had been, and continued to be, surreal.

"I'll get some ice for your foot," Carl said, heading to the kitchen. Lisette heard him refill his empty glass with ice and then the sound of ice plopping from the dispenser into a plastic bag.

Maria and Lisette continued to thumb through the pictures from the night.

"Send me that one," she whispered to Maria, indicating a close-up of Shane mugging for the camera, "and that one," a shot of Shane in motion, both feet off the ground like a thoroughbred racehorse in full stride, hair flying.

"How 'bout I send them all," Maria offered with a devilish grin.

"Ok, fine," Lisette said as Carl re-entered the room and handed Maria the bag of ice.

Maria's phone rang and the high-pitched shrieks of teenage girls could be heard across the room even though the speaker was off.

"You guys," Maria implored into the phone. "Hold on."

She turned to her parents.

"They saw us onstage, Mom," Maria relayed. "Let me call you right back," she said into the phone, ringing off. "This might take a while," she told her parents. "My battery is low. I think I'll go to my room and plug in."

Maria backed up the stairs on her butt and hopped into her bedroom, Lisette and Carl following with crutches, ice bag, and parental concern. They settled her into bed, with extra pillows under her foot. The phone call quickly resumed in that high register of teenage girls drunk with excitement. "I know, can you even believe it?" Maria was asking as they shut her door behind them. "Dudes, he was sooooo nice!"

Carl sipped his drink and looked over the glass at Lisette in her ballet togs.

"You went to the concert dressed like that?" he asked.

"I know," Lisette said. "These shoes are ruined."

"You're practically naked," he said.

"You should have seen what the other groupies were wearing," Lisette giggled, trying to deflect his criticism with a joke. Twelve years older than Lisette, Carl could be a real prude sometimes.

"Why didn't you call me?" Carl asked.

"I thought you were in South America," Lisette said. "What are you doing home?"

"There was a coup or something. . ."

Carl was nothing if not vague about his work as a pharmaceutical rep. He traveled a lot, especially the last two years, when he'd been gone nearly eight months out of the year. Lisette had raised their daughter practically as a single mother. She sometimes felt resentful when she saw fathers dropping their children off at school or picking them up from the conservatory. But over the years, she had come to feel a sense of relief when Carl packed his bags and flew off to sell drugs all over the Americas. Ultimately, she valued the independence his travels afforded her. She and Maria got along just fine without him, a fact she would never share with Carl. Over the years, the house started to feel crowded when he was home, like having company. The manly evidence of his presence – toilet seats left up and dishes in the sink that never made the final leg of the journey into the dishwasher – were annoyances she bore in silence, not wanting to start arguments in the rare time they had together. But sometimes she gave him the finger behind his back! The dog treated Carl like a workman on the premises, keeping a wary eye on him but not greeting him as a familiar. Once he pooped in Carl's shoes when he returned after two weeks away.

"Can I make you a drink?" Carl offered.

"A glass of wine would be great," Lisette said. "There's a bottle of white in the fridge."

"Be right back," he said, looking meaningfully into her eyes.

Ah, the "look." There will be sex, she noted.

"Thanks," she said, drifting toward the shower.

She inspected the pink ballet slippers. Beyond repair, she thought, thanking them for their service and dropping them into the trashcan. She peeled off her leotard and tights and stepped into the hot water. As the steam rose around her she flashed back to the stage, the ridiculousness of the fog machine wrapping the band in someone's idea of theatrical mystery. She smiled at the wonderful dementedness of rock 'n' roll as she picked the pins out of her hair, letting the rushing water part the white streak and roll down her body. She thought about Shane Stewart's hands.

Hands are as important to a dancer as feet. Maria Tallchief, in her older years, refused to be photographed without gloves because her once-beautiful hands had become knobby with arthritis. Lisette noticed hands. She studied them on people, in sculpture and paintings. She understood the truth that "you can tell a lady's age by her hands," but actually preferred hands that testified to their usefulness, that told stories of skills mastered, of life lived in gardens and kitchens and toil. Shane Stewart had such hands.

"Christ, woman, stop thinking about Shane fucking Stewart," she caught herself. "Snap out of it!"

She emerged from the shower to find a glass of wine on the two-sink vanity. She wrapped herself in a towel, sat down on the toilet seat and took a deep drink. The wine was crisp and tart. She took her time brushing the knots out of her wet hair, blotting it with the towel.

She studied her body in the mirror. Her neck was still holding, no crepey turkey neck. Her shoulders were straight, collarbone prominent and graceful. Her full breasts had begun to yield to gravity, faint stretch marks on her abdomen the eternal reminder of motherhood. Overall, holding together well for a woman of 57, she concluded. "Freakish" is how her friend

Chris described Lisette's youthful-looking body. Ballet kept her toned and firm. She had studied with ballet teachers who had become plump, and not one had made her peace with it. Some were bitter, regarding it as their bodies' ultimate betrayal and hiding under long skirts. Lisette accepted that she was not as strong as she once was. That is to be expected. No athlete retains the raw, bold strength of youth forever. But she figured if she ever had to wear the long skirt, it was time to turn in your ballet slippers.

What would Shane Stewart think of this, she wondered, turning sideways and sucking in her stomach. And these feet, she thought, considering her bunions, the bane of dancers. She smacked herself in the head: Stop! He's probably never seen a naked woman over 30. He probably has every kind of sexually transmitted disease known to science. He … STOP!

Lisette had actually embarrassed herself. She was acting like a starstruck kid. The man had been kind to her daughter. That was all. They would tell the story from time to time and get a kick out of it. The end.

Lisette stepped into the bedroom to the sound of Carl's snoring. A half-full glass with a few shards of melting ice sat in a puddle of condensation on the night table on his side of the bed. She used her towel to blot the table and tossed the rest of the drink down the sink. He must have had more than the three she counted. He would be out of sorts tomorrow.

It wasn't too late on the West Coast. She wrapped herself in her bathrobe, took her wine, and quietly crept downstairs to call her oldest friend in LA.

"You're up late on a school night," Chris greeted her.

"You'll never believe where I was tonight," Lisette said.

"Do tell," Chris said. "Should I pour a glass of wine?"

"Yes. Please join me," Lisette replied.

When Chris moved to Los Angeles 10 years earlier, the time difference of a mere two hours put a crimp in their near-constant contact. But the two friends kept in touch with regular "wine chats" and stayed fully briefed on each other's exploits. Chris's job as a party planner for the rich and famous provided more stories that rose to the level of exploits. Tonight though, Lisette thought, I've got the goods.

"I was at a rock concert," Lisette started.

"What?" said Chris. "Who?"

"Not the Who," Lisette said, "another band we saw back in the day, though. Guess."

"Like that narrows it down," Chris scoffed. "Give me a hint."

"Thunder…"

"…Struck! AC/DC!" Chris shouted.

"No, but close," Lisette replied. "Guess again. Hint: You wore a scarf as a halter top and a skirt the size of a headband."

"Thunder Thighs! Disgracefuls!" Chris chortled with glee. "Oh my god! I've been reading the tour reviews! Is Shane Stewart really still a babe? And he can still wail?"

"Total babe, total wail. His voice was so fine," Lisette intoned. "Wait a second, I'm sending you a picture."

She had recently learned how to access other smartphone features while simultaneously talking on the phone. Chris was impressed.

"Here it comes," she announced. She had sent the close-up Maria took.

"Oh. My. God," Chris responded. "How were you this close?"

Lisette told the story.

"When you hang up I am calling child protection services," Chris threatened. "How dare you imperil my goddaughter! She'll probably walk with a limp the rest of her life because her mother is a shameless ho!"

"She's fine," Lisette reassured her. "She's probably still on the phone with her girlfriends or posting on Facebook."

"I'll check out her posts. Did she get any pictures of the rest of the band? I seem to recall sleeping with the bass player. I'd like to see how he's held up. . ."

"Remember me? Where's the beer?" Lisette snorted, shorthand for their favorite overheard backstage greeting.

"So my precious goddaughter's pain and suffering lands the two of you on stage with the Disgracefuls, and you left before it ended," Chris ribbed her. "You couldn't put off the X-rays until after the victory lap?"

"Like I would go backstage after in my leotard," Lisette pooh-poohed.

"As opposed to a scarf and a headband," Chris giggled. "Tell me more about Shane. That was super nice of him to take care of you two the way he did. Did his pants make it to the end of the set?"

"They were still holding together when we left. And he seemed to truly appreciate my superior skills with a needle and thread. He, um, dedicated a song to me."

"What?" barked Chris. "Good lord, woman – you buried the lead! Shane Stewart dedicated a song to you? By name? What song?"

"He dedicated it to 'Lisette, emergency seamstress'," Lisette elaborated.

"What song?" demanded Chris.

"'You Shook Me' – Zeppelin version," Lisette answered. "Slow and dirty."

"Mercy," Chris breathed, "Of all songs. Don't tell Carl!"

"Don't worry."

"Hey, I miss you," Chris said. "When can we get together?"

"I just started the new semester, but I have three-day weekends," Lisette said. "Come east, we can blast up to the beach."

"Chica, I live at the beach, remember? And the water here is warm, unlike a certain big honking lake. . ."

"Unsalted, shark-free," Lisette quoted a popular Great Lakes t-shirt.

Growing up outside Detroit, the two friends had explored every beach town in the state of Michigan. Their favorite was on the southwest corner, on Lake Michigan. They waitressed summers there during college and played guitars and sang Beatles songs during happy hour as an acoustic duo, "The Fab Two." They'd gotten guitars for Christmas when they were high school sophomores and over time learned enough chords to flesh out a set list. Chris's confident, clear soprano handled most of the Paul leads, while Lisette added harmonies and took over a couple of John songs. "You Can't Do That" was her signature turn in the spotlight. It was a happy time and place for two young women on their way to becoming. Looking back, they realized how they empowered each other. As adults, they often wondered out loud where they'd be without the other's influence. And they never, ever were shy about breaking into song for any reason or none at all.

The place and time remained a part of them. Ten years before, Lisette used a small inheritance from her mother to buy a broken-down wreck of a cottage there, adjacent to a nature preserve. At the time, she was thinking of divorcing Carl. She thought she might open a small dance studio there, live a small-town life. She ultimately decided that for Maria's sake, she'd stay in the marriage. A child of divorce herself, she wanted to spare Maria that pain and woe, upheaval and self-blame. Ultimately, she decided divorce was too much trouble when Carl was gone most of the time anyway. She sucked it up. Carl didn't suspect anything was wrong, much less the depth of her unhappiness. She did not feel noble about it, in fact she felt like a sell-out, a coward who easily settled for the comfortable life and the path of least resistance. Maybe she was even a conniver. It wasn't as if she actively disliked Carl. But she certainly couldn't support herself, much less Maria, as a part-time ballet teacher in the manner that Carl provided. She supposed she was Carl's "trophy wife." His first wife, Edie, had been his college sweetheart. They had two children together who were now in their 40s and he paid alimony forever. That's one thing about Carl, he was a good provider. He was predictable, always the same. After a childhood of fighting parents, she dreaded confrontation and avoided it at all cost. They had settled into a transactional relationship, and that remained the status quo.

Over the years, she poured her energies into repairing and improving the cottage, using her own earnings. She had never put Carl's name on the deed. It stung her when he referred to it as "the dump." More than once he had encouraged her to trade up to a condo in a gated community on a golf course. He did not understand her infatuation with the humble cottage nestled in the dunes amid a crazy jungle of roses, hydrangeas, butterfly bushes and clownish sunflowers that grew to 10 feet. By dismissing the place, he cut himself off from some of the best aspects of Lisette, her quiet beauty reflected in creating a sacred space, a sanctuary, an escape from the demands and tedium of life. "If you don't get this, you don't get me," Lisette had decided. His criticism created an emotional wedge, the kind that can fossilize into emotional estrangement.

As the years passed and she grew into middle age, she loved her cottage ever more for the independence and balance it afforded her. How could such a tiny space be so expansive to her heart and mind? She yearned for it if she couldn't get there a couple times a month, dreamed of it, imagined she heard the waves at night. She caught herself singing on mornings when she packed an overnight bag and a cooler. In the two-hour drive from Chicago, as the landscape slowly transitioned from billboards to trees and farmland, she could feel herself exhale. She loved that Maria and her friends felt the same attachment to it.

"Come see me anyway," Lisette said. "We can freeze our asses off."

"I'll check my ass-freezing calendar, see if I have any openings," Chris said. "Give Maria my love and extend my condolences that her mother is a ho."

Hanging up, Lisette crept to the kitchen and retrieved a pack of Marlboros from the very back of the junk drawer, tapping out one before returning the pack to its hiding place. She softly called the dog and they stepped out into the cool fall night. While Misha sniffed around, Lisette lit up, inhaling with deep satisfaction. Her secret vice was a complete contradiction of her seemingly virtuous and healthy lifestyle, another secret she guarded. She felt the nicotine rush to her brain. She looked at the stars and replayed the crazy twists and turns of the day. A delicious shiver ran through her entire body. All things considered, Shane fucking Stewart had made a pretty big fuss over her, she decided, and she liked it. She was smiling as she ground out the cigarette in the grass and still smiling when she stepped inside to flush the butt away and wash her hands.

She was deeply tempted to Google "Shane Stewart girlfriend" but ordered herself to "grow up." She headed upstairs to bed where Carl snored on, unaware that some profound shift had been set in motion.

Chapter 3

The encore had been one for the ages, Shane reflected. The reviews would proclaim it so, along with all the usual crap about him being the Energizer Bunny, the elderrocker who kept going and going and...

Forty years he'd been doing this. Forty fucking years. Remarkably, the music still mattered. It mattered to his contemporaries, who grew up on it and continued to live out their eternal adolescence through the "classic rock" radio format. Real rebels. It mattered to their kids, who grew up on what their parents listened to and ultimately embraced the Disgracefuls as their own. The kids were the ones up front now, though it was anyone's guess how they could afford the seats.

The live experience had changed so much. Fans spent hundreds of dollars for premium seats only to watch the show through their smart phones, totally defeating the notion of the live concert experience. He used to love interacting with the audience, seeing their joyful faces and outstretched arms. Now a sea of glowing screens lifted toward him, not human hands holding lighters aloft. The in-the-moment intimacy of live performance now had a filter of remove, the priority had become capturing video to post and share, bragging rights that were more about the concert-goer than the concert itself. It was ass-backward.

Backstage after the show was the usual stream of ass-kissers, autograph seekers and selfie artists. Tiffany was drunk and loud, working the room with a proprietary air as if she herself had just performed, unaware that one nipple had worked its way free from her ridiculous dress. "Why am I with this woman?" he wondered, not for the first time. She had a magical va-jay-

jay, that much was true. At the beginning, when she was his assistant, she was efficient and capable. She had a sharp wit. She had steadily "improved" herself during her time as his assistant, first changing her hair color, then "fixing" her nose. It was anyone's guess what she had injected into her face as she morphed into a magazine version of her original self. They became romantically involved after a late-night meeting that included several bottles of red wine. A year later, she had delegated most of her duties to other assistants and spent her time shopping, dressing up, and insinuating herself into the entourage at a higher level in the pecking order. She was four years older than his youngest daughter, a source of friction in the family. He didn't need to read the celeb news – he realized he was a rock and roll cliché. It embarrassed him on one level, but also provided cover when women hit on him. Which was a pretty constant thing. He hated to admit that he had reached an age when the promise of sexual favors didn't hold as much excitement. He had chased women all over the world. Or rather, women had chased him. The world was chock full of magical va-jay-jays. He knew that for a fact.

Tiffany approached him with a drink in one hand and a chocolate-covered strawberry in the other. As she leaned in to offer him the strawberry, he allowed her to pop it into his mouth as he gently and ably tucked her breast back into her dress. A jutting spike on the dress jabbed his hand, drawing blood.

"Ack – I'm impaled," he barked.

"Oops," she said, swaying on her sky-high heels and giggling.

"Honestly, that dress is a weapon," he said, stepping away from her. "I'm going to have Derek take you back to the hotel so you can take it off."

He punctuated the words "take it off" with one of his signature eye twinkles, intending it as code for "to be continued," but it was false. He knew she'd be passed out cold when he returned, and that, he thought, was preferable to her current condition. She was an annoying drunk.

"See you back there, darling, I won't be long," he said, turning her over to Derek with a pat on her behind, like a parent sending a reluctant child to bed. Under the dark chocolate, the strawberry had been sour, he observed. So was his mood. He suddenly, desperately, wanted to be far from the noisy party, to be alone.

Shane slipped out and found his limo idling outside the door. He instructed his driver to take him to the Chicago lakefront. The limo was the only car in the North Avenue Beach lot. He got out, asking the driver to wait, he wouldn't be long, and walked to the waterfront. What a city! Turn west and feel like a speck at the base of a brawny urban skyline. Turn east and see nothing but water and the night sky. He felt the same sense of wonder he'd experienced the first time he saw Lake Michigan as a child. He'd grown up in Indiana, which had its own chunk of the lakefront.

He looked at the stars, dim but visible beyond the pinkish glow of the city lights, and thought of a ballerina with a shocking white streak in her dark hair. He imagined her dancing. To "Creep" by Radiohead.

Chapter 4

The next morning Maria insisted on going to school even though Lisette offered her a sick day. Maria's ankle was impressively swollen and darkening to a putrid shade of deep purple. The bruising seeped through to the sole of her foot. It looked hideous.

"Everyone knows we were at the show last night – they'll think I missed school because I was out late," Maria said, sounding like the disciplined, straight-A student she was. "The volleyball team has practice after school. I should go and watch."

Lisette suspected Maria couldn't wait to get to school, the center of her social life, to tell the Disgracefuls story to her classmates and show her pictures, proof of events the night before.

"Well call if you need to come home," Lisette instructed. "Or get a Lyft. I have senior ballet until 7." Lisette dispensed one of the prescription strength ibuprofens from Urgent Care, and shook out another for Maria to put in her pocket for 8 hours later.

Carl had left a note about a meeting downtown. He'd left early.

Lisette carried Maria's school bag out to her carpool while Maria swung along on her crutches. "I get front seat until I'm off crutches," she announced. Belinda, a mopey sophomore, sighed as she resituated herself in the back seat.

Lisette checked seatbelts and watched them pull away, ever on watch for careless driving, and noticed the senior behind the wheel did not signal as he pulled away from the curb, but did look over his shoulder, which Lisette decided was more important. The bass started bumping when the car was a half block away. She recognized the Disgracefuls tune. Maria had probably launched into the story of the night before.

It would be a long day. She had beginning, advanced, then the senior dancers, not senior in ability, but age. Lisette had started the class two years ago in response to hearing so many older women tell her how they'd loved ballet as girls and wished they could still study. Now the class was up to 12 women, from their 40s up. Some were mothers of Maria's friends, part of her social network. Her oldest student, Evelyn, was 72.

Lisette loved this class best of all. They worked hard, truly applied themselves as she explained how the various exercises benefitted their mobility and strength, calling out the muscles and joints they were working. Sometimes the entire class erupted into hysterical laughter at comments the women made about their bodies and the challenges of aging knees and hips. Sometimes it was a challenge to get their focus back, but that struggle was part of the mental discipline of ballet. Many of the older students agreed that their brains worked better as a result of the class. On a lesser level, they constantly shared insights on various brands of slimming undergarments they wore under their leotards. Lisette wondered how they were able to move with their flesh bound up so. She remembered dancers from her own days who took turns wrapping each others' midsections in plastic kitchen wrap to promote fat burning. Spanx were preferable to a plastic tourniquet, she supposed.

With the house to herself, Lisette poured a cup of coffee and sat down at the computer. Abandoning her willpower of the night before, she Googled images of "Shane Stewart girlfriend."

Up popped pictures of Shane and the blond Lisette recognized from the first aid tent the night before. Her hair was dark in some of the pictures, and over time, Lisette realized, she had morphed into someone more polished, more symmetrical. She'd definitely upgraded.

Lisette switched from "images" to "news."

"Oh come on," she berated the screen. "Are you kidding me?"

Tiffany Taylor (perfect name for a pole dancer) was Shane's "assistant" before she was his girlfriend.

"Shane Stewart Engaged?" read a headline from a French gossip magazine, dated two months before.

PARIS (AP) – Rocker Shane Stewart toured the City of Lights with girlfriend Tiffany Taylor to celebrate her 29th birthday. Stewart, 61, is on a

European tour with his band, the Disgracefuls. Taylor was sporting a dazzling ring on her left hand. Asked whether the couple was engaged, the twice-married Stewart had no comment.

"What are you doing?" Carl's voice startled her into a choking fit that sent coffee shooting out of her nose and onto the keyboard.

She clicked the page closed as she frantically mopped coffee off the keyboard with the sleeve of her robe while holding a finger up in the "one minute" sign as she coughed and sputtered and Carl crossed the room.

"I didn't hear you come in," she said, "you startled me."

He nuzzled the back of her neck.

"Meeting ended early," he said. "Sorry I fell asleep last night. I missed you."

She felt both embarrassed at her guilty search and annoyed at the interruption, which Carl obviously hoped would lead to quick sex before she left for the conservatory. She knew how to make it quick, she could practically make Carl come on command with this thing she did that rendered him helpless every time.

She let him take her hand and lead her upstairs, where she let him fuck her. Seven minutes later, while he fell into a twilight sleep as he always did immediately after sex, she rolled out of bed and got into the shower – after deleting the history of her illicit Google search.

Deleting the search history was like closing a book. She seriously needed to get a grip, put to rest her rock and roll fantasy.

Arriving at the conservatory, her imagination was whirring away on new steps for a dance the seniors were working on, adding a new part each class. "Ms. DuPre, wait!" the receptionist called after her as she headed toward the stairwell. "You have a delivery!"

She turned back and saw the tiny receptionist teetering under a tall, paper-wrapped package that could only be flowers.

"Oh! How lovely," Lisette said, smiling. She loved flowers! She hoisted the package and once again headed for the stairwell. The receptionist held the door for her. Lisette turned on the lights of the studio with her elbow and set the clunky package on the floor, thinking "Carl has his moments…"

She tore off the paper to reveal two dozen red roses in a clear glass cylinder. Each was perfect, at least two feet tall. She added water from the drinking fountain to the vase and returned the flowers to it, plumping them to a dense red halo over the crystal base. Finally she removed the card.

"Thanks again for saving the day," it read. It was signed "Shane Stewart and the Disgracefuls."

Lisette was stunned, disbelieving. She turned the card over in her hand. She read it again. Was someone pranking her?

She pulled her phone out of her big black bag.

"Real funny, Chris," she said when her friend answered.

"What?" Chris asked.

"I think you know," Lisette said. "Come clean."

"I have no idea what you are talking about," Chris replied. "What is going on?"

"A certain delivery ring any bells?" Lisette probed.

"Honestly, woman, I have no clue what in fuck you are talking about," Chris repeated. They had refined the art of swearing in Catholic high school.

"Well I have two dozen long-stemmed red roses on the piano that have your evil fingerprints all over them," Lisette argued, "even though the card says they are from Shane fucking Stewart and the Disgracefuls."

Chris was silent.

"I did not send you flowers, Lisettte," she said quietly. "I did not prank you. Though I wish I had thought of it. Wow. Does the card say anything else?"

"Wait, here, it says 'Thanks again for saving the day'," Lisette read. She glanced at herself in the mirrored wall of the dance studio. Her face was nearly as red as the roses.

"Wow," Chris repeated. "Lisette, I swear I did not prank you. And why wouldn't he send flowers? You did save the day!"

"But how could he possibly have found me?" she wondered.

"Ever hear of social media?" Chris retorted. "Facebook? Instagram?"

"I hate that shit," Lisette said.

"Yeah, but I just called up your Facebook page and it says right there where you teach. Did the flowers come to home or the conservatory?"

"Conservatory," Lisette mumbled.

"Send a pic," Chris ordered. "Pronto. Gotta go."

"Bye," Lisette said, but Chris was already gone.

The flowers were truly exquisite, reflecting a pool of deep red onto the glossy black grand piano. Lisette couldn't hold back a sly smile. She positioned the card against the vase and snapped a picture, then fired it off to Chris.

Chris texted right back: "See, not all rock 'n' rollers are assholes!"

The young students did not notice the flowers, but the seniors spotted them straightaway.

"Ooh," cooed Evelyn, "somebody's been good. Is it your birthday?"

"No," Lisette said. "I did a good deed and these appeared."

"Thanks for saving the day," read Maddie, a 50-ish woman who complained about never losing her "baby weight" and whose baby was in his late 20s. She hoped an hour of ballet twice a week might be the magic bullet.

Shit, I left the card out, thought Lisette. Maddie flipped it over.

"Shane Stewart and the Disgracefuls!" she crowed. "Are you kidding me?"

Lisette felt the color rise once again in her face.

"You've heard of them?" she asked.

"You'd have to live under a rock not to know who they are," Maddie retorted.

"Even I know who Shane Stewart is," said Evelyn. "I see him on the chat shows. What a charmer! Even with that crazy stuff all stuck in his hair, he's a babe."

"I went to a ton of their shows in the late '70s," Maddie said. The other ladies had gathered around. They were passing the card among them. "They played my college once when they were just starting out, before they got really famous."

Maddie looked off, and her dimples deepened.

"I actually partied with them once after a show at the old Chicago Stadium," she said. "What a time!"

"You partied with the Disgracefuls, dear?" Evelyn said, impressed. "What was that like? How did you get backstage?"

"It was kind of surreal," Maddie said. "We went back to a big suite in some fancy hotel downtown, probably the Palmer House because I remember looking out the window onto Grant Park. It was fun – musicians are fun."

"How did you get backstage?" Evelyn persisted.

"Blew a roadie," Maddie said, matter-of-factly.

There was a collective intake of breath, followed by an explosion of laughter.

"Oh dear," Evelyn gasped, "I think I peed a little."

The women, including Evelyn, erupted into new gales of laughter. The class had run off the rails before it even started. Intermittent giggles bubbled up and were stifled throughout the hour, aftershocks of Maddie's frank admission. Maybe I'm not crazy, Lisette thought. Maybe celebrity makes everyone a little nuts.

The roses remained in the studio, on the piano, opening a bit more each day and filling the space with their fragrance. Each day, Lisette was delighted all over again. She gradually accepted that they had in fact been sent by the band. Probably Derek, she thought. She snipped the stems and refreshed their water every day to make them last. A week later, the red reflection on the piano had been replaced by a pile of fallen petals. She retired the vase to her storage closet and the card, with a few petals pressed inside, to a zippered pocket inside her big black bag.

Chapter 5

Fall came in earnest with a blaze of Midwestern colors. Maria was cleared to resume volleyball, with an ankle support. She and Lisette piled off to Michigan after school on Fridays a couple of weekends to putter around and ready the cottage for winter.

Carl called from Bogota to ask Lisette about plans for their annual New York City trip at Thanksgiving.

"What would you think about staying home and having Thanksgiving here?" she asked. "We could invite a few people, I could make my mother's cornbread stuffing, bake a pie…"

"Lizzy, you know the bonus meeting is always that week. I have to be there. It's an opportunity to go as a family," he said, making his case. "We have tickets to the Met. We'll go shopping. You can take Maria around Columbia and NYU…"

Lisette sighed. The "bonus trip" repackaged as a family Thanksgiving. Giving thanks for Carl's bonus. Every year she hoped it would be different, but Carl prevailed with his own version of the ideal Thanksgiving: the opera, dinner at the latest chic restaurant, the parade, the throngs. A native New Yorker, he considered Chicago somewhat provincial. His responsibilities to the Midwest regional office kept him there.

How Lisette longed to put her culinary chops to use with a dinner for 10 – or 20! She had grown up cooking alongside her mother and was confident serving a crowd. After her dad left, her mother had made Thanksgiving her annual gathering of odd ends: elderly relatives, friends from her Divorce Isn't Death support group, co-workers with no family nearby, the parish priest. Lisette always invited a few friends, college pals who couldn't afford to travel home, boyfriends, teenagers feuding with their families. Thanksgiving is the best holiday, she thought: no presents, no unrealistic expectations. Just great food and the company of others. A holiday dedicated only to gratitude.

Her favorite Thanksgiving was the year she and Maria and assorted friends celebrated at the cottage a week early. All day the place smelled like heaven as the 20-pound turkey sizzled and spat in the oven. The logistics of preparing all the dishes in the tiny kitchen were truly an exercise of "firing on all burners." Potatoes and rutabaga at the boil, cranberries popping, pies baked earlier cooling on the windowsill. After dinner, they'd walked the beach and played softball in the sand until they were half frozen and it was too dark to see the ball. Back inside, every surface of the little place, every nook and cranny it seemed, was covered in sleeping bags. At midnight, the kitchen came back to life with people eating turkey sandwiches piled with stuffing and cranberries and leftover pie – people who just hours before had sworn they'd never need to eat again. That was Lisette's version of a perfect Thanksgiving. Even with no dishwasher.

"It will be great, you'll see," Carl cajoled. "It's a classic opera with a corps de ballet. You'll love it."

Some people who traveled a lot for work were happy to stay home when they could. True, Carl needed to show his face as annual bonuses were awarded, but his ideal Thanksgiving in New York City scenario seemed ostentatious and empty to Lisette. Next year Maria would be coming home from college for Thanksgiving for the first time. Maybe that new dynamic would finally allow Lisette to get her way. Next year then. For sure next year at home.

But the funny thing about years is they come and go. How many years had she not been in love with Carl? How many years had she coasted along, thinking about but never making a major change? How many years had slipped by with enough joy to tide her over, but not fill her up?

She felt ashamed about the lack of fulfillment she felt at times. She had things most people would envy, a great teaching job, a beautiful house, friends, a beach cottage, a comfortable and highly desirable lifestyle, her fantastic daughter. Was she a sell-out, a coward? Was she using Carl? Was she calculating in ways other than tallying up years spent in service to the marriage?

Because Maria was her greatest joy, for Maria she perpetuated this life. That was her bottom line. The pure love and devotion she felt for her daughter made it possible to live without romantic love. Families require sacrifice. It goes with the territory. Maria had told her once when she was having a bad day: "Mom, every day can't be awesome." Had she reached the full measure of her life's awesome days? Did she have unrealistic expectations? Did being a grownup mean foregoing awesome days and settling for a safe and stable life? Some internal timepiece was calculating: Just a few more years until Maria was on her own, maybe Lisette could be, too.

So she booked the flights and the suite, made a reservation for Thanksgiving dinner at a farm-to-table restaurant in the Village that received a gushing review from the Times, and braced herself for the Thanksgiving travel crowds.

Chapter 6

Shane awoke in a hotel room. As his brain slowly lifted to consciousness, he was aware of the usual aches and pains from performing the night before at…Madison Square Garden. He was in New York City. He was at the Plaza. He was starving. He rolled over and dialed room service.

"Send coffee and eggs, scrambled, and bacon," he said, his voice raspy from the show. "And juice. Do you have V8? Good. And a bowl of lemon wedges and a pot of tea."

He loved New York. Here, he was able to walk the streets without feeling conspicuous, and didn't mind when people snapped his picture from a respectful distance. He was mostly obliging for more forward fans who asked for selfies.

He was alone, having sent Tiffany home to her family in San Diego for Thanksgiving. It felt great to be unencumbered. He smiled at the thought of two days off and knowing he would see his daughter today. Next week would be talk shows in the city before the tour moved on to Boston.

He turned on the television with the remote and notched the volume down low to hear the door. The screen showed the time was a little after noon. He'd slept almost nine hours. One goal achieved, he thought. He was really working on his health, specifically sleep, exercise, and protein. No late afterparties, no hard drugs and no hard liquor. Just wine and a little weed. No shame in that, it was downright pious compared to how he'd lived into his 50s. That goddamned 60th birthday had been a cruel bitch emotionally. But he'd also been surprised by a sense of relief, that it was OK to rein in the lifestyle. Drunk doesn't look good on anybody, but it looks worse the older you get. At this age, there is really no difference between a drunken rock star in a $2,000 a night suite and a homeless alcoholic on the street. He came to that conclusion after an old wino hit him up for cash on the street late one night. Shane had looked into the man's cloudy eyes and seen himself.

The doorbell of the suite chimed. Shane rolled out of the barge-like California king bed and thrust his arms into a thick terry robe with the hotel's logo. He rolled his shoulders and stretched his neck as he walked into the living room and answered the door. "Good morning, sir," the waiter greeted him, rolling the breakfast cart to the table by the window. As the waiter set the covered dishes and the New York Times on the table and poured coffee, Shane opened the drapes and peered down onto 5th Avenue. He handed the waiter a generous tip and he trundled off with the cart and a cheerful "Thank you, sir!"

The coffee was nirvana, black and rich. Shane felt himself come to life as he sipped and savored it before attacking the breakfast. He squeezed two lemon wedges into the V8 and drank half of it down lustily.

The room phone rang.

"Hi, Dad," Autumn said. Shane's kids knew better than to call before noon. It was 12:30. Autumn, his youngest, was an art student. Now 24, she had enrolled in college after a few years of trying to make it as a musician. She would always love music, and she had great pipes. But ultimately, the life was not for her, she decided. Too many pitfalls, even though she would never be a typical starving musician, what with her daddy being rich and her mama good looking. Ultimately, she came away from the experience with heightened respect for her father's career and what it took for him to keep at it all these years.

"There are a couple of galleries I'd like to take you to," she said. "And a friend of mine has a show in Chelsea opening tonight, there's a reception at 6. Feel like arting it up?"

"You bet," Shane replied, timing out a workout and massage in his head. "I could meet you at 3, does that work?"

"Yes, that's good." She hesitated, then added, "Dad, will it be just you?"

"Yes, just me," he said. "Tiffany is in California with her family."

"OK, great," Autumn said, relief evident in her voice. Tiffany was probably having some more work done, she thought spitefully.

"See you soon, lovie," Shane signed off.

After his workout and massage, Shane returned to the suite for a quick shower before meeting Autumn. It struck him again how weird it felt to be alone. Managers, publicists, roadies, assorted members of the constant entourage had the rest of the holiday weekend off and had scattered to the winds to wherever was home. As he shaved, he checked out the new white streak over his forehead. At his request, his hairdresser had bleached it, but the inch at the hairline was his own natural growth. Many of his contemporaries – Bonnie Raitt, Steven Tyler, Joe Perry, and Sir Paul – were sporting the "shock" – a white streak that afforded a minimalist acknowledgment of their age while continuing to dye the rest of their hair.

"That ballerina really got to you," Derek said the first time he saw it.

"Who are your influences?" Shane had replied in an Irish accent, laughing off Derek's observation with a quote from one of their favorite band movies, "The Commitments."

"Right then," Derek said, looking at Shane knowingly. "She was truly fine. Do you think of her?"

"Do you?" Shane retorted.

"Every night," Derek said.

"Piss off."

Shane chose a low-key, blend-in-with-the-crowd ensemble: black t-shirt, jeans, vintage high-top Air Jordans for walking the city. Remembering the reception, he added a gray pinstripe vest, a tasteful deep purple scarf, and a black wool jacket from Versace. He pulled back his shoulder-length hair and twisted it behind him, pulling it up and catching the hank of hair inside a newsboy cap. Certain pieces of jewelry he never took off – they were part of him: a chain with a small Madonna, a small gold hoop earring, a pinkie ring with the birthstones of his children that the girls had given him for his birthday one year. He tucked his money clip in his front pocket, his room keycard in the inside pocket of the jacket, his cell phone in the back pocket of his jeans. Away from the stylists and designers, I can still dress myself, he thought. He found his sunglasses on a table inside the door and left the suite.

"Good afternoon, Mr. Stewart. Cab?" asked the doorman, whistle at the ready.

"Thank you, sir," Shane replied. He went out of his way to be respectful to service staff in any capacity. He remembered the days when the band first got together, when they were forced to load in and out through the kitchen, a not-so-subtle reminder that they were hired help. His father, a university professor, taught Shane that there was dignity in all work well done.

He spotted Autumn waiting on the sidewalk, talking on her cellphone and tipping her face to the late November sun. He broke into a broad smile at the sight of her. Exiting the cab, he swept her into a warm embrace, twirling her around once before planting a kiss on her cheek.

"Hello beauty," he said. "See why this season was named after you?"

Autumn rolled her eyes behind her mirrored sunglasses. "Dad, you are so corny," she said, obviously delighted to be in his arms. "Mom says hi, by the way."

"How is she?" Shane asked. Autumn had inherited her love of art from her mother, Suki, a painter Shane had met in the Netherlands. She was and continued to be a free spirit.

"She's good. She's in Rotterdam at the moment," Autumn reported. "She has two pieces at this gallery!"

"Let's take a look then," Shane said, taking her arm and guiding her toward the door. He noticed a bookstore across the street. "Mind if we stop there after?"

"Sure, that'd be nice," she replied. "We can get a coffee."

While Shane and Autumn were looking at art, Lisette and Maria were shopping for boots. Chicago winters required multiple pairs, from utilitarian Uggs to dashing fashion statements. Lisette was determined to find something unique to brighten up the long winter months. The concierge at the Four Seasons had provided a short list of shops that might have what she was looking for: high, above-the-knee black leather to wear over jeans or under a skirt. Her long legs would balance the dimensions.

Lisette scored at the third shop, finding exactly what she had in mind in black suede with a block heel and serious tread on the soles. Traction was everything in Chicago in winter.

"Mom, you're an Amazon," Maria said, standing eye to eye with her mother though Maria was in her stocking feet. In the boots, Lisette was suddenly four inches taller. "Those are excellent!"

"Should I get them in raspberry, too?" Lisette asked.

"If you don't you'll regret it later," said Maria. "You always say how hard it is for you to find shoes that fit your weird feet."

Maria, who traditionally spent October to April in Uggs, tried on a pair of deep brown riding boots with buckles at the top and around the ankle.

"These are nice and flat," she said, wiggling her foot in circles. Her ankle had healed.

Lisette eyed the large boot boxes stacked on the counter, a small city unto themselves, and thought about the plane ride home.

"Can you ship these?" she asked the clerk.

"Of course," the saleswoman obliged.

"Not mine," Maria said, "I want to break them in. Can I wear them?"

Lisette provided the shipping information and the clerk cut the tags off Maria's new boots. The two left the shop, Maria swinging the large shopping bag containing the boot box, her shoes now rolling around inside it.

"Thanks, mom," she said. "I'm so excited about these boots! I will have them forever! They'll just get better the more beat up they get."

"I'm glad you like them, Maria – oh, let's stop in that bookstore," Lisette suggested, pointing to a shop across the street. "We can pick up some reading for the plane."

Lisette had read a review of a new Led Zeppelin biography that was hailed as the definitive account of the band and was interested in checking it out. Ever since the Disgracefuls show, memories long dormant had floated to the surface. Not just concerts and different bands she'd loved, but memories from her teens, listening to boys in bands practice in basements and garages, countless nights jamming Beatles tunes with Chris. It was as if she had locked that part of her in a box labeled "The Past," never to be disturbed again, but the contents were determined to leak out. "Why does it still matter?" was a question she kept asking herself. "Why shouldn't it still matter?" was another.

No memory loomed larger than Zeppelin. She and Chris told the story of that tour for years. "Epic" was their code word for an experience that continued to resonate with them though the band had been history for nearly 40 years.

She felt strangely guilty about her renewed interest in rock, as if she should have grown out of it by now and should be content to sit between Carl and Maria at the Met, being *appropriate.* She realized she had no control over her subconscious, and that it was influencing her conscious. She wanted to read the book, look at every archival picture, and devote an entire wine chat to it. She'd order one for Chris as a surprise, she decided.

"Do you have the new Led Zeppelin biography?" Lisette asked at the counter.

"There's a big display in the music section," the clerk said, pointing.

Maria looked at her mother with questioning eyes. "Led Zeppelin?" she wondered aloud. "Who are you?"

"Don't you worry about it, missy," Lisette said, laughing. "Better yet, ask Aunt Chris about it sometime."

A tall man in a newsboy cap was thumbing through the tome at the display table, bending over to inspect a page of photographs. He looked up as they drew near.

"Lisette?...Maria?" Shane sputtered.

"Oh my goodness," Lisette squeaked. Maria's jaw dropped.

"Wow, um, hi Mr. Stewart," Maria said, recovering.

"Shane," he corrected her. "Though I appreciate your manners."

He looked piercingly at Lisette, completely unglued to see her in such an unexpected context. She looked lovely, her hair loose, the white streak framing her face. She was wearing red lipstick that accentuated her pale beauty. She literally took his breath away. He wondered if this was really happening or if he was having a mini-stroke. He could hear his heart pounding "swish swish" in his ears. Could be a stroke.

Lisette had a sudden wish that she had worn the raspberry thigh-highs and internally slapped herself for the thought.

"What a surprise!" she said.

"You never know who you might run into in New York City," he said, smiling delightedly. "How's the ankle, Maria?"

Maria held out her newly-booted foot and made a few circles. "All better," she said.

"Nice kicks," he complimented.

"Thanks," said Maria. "We just got them – across the street."

A young woman in a beret, peering over mirrored sunglasses halfway down her nose, came toward the trio with a coffee in each hand.

"Oh no, not again," thought Lisette.

"Here you go, Dad," she said, handing one cup to Shane.

"Ladies, this is my daughter Autumn," Shane said. "Autumn, these are friends of mine from Chicago, Lisette and Maria. Lisette saved the day before our show there a couple of months ago."

Out of the side of his mouth, *sotto voce*, he confided to Autumn, "I split my pants."

"Oh dear!" Autumn laughed.

Maria was checking out Autumn's chic New York style and concluded she needed to add a beret to her collection of winter hats. She also admired Autumn's black lipstick, but doubted she could pull it off herself. Still, she vowed to at least try it at the makeup counter next chance she got.

"I couldn't find the seamstress," Shane continued, "so I went into the first-aid tent figuring they would have a needle and thread. Lisette was there with Maria, who had sprained her ankle. And Lisette fixed my pants for me."

"Your dad was so great," Maria told Autumn. "He got me a wheelchair and we got to watch the show on stage. Until we had to go for X-rays."

"Da-ad, you little angel," Autumn said in a sing-song voice popular with young women when expressing appreciation. She made a smushy face, indicating "precious!"

"It was wonderful," Lisette said. "Really wonderful."

Oh god, what a spaz, she criticized herself internally. She was shaking like a leaf.

"Did you get the flowers?" Shane asked.

Maria looked confused. "Flowers?" she said.

"They were beautiful," Lisette interjected. "I was, um, surprised."

"Well you truly saved the day," he said. "It was the least I could do."

Lisette ignored Maria's inquiring glance.

"The studio smelled like a rose garden," she said. "They lasted forever. It was awfully nice of you."

"Are you an artist?" Autumn asked.

"Not an 'art' artist," Lisette explained. "The ballet studio. I'm a ballet teacher."

"You should have seen her at the show," Shane said, "she was wearing her ballerina outfit – pink tights and those little slippers. And a teensy weensy little ballet skirt. I convinced her to stay by assuring her that many people would be dressed way stranger than that."

Lisette blushed.

"That's the truth," Autumn confirmed. "Especially Tiffany."

Shane shot his daughter a sharp look.

"So how long are you in New York?" he asked.

"Just until tomorrow," Lisette said.

"What are you doing tonight? Autumn is taking me to a reception for a new show at a gallery nearby. Maybe you would like to join us…"

"That sounds so fun," Maria said.

"We have the opera tonight," Lisette reminded her.

"Ugh," Maria responded.

"Quite the music lovers, you two," Shane said. "And across ages and genres, too. You're buying the new Zeppelin biography?"

"I was a huge fan," Lisette said. "Saw them only once before, you know…"

"I know," Shane said. "It still hurts to think about it."

"Did you know them? Were they friends?" Lisette asked.

She could tell by the pain in his eyes that he did, and they were.

"I still see Robert on occasion. We're both still rockin' it," he said, lifting the mood.

"Any pictures of you in there?" Lisette asked, nodding at the book.

"Don't know," Shane replied, grinning. "I'll need my reading glasses for deeper study."

The four stood awkwardly as the conversation paused.

"Well, it was amazing to run into you ladies," he said, using the plural though his hazel eyes were locked on Lisette's misty grays. Holding the gaze, he reached out, picked up her hand, and pressed his lips to the back of it. "Amazing," he repeated, still not breaking eye contact.

"You never know who you might run into in New York City," Lisette agreed with a bright smile, holding his eyes with her own. The three women exchanged "so-nice-to-meet-yous" and Maria and Lisette took their leave.

"Mom, you didn't tell me Shane Stewart sent you flowers," Maria scolded her mother once they were out on the sidewalk, each lugging a copy of the heavy book.

"Well I thought Aunt Chris was pranking me," Lisette said, "as you know she does."

"Mom, I get the feeling he really likes you," Maria said thoughtfully. "He remembered our names and everything. That's weird. He even invited us to go out with him and his daughter tonight."

"Don't be silly, Maria," Lisette said. "He's a famous man – famous for being a rock star and famously charming. He's charming."

"Seems like he wants to be your Prince Charming," Maria said, elbowing her mother in the side and making her sway.

"As if!" Lisette retorted.

Their laughter bubbled up, they linked arms affectionately, and walked briskly into the chill November dusk.

Meanwhile, Shane and Autumn walked in the opposite direction to the reception. Shane was thinking he needed a glass of wine to calm what might be arrhythmia. "Arrhythmia" – interesting song title, he mused.

"Dad," asked Autumn, "does Lisette have anything to do with your new white streak?"

"It's a Baby Boomer thing," he said. "A lot of us are sporting the streak these days."

Autumn was not convinced. But she did appreciate her father's acknowledgment that he was of that generation. If he was to find a nice woman his own age, she thought, it would make her life less complicated. She could barely tolerate the annoying Tiffany and couldn't understand the attraction. Her father was a smart guy, way too cool to have fallen into the cliché of banging his assistant. Her mother and her stepsister Priya's mother Jill, who had been Shane's high school girlfriend, were the only women in his life who seemed semi-normal. She understood that his touring schedule made it complicated to have normal relationships. She sighed and resolved to enjoy the here and now, walking the streets anonymously with her famous father's hand wrapped tightly around hers.

Chapter 7

Carl was already dressed for the opera when the two returned to the suite. Lisette felt strangely uncomfortable, as if she was coming home from an illicit tryst. Maria spilled the beans instantly.

"Dad, you'll never believe who we saw today!" she said. "Shane Stewart! And he remembered us – even our names!"

"You two are pretty unforgettable," he said, noticing the blush creeping across Lisette's face and the red lipstick, which was out of character for his wife. It made her look like a New Yorker, he thought approvingly.

"We were in this bookstore and there he was, buying the same book!" Maria continued. "It was so random! We met his daughter, too. Mom, do you think we could get me a beret? Autumn looked so, so, put together. It was super chic."

"You two had better get ready if we want to see the first act," Carl prompted them. For the second time that day Lisette wished she had the raspberry boots already. They would be an ideal silent protest for a night at the opera. In the next second she wondered why she was acting like a recalcitrant teenager. She vowed to improve her attitude and willed herself to be enthusiastic. It was the Met, for crying out loud. Get with the gratitude program!

"We'll be quick," she promised, dropping the heavy book on a table on her way to the bedroom, where her little beaded black evening dress hung waiting. She caught her reflection in the bathroom mirror and was glad she had let the Lancome lady insist on the red lipstick. It was a significant departure from the subdued tones she usually wore. She decided that she would wear red lipstick every day, even teaching days, to make the day more exciting – make her more exciting. It made a fashion statement.

"Led Zeppelin?" Carl inquired when she stepped out of the bedroom and turned her back so he could fasten the hook above the zipper.

"I know, crazy, huh?" Lisette said. "Chris and I loved that band, and according to the Times, this is the authoritative biography. I bought one for Chris, too."

"What is up with this new interest in rock music?" Carl asked. "Are you planning to become a Deadhead?"

"Of course not, silly," she said, straightening his tie and brushing off the shoulders of his jacket. "It's more like an old interest. Maria, we're ready to go!"

The two parents watched Maria emerge from her bedroom, hopping into her shoes. Her actions were childlike, but there was no denying she was on the verge of womanhood.

"What?" she asked her smiling parents.

"You look so grown up," observed Carl.

"Mom bought me eyeliner and mascara at Bloomingdales! Isn't it awesome?" Maria enthused, batting her lashes for effect. "Mom got a lipstick."

"I noticed," Carl said. "You are both stunning. Everyone will think I'm a 'baller'."

The women laughed at his unexpected stab at being hip. They put on their overcoats and set off for the Met.

At the reception, Shane played with the thread of a melody in his head as he looked at art. He had practically gulped his first glass of red wine to calm himself after the surprise of seeing Lisette. Now, as he nursed a second glass, he noted that his heartbeat and breathing seemed to have returned to somewhat normal. He moved from piece to piece thinking about words and phrases that rhyme with arrhythmia. "When I see ya, I get arrhythmia," he toyed with words in his head. "I can never free ya. Come over he-ah. Give me that arrhythmia." Aphrodisia, bougainvillea.

Horrible, he concluded. Maybe "arrhythmia" would be the chorus. Just the word, repeated. The song would need a heavy drum heartbeat. Maybe it would start slow and gather speed. He thought about other desperate love songs, "Layla," "Something." Oh god, he realized, they were both about the same woman. Was he developing a fixation? Was he becoming a hypochondriac? Why was he acting so freaking…moony?

"Dad."

Autumn was at his elbow.

"See anything you like?" she asked. "Feel like supporting the arts?"

"Ah, my lovely," he said, taking her arm. "I have no more wall space. What about you? Anything strike your fancy?"

"There's a landscape I adore," she said, "though I can't understand why. It's strangely compelling, gripping, but it's like Wisconsin or Michigan or someplace. The trees are turquoise and purple, coral and yellow and lime."

"Let's take a look," Shane said. He'd spent plenty of time in both states, a prodigious tally of a native Midwesterner who'd been on the road for 40 years. His Midwestern fans were both rabid and loyal.

He agreed with Autumn. The landscape was soothing, yet full of mystery. The sandy path leading through the woods was expressed in shades of purple.

"It's an autumn scene, the leaves are changing," he observed. "Painted just for you, my sweet. Would you like to have it?"

"Oh Dad, I love it," Autumn enthused. "I have just the place for it."

They chatted briefly with the artist about the medium and her color choices, then arranged for the painting to be delivered to Autumn's flat when the gallery show ended. The artist gleefully placed a "sold" sticker on the information tag next to the piece. She had recognized Shane instantly, but managed to maintain her cool. She was secretly thrilled to have sold the piece to someone as famous as he, and she loved the "autumn" connection.

"What was your inspiration?" Shane asked, one artist to another.

"I went to art camp in Michigan when I was a teenager," she said. "There's a special kind of light there, near the lake, that I tried to capture. The sky and the water seem to reflect off each other. Everything seems crystal clear and golden. The empty sky in the corner hints that the water is just beyond the woods, that the path leads to the lake…"

If Lisette had gone to the reception instead of the opera, she might have engaged in a bidding war for the landscape. It resembled her cottage property so closely she would have inspected the undergrowth for a concealed fox or a deer, frequent visitors that delighted her.

Shane and Autumn had dinner at a bistro near the gallery, then he walked her to her place, she carrying the leftovers, enough for another feast later.

"This was really nice, dad," Autumn said, smiling up at him. Without her sunglasses, her hazel eyes were expressive. "I love spending time alone with you – without Tiffany. I just want you to know how I feel."

"Which is?" he asked.

"Uncomfortable around her. I feel like she's always trying to insinuate herself into our family."

"Is it the age thing?" he asked.

"Well, duh, that's awkward," Autumn said. "It's like you're dating one of my friends. But mostly it's that I don't find her very interesting. What exactly is the attraction, Dad?"

"I've been wondering that same thing myself," Shane admitted. "It sounds lame, but she's there, she's around, you know, a familiar. And she knows everyone, she gets things done that need doing. God, that sounds like she's a convenience. She likes the music, and she likes traveling…"

"You could say the same generic things about anyone in the Disgracefuls' entourage," Autumn countered. "What makes Tiffany special? What's the emotional connection? Do you love her?" Shane felt like he was the kid and she was the parent. Shane was silent.

"Good questions, Autumn," he finally said. "I need to think them over. I don't have the answers. But whatever I decide, Tiffany will hear from me first. Not through rumor-mongering on the internet. Keep this private, between us, okay?"

"Dad, for a Disgraceful, you are quite the gentleman," Autumn said. "I won't say a word."

They were at her building. He swept her into a hug and said goodnight. From the sidewalk, he watched her safely board the elevator. Then he walked on, deep in thought.

Chapter 8

Lisette was on the verge of exploding. She was dying to call Chris, but between the opera, close quarters in the suite, then the inevitable race to the airport, there was no time or space. She and Carl had silent post-opera sex in the bedroom the night before while Maria watched TV in the living room. Carl knew Lisette found hotel rooms a sexual turn-on, and chalked up her responsiveness to that quirk. With Shane Stewart very much on her mind, Lisette felt like a fire was burning between her thighs. She welcomed the release.

"Call me Monday!!!!!" she texted Chris before powering down her phone for the flight.

All three seemed gripped in a case of Sunday Melancholia on the way home to Chicago. Carl was buried in the Sunday New York Times and Maria was rendered incommunicado by her earbuds, watching a movie on her phone. Lisette shut her eyes and replayed what she had titled (to herself) "an extraordinary encounter."

"What a dweeb," she chastised herself, the next second arguing internally, "but it was extraordinary! For me anyway."

What about Shane? He seemed excited to see her again. He had sent strong signals that he was interested in her, inviting them to come along to the reception. Or was it more like a play date for their daughters, an excuse for adult companionship? She overanalyzed every detail as she replayed the bookstore scene multiple times on the flight, lingering on the kiss on her hand in slow motion and wondering what those same lips would feel like on places other than the back of her hand.

Lisette was relieved that they landed with enough time to pick up Misha at the dog-boarder. He twirled in circles on his leash, all waggy-tailed and whining with delight, as Lisette presented her card and paid the bill.

"Were you a good boy at the Pet Palace?" she asked him in a stupid voice. "Did you play nice?"

She knelt down and put her forehead against his furry dome of a head and rubbed the sides of his neck. An avalanche of dog hair fell with every fond stroke and pat. A shepherd/husky mix with one blue eye, he was the sheddingest dog Lisette had ever known. He was completely devoted to her and she treated him like her second child. She was never afraid when Carl was away with Misha to protect them. On their daily walks, he would not allow strange men to approach her, standing firm, growling if necessary, until Lisette said "It's okay."

Once at home, they ordered Chinese food and prepared for the week ahead. It was back to class for Maria and Lisette. Carl had business with the regional office, where some new initiative was being cooked up to exploit the sick and dying.

Chris called at 11.

"It is 9 a.m. here and you are my first call on a post-holiday Monday. What's up with the five-exclamation point 'Call me'?" she demanded.

"Chris you will never believe what happened in New York," Lisette started.

"Let me guess, Carl decided to stay in his native habitat and you are free from the bonds of marriage?" Chris retorted.

Lisette wondered why that was her friend's first guess.

"I saw him again," Lisette answered. "Shane."

Chris was silent for a beat, processing.

"As in Stewart?" she clarified.

"Yes. Shane Stewart," Lisette confirmed.

"You're on a first-name basis? Where'd you see him? Madison Square Garden?" Chris asked. She lived in L.A., but kept close tabs on what was happening in New York. After hearing about the backstage episode, and the flowers, she had boned up on her Disgracefuls, visiting their website and checking tour dates. They wouldn't be in L.A. for two months, but she was already thinking about inviting Lisette for a visit so they could go. At a certain age, a woman's circle of rock 'n' roll concert-going friends tends to shrink exponentially. The two had once made a pact to keep rocking forever – or for as long as their favorites were still performing. It was a good plan, it turned out. Thanks to the casino circuit, bands of the past were reuniting with their fans in the present all over the map, and the small venues were way more accommodating than stadium shows, which are as much trouble as camping.

"No, at a bookstore in Chelsea," Lisette explained.

"Did he see you?" Chrisi asked.

"Yes! He remembered our names, both mine and Maria's. We met his daughter," Lisette continued. "Well at first I thought it was his girlfriend, but it was his daughter, Autumn, the one whose mother is an artist."

"Not the daughter with the high school girlfriend baby mama," Chris concluded.

"Right," Lisette said. "It was so crazy, Chris, I went in looking for the new Zeppelin biography and there he was, looking at the same book."

"Was he surprised to see you?"

"As surprised as we were to see him. I was a blithering idiot," Lisette confessed. "I totally forgot to thank him for the flowers until he brought it up."

"He knew about the flowers?" Chris probed. The two had decided that an underling, likely Derek, had probably arranged for the flowers.

"Yes, and now Maria knows about them and she's giving me the treatment."

"What did he say about the flowers?" Chris asked.

"Just that it was the least he could do after I saved the day."

"Did he actually say the words 'saved the day'?"

"Yes."

"That's exactly what the card said," Chris reminded her. "Shit, he must really have sent them himself. Lisette, what else did he say?"

"He invited Maria and me to go to a gallery opening with him and his daughter."

"And?"

"We had the opera."

"You had the fucking opera."

"Yes."

"And you went to the fucking opera."

"Yes."

"You are an ass and you have terrible judgment and I don't know why you are my friend. Tell me more."

"He said it was amazing to see us and he kissed my hand in parting."

"Did you just say 'in parting'?"

"Yes. It was quite gallant." She pronounced it "gal-AHNT."

"He looked into my eyes, took my hand, and pressed his lips to the back of it."

"What a player," Chris observed. She said it "play-uh."

"Oh and I got you a copy of the book, too. Look for a big heavy package stamped 'Media Mail,' arriving by stagecoach any week now."

"Lisette," Chris said seriously, "I don't mean to wreck your marriage or anything, but would you possibly want to come to L.A. and see the Disgracefuls when they are here in February?"

"You bet I would, more than possibly," Lisette said. "I might get there before the book."

"I'll get us invited to the meet-and-greet," Chris said. "We can say hello. I can reminisce with the bass player. And thanks in advance for the book. I read the reviews and it does sound cool."

"Chris, what is going on here?" Lisette wondered out loud. "Is this nuts?"

"Probably," her friend admitted. "But wouldn't you like to find out if you are star-crossed lovers? What if all these 'meet cutes' are signs from the universe? Speaking of which, I saw a guy who looked exactly like Carl at LAX last week at a rental car counter. I almost went up to him."

"Carl's a type. He looks like a lot of guys. It was probably Larry David you saw at the airport. And the news flash from the universe is you are nuts," Lisette confirmed. "I am hanging up on you now. This conversation will remain top secret. Do NOT say a word to Maria about the Disgracefuls."

"I won't. She'd feel obliged to come along as a chaperone for her ho of a mama."

Chapter 9

Tiffany rejoined the band in Boston, cabbing straight from the airport to the hotel. She was put out that they hadn't sent a limo for her. She loved coming down the escalator to baggage claim and seeing the drivers waiting with their hand-lettered signs: "Johnson," "Taylor," "Disgracefuls."

"Careful," she greeted Shane at the hotel, moving in for an air kiss with lips that looked like she'd been stung by bees.

She was smudged and wrinkled from her coast-to-coast flight. Shane noticed bruising around her newly puffy lips, despite her attempts to conceal it with makeup. She looked like Alice Cooper wearing wax Halloween lips.

"Good god, what have you done?" he asked.

"I paid a visit to mommy's beauty doctor while I was home," she said triumphantly, turning her face from side to side for him to admire. Her attempt at a smile looked painful. Shane worried her lips might burst. The rest of her face was strangely immobile, expressionless. Not Alice Cooper, he decided, more like the inflatable sex dolls the band used to fill with helium and set loose into the air at their shows.

"I need a nap," she announced in a pouty voice that matched her now perpetually-pouty visage.

"There's work to be done," Shane reminded her.

"Let someone else do it," she replied. "I'm exhausted from four days with my family. They actually made me play golf! At the country club!"

Tiffany's family had plenty of bread. If she was my daughter, he thought, I'd send her back to finish college and find an actual career. He'd met them twice, after shows both times. It was awkward to say the least. He felt like a lout meeting her father, a nice enough fellow his own age. Tiffany's mother, an older version of her daughter, had flirted aggressively.

"You should think about going back to school," Shane said, studying Tiffany.

"Where did that come from?" she demanded, immediately on the defensive.

"It's just that I worry about you wasting your life roaming around with a bunch of old men," he explained. "What kind of life is this for you?"

"You saw Autumn in New York, didn't you?" Tiffany said, teeing up for an argument. Every time Shane saw that little bitch Autumn he got weird like this. "She's back in school so now you think everyone should go back to school? I'm not your fucking daughter, Shane. I'm your…your girlfriend."

"And I want the best for you," Shane said, trying to smooth her ruffled feathers. His scene with Tiffany was unraveling. He didn't want her to go away mad, just go away. He should have worked up to the college thing, not blurted it out first thing. Poor strategy there. Was he that eager to be done with her?

There was a knock at the door and Derek entered.

"Good time?" he asked.

"Come in," Shane replied, glad for the diversion. "Go have your nap, Tiffany," he said, and she gave him a sharp look before leaving.

"How was your break, bro?" Shane inquired.

"Oh you know, I try to assimilate around the big gamey bird you Yanks make such a fuss over," Derek said. "I was kindly taken in by Eldridge's family."

Eldridge was one of the younger roadies, but by far the largest. That this young brother took up with the legendary Disgracefuls was a demographic anomaly.

"It was my first African-American Thanksgiving," Derek continued. "Man do they do it right: macaroni and cheese, collard greens, cornbread stuffing. My willy grew two inches."

"Now you have a massive four-incher," Shane ribbed him.

"How was your holiday, mate?" Derek asked. "PS: fuck you."

"It was nice. I stayed in New York and knocked around the city with Autumn, we went out to Montclair and had dinner with Suki's folks on

Thanksgiving," he said. "You'll never believe who I ran into in the city."

Derek raised his eyebrows, interested.

"The ballerina from Chicago," Shane continued, "in a bookstore in Chelsea. I was perusing the new Zeppelin bio and there she was, buying the same book."

"She still sexy?" Derek said lasciviously.

"Sexier," Shane said, his eyes glassy with memory. "I wanted to say, 'I didn't recognize you with your clothes on' but her daughter was with her."

"Good, right, keep it clean in front of the kids," Derek agreed. When a man tells another man what he "coulda shoulda woulda" said, it indicates that he's replayed the conversation in his head multiple times. Derek was on to Shane.

"Lisette, right?" Derek said.

"Yes. Lisette DuPre," Shane repeated, Frenching up the pronunciation.

"You got it bad?" Derek asked.

"Yeah, I guess I do," Shane admitted. "I asked her – them – to come with Autumn and me to a party at an art gallery, but they had tickets for the Met."

"Classy. What is her scene?" Derek asked. "Is she married?"

"I'm pretty sure she is," Shane replied. "She wears a ring, anyway."

"Too bad," Derek commiserated, pursing his lips and shaking his head sagely. "The good ones are always taken. That said, are you going to see her again?"

"I would love to see her again," Shane said. "But that doesn't seem likely. I really need to get my shit together."

"Meaning Tiffany?" Derek intuited. He'd felt the gathering clouds when he interrupted their conversation, and he'd known Shane a long time, long enough to sense when a breakup was imminent.

"How you planning to do it?" Derek asked.

"Don't know yet," Shane said. "But give it some thought, will you? You have a knack for these things. Help me plot it out."

"She won't be happy," Derek said.

"What else is new?" Shane said.

"Definitely time to pull the pin then," Derek advised, secretly delighting in the drama to come. He had never understood the relationship and had had quite enough of Tiffany Taylor for some time now. He would not miss her.

"Once the deed is done, how will you proceed with the dancer?" Derek wondered.

"Not sure," Shane said. But he definitely wanted to see where his infatuation might lead, he knew that much. He felt compelled to play it out.

"You could write her a letter," Derek suggested. "Girls love that."

"A letter?" Shane snorted. "In the age of technology?"

"You and she both grew up without all that bullshit," Derek said. "A letter is age-appropriate."

"A letter," Shane repeated, looking skeptical.

"Old school," Derek said simply.

Chapter 10

Christmas came and went. Lisette and Maria spent the long winter break hunched over college admission forms, drinking gallons of chai and logging hours on "virtual tours" of various universities. January brought the start of a new semester for both, along with pitifully short days and sub-zero temperatures. Lisette was living for the California trip to get away from the torture of winter.

"Chris, let's always have something to look forward to," Lisette had proposed in their last phone call. Just looking at her February calendar was therapy, even though her trip was just 24 hours. Carl would be in the middle of a two-week business trip and Maria would be on a school-sponsored senior tour of three colleges in Wisconsin, sparing Lisette any excuse making about why her trip was an old girls-only weekend.

Tipped off by a text from Chris, Lisette recorded a Late Show episode with Shane as a guest. She watched it furtively the next day when she had the house to herself.

"What the—," she said out loud to the TV as Shane came out and sat down in the interview chair. Shane was sporting a white streak in his hair! It looked good on him. She wondered if he'd had it when she saw him in New York and recalled he was wearing a hat. She did not take credit for influencing his hair color. A lot of Baby Boomers were doing the streak thing. Hers had started with a few white hairs at her widow's peak in her early 20s, about the same time her boobs came in, and both the streak and her chest had expanded over time. She never colored it – she thought it was unique and made her stand out in a group of identically dressed dancers.

The host was asking Shane about the latest Supreme Court nominee.

"It's a lifetime appointment, and the justices typically have a long shelf life," the host was saying. "Why is that, do you think?"

"Perhaps it's because they live such contemplative lives," Shane mused. "And I think it's safe to assume they have pretty great health insurance."

Wayne's World really had influenced the type of questions talk show hosts ask rock stars. It continued to be amusing to hear their unexpectedly articulate answers to social and political queries. Lisette suspected it was scripted, but maybe not.

Next the host asked Shane about his love life! Lisette turned up the volume.

"The tabloids say you are no longer romantically involved with your young assistant," the host prompted. "Is it true? Are you back on the market?"

"I'd rather not go into details," Shane replied. "We will continue to wish each other well. I'll just say that youth may have its advantages, but so do age and experience." He did that twinkle thing and she could hear a few squeals from the audience. After a commercial, the band played one of its classic ballads and everyone shook the host's hand as the credits rolled.

Weird was the only way to describe how it felt for Lisette to see and hear Shane, to see the evidence of his fame and reach, now that she felt a personal connection. She'd been written up on several occasions by the Chicago papers, and she did a stint as a dance and arts reviewer on public television. Friends gushed about it and a few strangers, too, but that was such small potatoes. When John Lennon said the Beatles were more popular than Jesus Christ, it was true.

In reality, Shane did not know her, he knew her name. They had shared 15 minutes of conversation. And with people that famous, who really does know them? How and where does the image intersect with the actual person? Where are the lines that separate the public face and the private individual? It all made her feel a little foolish, slightly delusional. She started to have second thoughts about going to the meet-and-greet. Nothing good would come from it, she thought.

Shane thought the show had gone well enough. He was ready for the Supreme Court question, he had a heads-up. The Tiffany question caught him off-guard, though. It had only been a couple of weeks since the official break-up, which had been sticky.

During one of their talks, Tiffany had actually appropriated a line from the movie "Something's Gotta Give," indicating her repackaged face and body and asking him, "What am I supposed to do with all this?" He'd seen the movie, too, and struggled to keep a straight face. She was ultimately packed off to California with a generous "severance package" and glowing references. He insisted that she keep the ring. He truly did wish her well, and hoped she'd go back to college and finish, she was a smart young woman. Word from L.A. was she was running with an up-and-coming band with a bright future. Maybe that's what she figured she was supposed to do with all that.

Chapter 11

Lisette dropped Misha at the Pet Palace before leaving for the airport. Her strategically-planned outfit – the raspberry suede boots, black leggings, a short-sleeved t-shirt under a long black sweater – was covered in dog hair. It was strategic in terms of leaving a very cold place for a warm destination as well as logistics of not having enough room in her carry-on roller bag for the boots. She was wearing a dark pink lipstick that matched the boots, thanks to a return visit to the Lancome counter. She soundly berated herself for it afterwards as evidence of further foolishness, a generational belief that a lipstick could change your life. Guilt was the cherry on top. She felt guilty for entertaining certain fantasies as if they were actual possibilities. All of this churned in her mind as she attacked the fur with a lint roller. Six sheets later, fur-free, she left for the airport.

Exiting the airport in L.A., she breathed in the warm, moist California air, perfumed with overtones of jet fuel fumes and car exhaust.

"You are an angel to pick me up," she greeted Chris as she pulled up at curbside.

"No feet touch the ground here," Chris said, leaning over the passenger seat to hug her friend. "Love the lipstick!"

Lisette was starving after the four-hour flight and the two stopped at a restaurant on the way to Chris's apartment. Lisette ordered chilaquiles verdes – she loved Mexican food, especially in California.

"Bloody Mary?" Chris asked.

"Not for me," Lisette said. "With the time change I'd be down for the count by showtime."

Chris ordered one for herself and an American breakfast.

Sitting outside in the sun, Lisette felt herself unwinding. She removed her sweater and wished she could peel off the boots. She had flip-flops in her suitcase. They'd feel great.

"So what would you like to do between now and the show?" Chris asked, running her fingers through her streaky blond curls. "Need to do any shopping?"

"I would just love to be outdoors and drink in the warmth," Lisette said. "This is my big escape from the Arctic tundra. Why don't we go to Long Beach or Venice and put our toes in the sand? It's been a while since I enjoyed your fly-infested Pacific kelp."

"You bet," Chris said. "You know, when I first moved out here I was so determined to spend time outdoors, live the California lifestyle, hiking, biking, all that business. But with work being so busy, I never got it together."

"But you also didn't get eaten by a mountain lion," Lisette joked. "The outdoor lifestyle here is rife with perils: rattlesnakes, bears, serial killers…" She shuddered. "Give me a Midwest possum over a bear any day."

"So, Lisette, are you ready to rock?" Chris asked. "Oh, and did you see Shane on 'The Late Show'?"

"I did. He was good," Lisette said. "Quite charming. Did you watch?"

"Yes, strictly for research," Chris said, navigating a huge skewer of pickled vegetables in her drink. "God, a person could lose an eye," she observed. "I thought they nailed 'Serene.' For a bunch of geezers, they still rock! It's that Malcolm Gladwell 10,000 times thing."

Both women were aware of the effervescence bubbling up inside of them at the prospect of the show that night. Lisette couldn't blame it on the green sauce, her breakfast was just arriving at their table.

"I'm excited," Lisette admitted. "But I'm having second thoughts about the meet-and-greet, Chris."

"What? Why?" Chris asked.

"I don't know, I feel guilty, I guess, and I don't want to embarrass myself," Lisette explained. "I mean what do I expect to come from it? I'm an old lady with a silly crush."

"First, stop overanalyzing," Chris ordered. "It's only rock 'n' roll, my friend. Second, why are you casting yourself as 'old' when you are younger than the band? WE are younger than the band. We are not old, just older. We have 40 years of history with their music. Can we leave it at that? Honor the history and the fun? It's just us writing a postscript decades later. Don't take it so seriously. I'm sure they don't."

"I guess you're right. It's just saying hello," Lisette said. "I'm such a spaz."

"Yes, you are," Chris confirmed, looking into her yellow backpack and rummaging around. She pulled out two laminated meet-and-greet passes on lanyards. She dangled them in front of Lisette.

"For your information, the meet-and-greet party, such that it is, is actually my gig," Chris said. "So for me, it's part of my scope of work to go to the event. There are many important details to check on at the venue – cold beer, deli trays, press access, photographers to take fan pictures. We are totally legit."

"Well that's comforting," Lisette said. "Promise we'll go home together."

"Of course," Chris smiled. "This is why I never got married. Too much goddamned angst."

They dug into their plates and munched thoughtfully.

"Why does Mexican food taste so much better out here?" Lisette wondered, shifting the conversation away from marriage. "These are insane."

"It's the soil, the weather, the proximity to the motherland. Muy autentico," Chris said. "Lisette, you are a treasure. You care so deeply about things. You are so relentlessly responsible. Just have fun, sweetie. Just have a little fun."

And that is what they did for the rest of the day. Lisette swapped the boots for flip-flops in the car and the two friends walked the Southern California beach, laughing and blabbing. Lisette kicked off her shoes and let a few cold waves roll over her bare feet just for the joy of it. Was there any place more nurturing to the human soul than a beach? As they wandered, many tales were told that started with the words "remember when." Other pieces of conversation started with "what if?" What if Lisette lived in L.A.? What if Maria went to UCLA? What if the bass player remembered Chris and had been pining for her all these years?

One thing they did not discuss was cancer.

When Chris was diagnosed with breast cancer three years before. Lisette made it her personal mission to be the point person in Chris's support system, traveling multiple times to L.A. to nurse Chris through the chemo, the worst months of that awful year. As sick as the treatment made Chris, despite their tears and fears, the two friends still managed to laugh at each other's grim jokes.

"I can finally wear a cat suit," the formerly buxom Chris had proclaimed after losing 15 pounds due to chronic nausea and stress. Lisette went out and bought them matching black lycra cat suits. They threatened to wear them out on the town, but lounged around in them at home instead. Thanks to Lisette's home cooking and new anti-nausea drugs, Chris turned a corner soon after. Lisette went home for good when Chris was well enough to handle the radiation treatments on her own. After a lumpectomy, chemo, and radiation, she was given a clean bill of health.

Lisette had brought Maria along on two trips. She thought it was important for a typically self-absorbed 14-year-old to understand what it meant to be a true girlfriend, and not shield her from witnessing Chris in illness. Shit happens, and serving people here on earth was Lisette's religion. It had been important to model that for Maria. Lisette let other people speculate about god and the afterlife.

Part of the wisdom Chris had taken from her life-changing cancer experience was a reaffirmation to have big fun, love life, and pursue possibilities. Those were the very things on Lisette's mind now, dangerous ideas to her. She didn't want Chris to tip her delicate balance, to make her reckless based on the notion that we never know how many chapters we have left. So, other than Lisette asking "How's your health?" and Chris assuring her that everything was still fine, the word "cancer" was never spoken.

Chapter 12

Lisette felt tired from spending the morning in the air and the afternoon out of doors. The sun had left her with a slight glow. Feeling its warmth on her face and the wind in her hair had been worth the trip. Late in the afternoon, Chris reminded Lisette that the meet-and-greet was before the show, so they should be at the venue early. It would be bad form on many levels to tell her cancer survivor friend/hostess/partner in crime that she could use a nap, so she revived herself with a shower and iced coffee.

"Those boots are staying in Cali," Chris proclaimed. "I'm stealing them while you sleep and hiding them in a creepy place with lots of spiders."

"And sending me back to Chicago in flip-flops?" Lisette asked.

"There's always one asshole in flip-flops and shorts on every flight to a cold destination," Chris said. "You can be that asshole for once."

"You don't think they're 'out of season' for L.A.?" Lisette wondered, pointing one booted toe forward in *tendu* front.

"No, they give you an international flair," Chris assured her. "It's already cooling off and it will get chilly as soon as the sun sets."

Lisette picked a few embedded Misha hairs off her sweater before putting it back on. She refreshed her minimalist makeup and was ready to go.

"Ta da!" Chris announced, bouncing into the living room. She was wearing a vintage Disgracefuls t-shirt and black jeans, capped by a very soft, and very expensive, leather bomber jacket.

"It can't be – is that your original t-shirt?" Lisette asked.

"The one and only," Chris replied. "I'm so glad I never cut it up during our Flash Dance phase or gave it away. I was afraid it might disintegrate in my fingers when I took it out of my trunk of old goodies. But it survived disinterment and a hand washing!"

"What a classic, I wonder what ever happened to mine," Lisette said, admiring the now-ashy black tee with the Disgracefuls' logo in faded red. She had a vague memory of Maria, at 2 or 3, bouncing around the house in hers, the shirt floor-length on the toddler. Chris's was tight, hugging her in all the right places. She looked authentically rock-a-licious, while Lisette looked sophisticated. Her dark hair and white streak were fashion statement enough. She had learned not to overdo with accessories and colors, and she generally hated anything with a logo. Her style was more streamlined. She wore Tahitian pearls the size of small marbles in her ears.

"Ooh la la," Chris commented upon seeing them. "Nice."

And with that they set off into the evening and whatever adventures it held in store.

The outdoor concert venue was clean and spacious, with a row of palm trees at the back edge of the lawn. Chris's laminates were like kryptonite. She flashed hers at every turn and security agents practically dropped and rolled on their backs. They quickly reached a small parking lot behind the stage where huge equipment trucks and limos were already parked. Lisette's heart beat faster at the sight of the limos.

"They're here," she said, a bit breathless.

"Keep it together, chica," Chris advised, banging on a metal door with her closed fist until it opened. They proceeded through the door into the inevitable cinderblock hallway filled with flight cases, turning several corners before emerging into a bright outdoor patio where a hundred or so raucous fans milled about like cattle in a stockyard.

Chris was wearing sunglasses as the long rays of late afternoon cut across the space.

"I don't see them," Lisette said into her ear. Music was blasting from speakers mounted to the rafters.

"They have to make an entrance, darling," Chris replied. "It will be soon, the beer's getting low. This is the intentional stoking of anticipation. It's all very strategic."

Chris went off to assess the party provisions and sent a young guy from her agency to a truck in the parking lot for several more cases of beer and water and some bottles of wine she had reserved for her personal use. The first notes of the warm-up band interrupted the recorded music that had been playing when they arrived.

"Wait for it," Chris said, rejoining Lisette with two clear plastic cups of chilled white wine. Handing one to Lisette, she explained, "Any second now, the Disgracefuls will walk through that black door right there. All of this is timed out – when the warm-up band starts playing, the headliners arrive at the meet-and-greet. They will stay until the first band finishes. So be sure to get your picture taken early if you want one! We will be graced by their presence for about 45 minutes. And here they are…"

Chris's voice was swallowed by a huge cheer from the corral of fans, hangers-on, winners of radio contests, disc jockeys, rock writers, record company people, assorted friends and family members of the band. "Whoo hoo!" a large biker guy behind Lisette yodled into her ear, followed by an ear-splitting whistle.

"Take these," Chris said, handing Lisette two soft blue Hear-Os. "They're the best," she said, rolling them into tiny balls and inserting them into her ears. Lisette did the same.

The crowd surged forward, Chris and Lisette hung back.

"Let him see you first," Chris said. "And no matter what happens, re-member, he's working. This is his job."

Lisette was surprised that she was able to hear Chris clearly through the protective earplugs, though she was speaking in a normal voice. She was surprised her wine glass was nearly empty. Chris topped off both their drinks and they both said "clink" as they touched their plastic cups.

Five security guards moved the five band members to different areas of the corral. Chris explained the protocol: It was smarter to separate them and allow fans to circulate among them than to from one long receiving line for the whole group. Fans tend to linger too long and people at the end of the line get stiffed and leave disappointed and pissed off.

As the crowd parted, she saw Shane at the same instant he saw her. His face expressed 1) surprise, 2) disbelief, 3) confusion – then split into a wide smile. He crossed the short distance between them in a few strides, throwing his arms wide a step from her and enveloping her in a quick hug.

"Lisette – what a surprise! Again!" he said, grabbing her hands and tak-ing a step back to admire her head to toe. "Nice boots! You're the towering inferno," he said.

Chris smiled as she observed the exchange, thinking that their dark hair and white streaks, head to head, reminded her of a Rorschach image. "Who are your influences?" she asked herself in an Irish accent, quoting one of her favorite band movies, "The Commitments."

"This is my friend, Chris," Lisette said. "She's the party planner."

Chris and Shane shook hands awkwardly.

"Are you responsible for this?" he asked Chris.

"For the party or for bringing Lisette?" she asked.

"Um, both, either," he said.

"Both," Chris confirmed, to which Shane responded by sweeping in low with another quick hug, whispering "Thank you" in Chris's ear.

The security man and a publicist for the band's record company interrupted.

"Shane, we need you over here," the publicist said, handing him a large black Sharpie marker.

"Right, of course," he said. "Ladies, duty calls. But I shall return."

He walked back into the throng, smiling over his shoulder at the two, and confronted a winding line of fans with album covers, photos, and t-shirts to be signed. He called back to Chris: "Nice shirt, by the way."

Chris turned to Lisette.

"Wow," she said, then repeated, stupidly, "wow."

"I'm not sure what I expected, but it wasn't this," she said.

Before Lisette could respond, a jolly voice nearby called "Lisette!"

It was Derek.

"Jesus, Lisette, you know more people here than I do," Chris spurted.

"What on earth are you doing here?" asked the Englishman. "Did you get the letter?"

"Letter?" Lisette asked.

"Oh nothing, nothing at all, never mind," he said lightly, then asked, "And who is this, then?"

Lisette introduced Derek to Chris, and Derek made a huge fuss over her original Disgracefuls t-shirt.

"Even I don't have one of these," he said, pretending to inspect the red logo but really checking out Chris's breasts. He asked Chris rapid-fire questions about their friendship, their association with the band, and other personal details, backpedaling at full throttle to cover his "spoiler" about the letter, which until then had remained top secret between him and Shane.

"So how have you been? How's Maria?" Derek asked Lisette. "Shane told me he ran into the two of you in New York."

"Yes, at Thanksgiving," Lisette said. "It was so random. I couldn't believe he remembered us!"

"You made quite an impression," Derek said, offering up his own version of a twinkle, which came off as a possible wincing gas pain.

"I can't imagine why," Lisette said.

"Look at these people," Derek said, his hand sweeping backward to indicate the fans now in lines like ants collecting autographs and taking selfies. Their age range was broad, from weathered gray-bearded bikers to nubile young women in bustiers. There was quite a bit of leather, quite a lot of tits. Shane, in fact, was signing a woman's left breast at that very moment. "You sort of stand out in this crowd, Lisette."

Chris listened with an amused smile on her face. Lisette really didn't get it. She didn't understand her impact. She'd been in mommy mode for 17 years. Her life had taken that sudden turn when she was 40, and she had devoted herself to the journey ever since. Maria was dearly beloved. Chris thought Lisette's rediscovery of the joy of rock 'n' roll was some sort of midlife crisis that had everything to do with Maria leaving the nest. Mother and daughter had the exciting concert experience together. Maybe for Lisette the Disgracefuls were a lifeline of sorts that tethered her to Maria as well as her own past, helping her reclaim her long-back-burnered self.

Meanwhile, Lisette thought of herself as a suburban matron who took impeccable care of her teeth, plucked her chin hairs, and moisturized religiously to keep her wrinkles at bay. She was rarely flashy, and a general failure at acknowledging her own assets. The ballerina thing alone was a huge accomplishment. Chris had watched her perform many times in complete awe. Of all the little girls and boys who study it, only a very few possess the talent, discipline, and dedication to ever dance professionally. Of the scores of dancers who applied for the conservatory teaching position, Lisette had prevailed.

Chris knew her friend's dance floor moves as well. She and Lisette had practiced together countless hours to get them just right. Chris worried that over the years Lisette had become boxed more and more into the strict parameters of ballet to the point of becoming rigid. It was a metaphor for her life, keeping within the positions and movements with strict conformity, just as marriage and motherhood had kept her playing by the rules, doing all the right things. Of all the things Chris had been looking forward to this night, dancing with Lisette to the Disgracefuls again – on their own terms

– was at the top of the list. It was the surest way to resurrect the original Lisette.

Maybe Lisette's cluelessness was the key to her charm, Chris thought. She was humble. In an age of reality TV and social media full of people screaming "look at me!" that was a rare quality. Especially so backstage, where fans feasted on the fame of their idols to nourish their own self worth.

The publicist was making the rounds, letting the band members know "10 minutes" so they could speed up the process to accommodate the hungry horde. Chris used her 10 minutes to track down the bass player and see how he'd held up over the decades.

"Not only did he not remember me, he wanted to show me pictures of his fucking grandchildren!" Chris reported back, miffed. She continued her armchair psychology, analyzing out loud this time.

"Musicians are damaged goods. They start young, before their brains are fully developed, then they pickle themselves with drugs and alcohol, and all their motivation becomes extrinsic. They need everything they do to have someone watching them and cheering. They change a light bulb and expect a standing ovation. It's tragic, actually."

Derek listened to her tirade wide-eyed. It was the opposite of the backstage ass-kissing he was used to hearing.

"Everything you say is true," he agreed. "I hope you enjoy the show just the same."

"Sorry, didn't mean to go off like that," Chris said.

"I rather appreciated your analysis," Derek said. "It was spot-on."

Shane reappeared at Lisette's side.

"Gotta go, will I see you after?" he asked. "Please say yes."

"Yes," Chris answered for them, flickering her "All Area Access" laminate.

"We can talk," he said, bouncing off. "Enjoy the show!"

The two women watched the band exit through the black metal door, fans still trailing them, asking for "just one more" selfie or autograph. Chris had gotten over her pique and given in to giddiness from the excitement and the wine. They finished the bottle before heading to their seats.

"Oh, I almost forgot," Chris said, reaching into an inside pocket of her bomber jacket and pulling out a crumpled joint. "I brought weed!"

"Can you believe we lived long enough to see it legalized?" Lisette remarked.

"Legal weed and a brother in the White House," Chris added. "We have much to be grateful for."

"Yes, we do," Lisette agreed, grabbing her friend in a warm embrace and rocking her back and forth.

Their seats were excellent, close enough to see everything on stage, far enough back to appreciate the mix. Lisette was grateful again for the earplugs. One of Chris's plugs had worked its way out and was protruding from her ear, which struck Lisette as hysterically funny. Or maybe it was the Cali Kush, which smelled like skunk and delivered a pleasant, floaty high in one hit. Lisette thought she needed to visit a dispensary and smuggle some back to Chicago.

The show started the same as before, with the Disgracefuls roaring through three hard-charging songs, Shane racing back and forth, covering every foot of the stage, before launching into a ballad that soared at the end with impossible bombast. The audience was on its collective feet, one with the band. Lisette grooved a while looking at faces in the crowd. There were plenty of people her age, she realized, and they were so into it! She noticed there was no cheering section at the edge of the stage this time, just empty space where she and Maria had stood four months before. No "You Shook Me" this time, either.

About 10 songs in, Chris nudged Lisette. "Let's walk around," she said. They walked the permimeter of the seating area, checking out the sound and the stage from various vantage points, ultimately reaching the lawn. They heard the first chords of one of their all-time favorites, Downward Dog, joined by drums and a heavy bass line.

"Let's dance!" Chris shouted.

Moving onto the lawn, Lisette noticed a full moon high in the pinkish brown auburn L.A. night sky. Under its glow, the two fell into their old dance steps on the grass. They wheeled like crazed Druids as the music pulsated in their chests. They were alive! They were joyful! They were free! They were together! They were transported back in time in the same moment that they were making a new memory. Every time they thought they'd heard every last one of their favorite songs, another would begin.

"That's enough for me," a panting Chris finally announced. They returned to their seats for the end of the set and two encores, a blaze of sparks and cannons shooting confetti that made them howl with both laughter and appreciation for the spectacle.

They stayed in their seats to recover while the amphitheater emptied, eventually rousing themselves and making their way backstage from the side. Roadies were already breaking down equipment, kicking up swirls of spent confetti as they moved quickly, intent on their work.

"We're looking for Shane. He wanted to see us," Chris told a security guard. He examined her pass and told her, "This way." They followed him through a narrow corridor crowded with people standing around talking. Lisette spotted the bass player. He was showing a guy something on his phone – probably the grandchildren pictures, Lisette suspected.

Finally the security man knocked on a door. It opened into a room with low-slung couches and tables set with fruit, savory snacks, chocolate, and ice buckets filled with drinks of all sorts. Chris gave the table a once-over and gave Lisette a thumbs-up. She helped herself to a bar of dark chocolate with sea salt and dropped it into her backpack.

"Where is he?" Lisette wondered. She did not see Shane. He had definitely asked them back – she hadn't hallucinated. He had said, "We'll talk."

At last she saw him in a dark corner, the back of his head anyway, the cowry shells confirming his identity. His sweaty shirt was stuck to his torso. He was engaged in an intense conversation with a young woman. He was looking deeply into her eyes, with his hands on her shoulders. He caught her in a long, intimate hug, then held her back to kiss her face before enveloping her in his arms once again.

"Chris, I think we should go," Lisette said, indicating the action in the corner with her head.

"Ooh," Chris responded, taking in the corner scene and drawing a hasty conclusion. "Okay, roger that, we are done here."

They were back in the corridor when they heard Derek's voice behind them.

"Leaving so soon?" he asked.

"Yeah, early flight back to Chicago tomorrow," Lisette lied. "Nice to see you again, Derek. Thanks again for everything, taking care of us in Chicago and all."

"Chris, do you have a business card?" he asked. "I have several large parties coming up that may require your talents."

Chris fished in her backpack and extracted a fancy gold card case, handing one business card to Derek. He took it with a flourish and bowed to Chris. As manager, Derek was not in the spotlight and had no pre-determined image to uphold. He preferred women his own age and never went hunting among "the kids" who hung around the band, dazzled by celebrity and always ready and willing for a meaningless romp. A professional woman with a gold business card case was his cup of tea.

"I'll call you," he said to their backs as they quickly made their way down the hallway and out the door to Chris's car. Chris spoke first.

"It's only rock 'n' roll, Lisette," she said, starting the engine. "All things considered, I still like it."

"Me, too," Lisette said, filled with relief that she had played out her little rock 'n' roll fantasy and could now get back to normal. "What a great show, what a great night. It was best that it ended before things got weird. I really don't know what I expected."

"It does suck, though, the young girls getting all the attention when the full-grown women have so much more to offer," Chris said. "I can't remember the last time a construction worker said something lewd to me. I never thought I'd miss that."

"Invisibility cloak," Lisette said, explaining simply "Harry Potter" when Chris looked at her curiously.

Inside, Derek sidled up to Shane and the young woman, still head to head in the corner.

"Hello, Priya," Derek greeted her. "How are you, sweetness?"

"Can I tell him?" Shane asked his oldest daughter. She nodded.

"Derek, Priya's preggers!" Shane announced, beaming. "I'm going to be a granddad!"

Chapter 13

Chris and Lisette were in a fugue state the next morning from the wine, the weed, and the emotion of the night before. It hadn't helped that Chris had remembered she had been gifted with an electric "pen" with a cartridge of hash oil. They'd stayed up late, first figuring out how to use the device by watching several YouTube videos, then practicing with the new THC delivery method until they were zombies.

"Who could have imagined this high-tech weed thing?" Lisette dreamily wondered aloud. They had a rambling conversation about rock 'n' roll movies and their female roles, good and bad. While they loved The Banger Sisters, their favorite fictional woman in rock was hands-down Joann Carlino from "Eddie and the Cruisers."

"She was in the band, she had a power position: 'Why not ask her, she has a brain?'" Chris quoted from the movie script. "She played a fine tambourine."

"And when Eddie storms out, she sings lead on 'Tender Years'," Lisette added.

"When we were the Fab Two, we had the power position," Chris noted. "It's way cooler than being 'with the band'."

"If I ever get a dog I'm naming her Joann Carlino," were Chris's last mumbled words as she drifted off to sleep.

"She's so cool," Lisette murmured, falling into blackness.

The next noon, back at the airport curbside, the short visit felt like time travel – 40 years capsulized in 24 hours. Lisette was looking forward to a nap on the plane. She reminded herself to buy a neck pillow in the airport.

"I'll call you later," Lisette said, making it easier to leave.

Chris watched her friend disappear behind the glass doors. She was looking over her shoulder before pulling away from the curb when she braked sharply. A man with a "Hertz" folder sticking out of his breast pocket was in her sightline, walking briskly toward the rental car lot.

"Carl?" she wondered out loud.

Before Chris became a party planner, she had been a newspaper reporter. A damned good one. Her specialty was crime reporting – she had even solved a few cases ahead of the investigating detectives. When technology imploded the newspaper business, and wave after wave of layoffs sucked the joy, irreverence, and lifeblood out of newsrooms, it got pretty goddamned depressing to wait for the closed-door meeting that meant her number had come up. She would be a fool not to have a Plan B. She thought about becoming a private detective. More than thought about it, she actually acquired her PI license and a concealed carry permit for a .38 Special. She also started working weekends with a friend who was a party planner and learned that business. She had never been afraid of change, merely preferred it on her own terms. Too many of her journalist friends had been left twisting in the wind, ranting on Facebook, or flacking for the agencies they used to cover. Grim times for the watchdogs of democracy.

Chris flashed back months before when she had thought she spotted Carl at LAX. This time she was sure it was him, though according to Lisette he was on a two-week business trip somewhere in South America.

Chris's suspicious mind went into overdrive. She felt the old excitement of the chase and started plotting her strategy as she entertained various scenarios: Carl had a secret second family. He was gone so much it was possible. That shit was more common than people thought. Or maybe he wasn't really a "pharmaceutical rep" – maybe he dealt in "pharmaceuticals" of the illicit variety and was involved with a drug cartel. She would follow Carl, she decided. She'd tail his ass.

Her heart was pounding as she circled around to the rental car lot, passing the signs for Enterprise, National, and Avis, slowing to a crawl as she scoped out the action in the Hertz lot. She quickly determined the flow of traffic, pulled ahead to the exit lane and waited in a spot that gave her a clear view of traffic going out. It was dark in the parking structure but Chris put on her sunglasses. She leaned into her back seat and retrieved a baseball cap. She tucked her blond curls up under the hat and waited.

In a few minutes, a white Lexus with Carl behind the wheel cautiously inched out of the lot, picking up speed at the exit ramp. Chris pulled out and followed. The Lexus headed away from the airport tangle toward the 405. Chris was glad she had a full tank of gas and an empty bladder. One could drive all freaking day on the 405.

She kept a distance of a good 10 car lengths, and switched to a lane right of the Lexus whenever possible to stay out of Carl's rear- and side-view mirrors. They were headed south, passing signs for the big beach towns: Manhattan, Hermosa, Redondo, Long Beach. On a Sunday afternoon, traffic wasn't too thick. They crossed into Orange County. After a while, the Lexus signaled to exit at Mission Viejo. Chris allowed a truck to pull in front of her, dropping back to make sure the Lexus took the exit.

This is where it gets tricky, Chris reminded herself. It's much easier to tail someone on the highway than suburbia. Seeing the Lexus turn left into a subdivision of thousands of near-identical white houses with terra cotta tile roofs, she slowed to deliberately catch the red light. She watched the Lexus make a right turn at the first side street. She had memorized the license plate. No good to come all this way, then be fooled by a different white Lexus.

Chris took the left arrow into the subdivision, then the first right, scouring the road ahead. No Lexus. She continued on, frustrated by the cul-de-sacs that splayed out from both sides of the street. She proceeded slowly, scanning driveways right and left, until she spotted it —there was the Lexus in the driveway of a house on a cul-de-sac called Briar Circle. Chris used her cell phone camera to enlarge the image and confirm the license plate. She snapped a few pictures of the car, the house number, and the street sign. She had an ex-boyfriend who was an FBI agent, but knew she could do her own title search. With only the address, she could find out who lived there, and from that establish a connection to Carl. Presuming the man was Carl. If she could confirm that, only if she could confirm that, would she tell Lisette. If she couldn't confirm it was Carl, she'd chalk up her detecting as practice for her dormant PI skills, and Lisette would never hear about it. Chris staked out the house for an hour. No one came or went. She finally left and headed back to L.A.

Back at her apartment, she checked her email and saw the photographer had sent files from the meet-and-greet. She quickly breezed through them, stopping to enlarge an image of Lisette and Shane from the night before.

Chris was in the background, grinning at the two of them standing face to face, their arms out, hands joined as if they were dancing a minuet. The Rorschach moment, she realized. She downloaded the jpg and saved it, but did not share it.

Chapter 14

When she deplaned in Chicago, Lisette was grateful that Chris hadn't made good on her threat to steal her boots. The "Hawk" was whipping off the lake and the landing was like a thrill ride at Great America. Just 24 hours earlier she had her toes in the surf, she mused, smiling at the memory.

She felt the creeping melancholia of Sunday night and fought it back by remembering dancing on the lawn with Chris the night before. What a blast it had been! She also felt like she had been let off a great big hook, sharp and shiny and dangerous. It had been a smackdown of sorts for the two old girls to feel shunned at the end. But she was relieved that an opportunity had not presented itself for her to be lured into anything scandalous with Shane Stewart. What a poser, she thought. Acting all thrilled to see her when he had a booty call lined up. What if something had happened? Would she be returning home on a flight of shame? She giggled at the thought of her requesting an airport wheelchair after a sleepless night of wild illicit sex.

Giggling is good, she told herself. She congratulated herself for making a healthy transition from fantastic possibilities to real-life parameters. Married women her age do not run off with rock stars. It simply did not happen. Still, the meet-and-greet was fun and exciting, not her usual Saturday night, that's for sure! She's glad Chris insisted they go. She'd call her friend for additional post-show analysis when she got home, after checking in with Maria on her college trip. Misha would have to spend one more night at the Pet Palace. It was past pick-up time. See, she thought to herself, you are re-entering reality. She congratulated herself once again on her stellar mental health.

Shane had been so caught up in Priya's baby news that Lisette had slipped his mind completely until he saw Derek. After he sent Priya off to get her important gestational sleep, he learned from Derek that the women had come round, but had quickly left.

"Why didn't you ask them to stay?" he demanded, angry.

"I tried, mate," Derek said. "The ballerina said she had an early flight and thanks for everything."

Shane quickly got a grip. Priya's news had trumped his own ulterior motives. His oldest daughter, product of his early first marriage to his high school sweetheart, and her husband had been hoping for a baby for two years with a few false alarms along the way. Finally it was a go. She was past her first trimester and everything looked fine. In six months, there would be a baby! It's a lot to wrap one's mind around, when children become parents. He'd wept with joy – and terror.

"Sorry, man," he told Derek.

"I'm sorry, too, mate," Derek said. "You see, I mentioned the letter to her at the meet-and-greet. So you have two things to be pissed about."

Shane drew a long breath. "What did you say, exactly?" he asked.

"I said something like 'Did you get the letter?' I was just so surprised to see her. I thought she had come because of it. Then she said 'What letter?' and I said 'Never mind' or something, then changed the subject and you all showed up and events sort of pre-empted that line of questioning. If it's any consolation, she seemed genuinely happy to see you. And you her. So that's where we stand."

"Derek you are a regular Friar Laurence with your bungling of my romantic life," Shane lamented. He decided to drown his sorrows in the stick-like arms of a supermodel who had been sipping champagne and staring at him for quite a while. He changed his shirt and approached her with his signature twinkle on high beam.

"Tell me something dirty in Ukrainian, Svetlana," he said.

"Vy krasyvi," she said with a smile. "Skil'ky vam rokiv?"

"Ooh," he said, taking her chicken bone of a wrist and lifting her hand to his lips. He didn't know or even care what she said, it sounded smokin' hot. It was something Svetlana herself had heard plenty in her brief lifetime: "You're beautiful, how old are you?"

Chapter 15

Carl carefully raised the front wheels of the wheelchair and gently guided the rear wheels down the front step of 465 Briar Circle. The two gray-haired people – the man pushing and the woman sitting – were smiling and chatting. Edie couldn't walk very far because of the MS, so for their afternoon rambling they took the chair.

It was heaven to be out in the sunshine and on the move, even if the movement for her was rolling. These little jaunts helped her stay in touch with her neighbors and the outside world. Her world had become somewhat narrow, but she thanked god every day that if she had to come down with a disease, at least it was one for which new treatments and breakthroughs were happening all the time. She was nearly 70, after all, and had been healthy until this.

Since her diagnosis, Carl had been an absolute angel. For an ex-husband to assume the role of caregiver was rare indeed, Edie realized. Who would have thought that a devastating diagnosis would lead to reconciliation? She was a lucky woman. She smiled at the memory of their tender lovemaking the night before. Had it been so good because they were in love or because they were technically committing adultery? Did adultery even count if it was someone you'd known for 50 years, been married to for nearly 20 of those years, raised two children together? She fucking deserved it after the devastation of the divorce.

They proceeded through the neighborhood, across a busy street, and continued on about a mile to their favorite sushi restaurant, Tank, nestled in an unassuming strip mall. They were regulars. The owner greeted them warmly and walked ahead, removing a chair from a table by the window to make room for the wheelchair.

After the waiter brought them menus and tea, Edie sat back in her chair. She was still a beauty, she observed, admiring her reflection in the window. The wheelchair was not visible in the reflection. They looked like any other couple out for a late lunch. She wanted to talk about something Carl was good at avoiding: the future.

"So what are you thinking about retirement?" she asked.

"Well, I had hoped the bonus would get me closer to the million-dollar mark, but my accountant says I should work at least two more years, with Maria's college and all," Carl said, rubbing his unshaven cheek thoughtfully.

"That has to be your first concern," Edie agreed. "Maria deserves everything that our kids got, and that includes college. But what about you? How long can you live this secret double life? When will you tell Lisette and Maria? About us?"

"I'd like to hold off until Maria is settled in at school," Carl said. "Maybe it won't be so hard on her that way. She'll be all caught up in her own life, more independent. I sure didn't expect to be actively parenting at this age."

Edie bit her tongue. She wanted to retort, "Then you shouldn't have married a younger woman to cure your mid-life crisis because the trophy wife always wants a baby."

Instead she agreed. "So true, but a lot of our generation is in the same boat. And not even talking about teenagers or college students, so many people have children moving back home to live in their old bedrooms or their parents' basements. Think of the Whitmans, with their kids, and their kids' spouses and children back home with them. Their house is insane! This economy sucks. I feel so bad for these young people who will never have pensions, maybe not even Social Security. They consider themselves lucky to find full-time employment with benefits and not have to work multiple jobs. We were so lucky to be able to move out and never go back."

She realized Carl hadn't answered her questions. She tried another tack.

"What's the deal with the 'one million dollars' being the magic number for retirement anyway?" she asked. "Seems like everyone over 50 has that number in their heads. They talk about it all the time. It's unseemly."

Carl was studying the menu, even though he always ordered the same thing.

"It's a nice round number," he said, "enough to live comfortably for our longer lifespans."

Edie was silent. She did not like to think about lifespans. The waiter returned and they ordered.

"Things are good here, Carl," Edie said. "It's taken two years, but the children – our children and our grandchildren – have gotten to know you again. You've made up a lot of lost time with them. And we are in love again, something neither of us saw coming. Why should we keep living on the sly like this? It's not fair to anyone."

Carl had wrestled with the situation for months and months. Nearly two years ago, when his son called him about Edie's diagnosis, and told him that she might lose the house, he had flown out to handle the situation. At first, he thought he would simply settle with the bank and help Edie with expenses. But one visit became five, then 10, tacked on to his frequent business trips without ever informing Lisette, in fact misleading her with daily texts from the road. And then one day he realized that the person he missed most when he traveled was Edie.

Chapter 16

Maria was definitely not going to college in Wisconsin.
"I should have gone with you this weekend and visited UCLA," she announced. "Wisconsin is like a smaller, uninteresting Chicago, with extra cheese. Friday night we went to a fish fry for cultural enrichment."

"We can go to L.A. again," Lisette replied. "That's easy enough. And there's still Ann Arbor, don't forget, which is arty and interesting and not like Chicago at all. Everyone says 'hi' on the street. It's a lot easier – and cheaper – to go to a school within driving distance. Remember, your brain is not fully developed yet. You may be several years into college before you even know what you want to major in, what your passions truly are."

"Then why do they always want you to declare a major?" Maria asked. "We are brain-deficient teenagers. We have no clue!"

"One of the many mysteries of higher education, my dear," Lisette replied. Secretly, nothing would please Lisette more than to have Maria choose University of Michigan, a three-hour drive from the cottage on the other side of the state. "Let's make time tonight to book those last tours so we're on track with final decision-making."

"Let's go soon – I miss Aunt Chris," Maria said. "How is she doing?"

"She is as fantastic as ever," Lisette said. "We had a blast-o-rama. Can you believe I had my feet in the Pacific Ocean yesterday?"

"No," Maria said, looking dreamily at the snow-covered landscape outside their windows.

"The snow at night is like looking at a negative," Lisette mused out loud, following Maria's gaze.

"What's a negative?" Maria asked. Lisette tried to explain.

"I can't say I would miss winter," Maria continued. "But I wouldn't be able to wear my New York boots in Los Angeles."

"You never know," Lisette said, smiling mysteriously.

"What?" Maria asked.

"Nothing," Lisette said, "just that it was chilly enough last night for me to wear boots."

"That was an all-time best purchase, our boots in New York," Maria decided. "And that Led Zeppelin book –I've been reading it, Mom. The pictures are amazing. I found Shane Stewart in it!"

"Really?" asked Lisette, and to show she didn't care one bit about Shane Stewart she circled back to Maria's question about negatives with a mini-dissertation about the photos in the book being from pre-digital technology, requiring film, dark rooms, chemical solutions and other boring details.

Lisette was about to launch into a Rock Photos 101 lesson about Linda McCartney when Maria popped up from the table, retrieved the book from the living room and returned with it open to one of the picture pages.

"See? Here," she said, laying the open book on the kitchen table.

There, in black and white, was Shane, impossibly young, breathtakingly beautiful, sitting with an acoustic guitar across his lap and a spiral notebook beside him, practicing what would become his signature smile/eye twinkle. He must have cut quite a swath, Lisette imagined, correctly.

"What a babe," Maria said with awe. "I mean seriously, Mom. It's weird that we kind of know him, and we were getting the same book, and then he turns up IN the book!"

"Don't' get carried away with celebrity," Lisette cautioned. "We met him, but we don't know him."

"We met him twice," Maria corrected her. "And he remembered our names. I follow him on Instagram."

Lisette could not correct the math without confessing that for her, the tally was three times. She felt guilty as hell.

She tried calling Chris but got her voicemail.

"I am safely back on the prairie," she reported, "despite the vomit comet landing we endured. It was so wonderful to see you, my friend. Let's never stop having illicit adventures, even when we are withered crones with dowager's humps on weekend passes from the nursing home."

Maria, listening in, cracked a smile.

Chris didn't answer because she was deep in a title search for 465 Briar Circle and was afraid Lisette would detect deception in her voice and pry out of her what she was holding back, which was pretty major. The house had been briefly on the market about two years ago, she noted, then the listing was withdrawn. The owner was Edith Anderson, same last name as Carl. Did he have a sister? Then it hit her: Edie. Carl was visiting his ex-wife! Christ, she thought as she let the call go to voicemail, how am I going to spring this on Lisette?

Chris listened to Lisette's message, waited an hour until it was too late to phone, and texted her back: Glad you are home safe, sound, withered. Thank you for a crone-i-licious adventure! I hump you!

Chris started a list:

What was C doing at house of ex-wife?

Did L know about it but not mention it for some reason? Why?

Did I see C twice at LAX/multiple visits to E?

Should L confront C? Timing!

What else did she need to know?

C's travel itinerary

Follow the money!

Making a list had always helped Chris organize her thoughts and figure out next steps. This was no exception. Her phone rang, startling her.

"Hello, Chris?" said the caller, who she recognized instantly as Derek from his gruff voice and English accent. "Derek Morgan here, from the Disgracefuls."

"Hello, Derek," Chris responded automatically, untangling her mind from the quandary she'd been contemplating.

"Lovely to see you the other night. A shame you couldn't stay," he said. "Listen, I have a party coming up and I could use your help. It's not for a couple of months, but what do you say we get together and run through some ideas? What do you think?"

"I think you're full of shit," Chris answered. "I think you want to go out with me but you're too chicken to ask, so you are making up a convoluted party-planning scenario."

Derek burst into laughter.

"Was it that obvious?" he asked. She could hear his grin over the phone.

"It was that obvious when you inspected my t-shirt like you were the fucking USDA," she said.

"What is that, like TSA?" he asked.

"Something like that," Chris said, "but usually involving meat."

"Sorry about that," Derek said, sounding contrite. "Couldn't help my-self. Didn't mean to be crude."

"Look, Derek, I don't date. I'm 57 years old and it just seems silly."

"Why?" he protested.

"You rock guys think a date is waiting around backstage after a show," Chris explained. "Been there, done that."

"Chris, I heard what you said the other night," Derek said, suddenly earnest. "It resonated with me. I deal with these personalities, the behaviors, every bloody day. People in this business tend to be complete wankers. I was thinking we could do something normal like people our age do, something not attached to the scene. Like go out to dinner, or go to the cinema or something normal like that."

"Don't you travel constantly?" Chris pointed out.

"Well, pretty much," he admitted.

"Then when would we have this normal adult get-together?"

"The Grammys are next week. We'll be in L.A. for a couple of days, how about then?"

"I'm doing a couple of the after-parties. I will be very busy," Chris said. "But if you are still here Monday, I might be able to see you."

"Splendid," said Derek. "I'll ring you."

And he was gone, leaving Chris shaking her head and staring at her phone.

She turned her attention back to the list. After the interruption, she once again turned her focus to her notes.

Two things became apparent:

She had to tell Lisette what she knew.

She and Lisette would need to feign ignorance while they gathered ad-ditional information.

Chris's mind was whirring ahead to obtaining financials and docu-menting Carl's trips to L.A. Only when they had all the details – complete records and a solid timeline – would they know the true extent of the situ-ation. They needed time for discovery and whatever steps had to be taken to ensure that Lisette's assets were protected, regardless of what happened with the marriage.

"Maria!" Chris thought with a jolt. "Shit," she said out loud.

The sooner the better, she thought, sending Lisette an invitation for a Google Hangout on Friday night. This conversation needed to be face-to-face. She remembered Lisette saying that Carl wasn't due home until the following week, so that would give her a couple of days to put on her game face. And, more likely than not, Maria would not be at home on a Friday night.

What a fucking shitstorm.

Chapter 17

Shane felt bruised after his night with Svetlana. Her arms held no comfort for him. Her body felt like gristle, her hipbones were scimitars. He was angry with Derek all over again for letting Lisette slip away. On second thought, he realized he was angry at himself for the supermodel. Pictures had been taken. It was probably all over Instagram, the girls would see it. Priya would realize he celebrated her big announcement by banging a supermodel. A new wave of self-loathing washed over him. It wasn't Derek's fault.

At least she was gone, he thought, remembering a kiss and a whisper that almost pulled him out of sleep earlier. He rolled over and ordered coffee. He opened the drapes while he waited. The bright L.A. sunshine hurt his eyes. He was glad they were headed to dreary Seattle next. Two shows there, then back to L.A. for the Grammys a week from today.

He was so tormented about the letter! He had taken Derek's advice, and why not? Derek was English, courtly, he inspired gentlemanly confidence and camaraderie. Surely he knew how best to approach a woman of substance. That was how he held Lisette in his mind. She was accomplished, an artist. She wore leotards to work, and a tiny wraparound skirt the size of a handkerchief. There was something hidden and rich about her that left him wanting to know more. He found her unique and classic. Just the thought of her grounded him. After sending the card, he started lifting intentions to her as if she was a deity, dedicating his day to her. That had run off the rails last night, of course, but that was a small glitch, the result of intersecting events. He'd try to do better today to be more worthy of her.

A knock at the door.

"Thank god, coffee," Shane announced to himself. His preoccupation with the letter had slipped him into the third person, he was narrating. He envisioned himself as a puppet or an actor in his own drama: Will he hear from her? Descending crescendo: Dum dum dum!!!

"To be continued," he said out loud, realizing that he had already opened the door, was looking into the wide eyes of the startled room service porter, and was stark naked.

"Sorry, sorry, bring it to the table," he said, turning neatly and walking with what he intended to be dignity into the bedroom, where his robe was on the floor. He bent over and picked it up. The waiter was gone when he returned. The coffee was hot. The day has broken. On a roll.

He sipped coffee and checked Instgram. It was worse than he feared. Svetlana had posted a video of him sleeping. She had publicly claimed him as a conquest. He felt profoundly violated, and foolish. While Shane had lived a very public life for a very long time, he had still not reconciled his fame with the intrusion and reach of social media. It had established a new set of values about public vs. private. It exposed a generational divide as it exposed its subjects. Nothing was private anymore because of his childrens' generation and their goddamned technology.

He felt tatty and used. He threw the phone onto the bed and headed for the shower. The band was meeting in an hour to go over material for a new album and set up a recording schedule.

Derek was standing in the sun outside the record company offices looking pleased with himself.

"Hello, mate," he greeted Shane cheerily.

"What are you so bloody happy about?" Shane asked. His foul mood had not lifted and he anticipated merciless ribbing from his bandmates about the Instagram post. Most of them had families and houses in L.A. They had slept in their own beds the night before, waking up refreshed and scandal-free.

"I got a date!" Derek announced.

"Good lord, man, will wonders never cease?" Shane said. "Who is this poor creature, your next victim?"

"Chris, Lisette's friend with the fantastic, um, t-shirt," Derek replied, making an effort not to descend to locker room talk. He was in training, he figured, or rather re-training. Too much time around the lads over years had significantly tarnished the manners his mother had prized so highly and pummeled into him growing up.

"What?" Shane yelped. "You let the ballerina get away while you were sniffing around her best friend? You wanker! This will never work."

"It worked," Derek said. "I called her saying I needed party planning services. She saw through the ruse straightaway and called me on it. It was a breath of fresh air to be dressed down by an honest woman."

"Older women do have uncanny radar for bullshit," Shane agreed, though his experience was limited to his two ex-wives. "My exes are like that."

"Older women are the last bastion of sanity," Derek "In fact, John Lennon had it right marrying a woman seven years older. It levels the balance of the actuarial tables and improves the odds she has some damned sense."

"Old Ben Franklin said as much in his day," Shane said. "He said older women are infinitely more interesting than young women and have a thousand skills that young women haven't learned."

"I, too, have read Franklin on the virtues of older women," Derek said. "He also mentioned that they are more discreet. And that was 250 years before Instagram."

Shane flinched as if stung.

"You saw it, then," he said.

"It's going 'round, yes," Derek confirmed. Then he asked with a lascivious leer, "And how was she then, the Ruski supermodel?"

"Hungry from the looks of her," Shane replied. "And sharp – not in the intelligent sense of the word."

Derek laughed.

"Right, mate, ouch," he said. "Give me a woman with curves and a nice plump bum any day. The mere thought of it makes me hard. Now let's act our age and be discreet. The pack awaits."

"Ugh," Shane grunted, bracing himself for the mockery that awaited him in the executive suite meeting/locker room.

It would be merciless, but at least it would be quick. Just some scheduling, share a few song ideas, then on to Seattle for tomorrow's show.

Chapter 18

When Lisette turned the lights on in the studio the next afternoon, she was surprised to see an envelope on the floor. It was addressed to her, hand-written in a loopy feminine script. There was no return address, but an Austin, TX, postmark. Unusual. She rarely received mail at the conservatory, didn't even have a mailbox. The receptionist must have slipped it under the door.

Lisette placed the letter on the piano and took off her coat. She hung her big black bag on its hook, then her coat over the bag. She sat down at the piano, took off her boots and slipped into her pink ballet shoes. The studio felt chilly, so she turned up the thermostat.

Returning to the piano, she picked up the envelope, which by its long narrow shape she could tell was a greeting card. She stuck her index finger into the gap and tore the top, extracting the card. It was a Georgia O'Keeffe cityscape, "New York – Night, 1926," a painting she knew well. O'Keeffe had painted her cityscapes as a newlywed, setting up her easel on the sidewalk to work. Lisette had a tiny print of one of the series on her wall for 25 years before learning who the artist was. "That looks familiar," she thought when she ran dead-on into the enormous original at the Art Institute of Chicago. Intrigued, she further researched the bounty of work from that period of the artist's life. Ultimately, "New York – Night, 1926" emerged as her favorite.

Opening the card, she saw the same girly handwriting inside:

Dear Lisette,

It was nothing short of amazing to run into you and Maria in New York. What are the chances?

I have thought of you often in the months since and I feel weirdly compelled to reach out to you. You are someone I would like to get to know. That's the only way I can explain it. Please indulge me. Could we meet for lunch next time I'm in Chicago?

I don't know what your situation is, but lunch is innocent enough regardless, right?

Hoping to hear from you,

Shane (Stewart)

A phone number "(cell)" and email address were included under the signature.

"Goddamn you, Chris," Lisette muttered. She dropped the card and envelope in the trashcan and started in on her choreography notes for the various classes, reading through the dances each group was working on and adding new ideas to the ends. A thread of a Disgracefuls song was in her head and she was suddenly conscious of it as she practiced the seniors dance in front of the mirror. A light went on in her head and she said "Oh!" out loud. She ran to her hook and extracted her phone from the abyss of her bag. She called up the tune on YouTube and laid the phone on the floor. She tried dancing the senior piece to the Disgracefuls song. It synched perfectly, changing the graceful intent and spirit of the dance into something fierce and unexpected. She could not wait to share the reworked version with her favorite dancers! Evelyn will definitely pee! After running through it a few times, she was satisfied on several levels, emotional, professional, personal. Fight fire with fire, she thought. Take that, Disgracefuls. I can face you head-on, on my own terms, with my own (he)art.

Fortified, she walked over to the trashcan and extracted the card for further study. Chris had truly outdone herself. Chris's handwriting was distinctive, very small and round, a unique hybrid of printing and cursive. This flowing script, so different from Chris's own, was a masterful forgery. Lisette herself had invented handwriting when she left notes from the Tooth Fairy on Maria's pillow or Santa on Christmas morning. And Chris, being a PI, likely knew a thing or two about handwriting analysis. If you let her get going, she was a walking forensics course about seriously gross stuff like how to tell if a body had been moved, rigor mortis, and the putrification process. Lisette shuddered.

Before she put her phone away, she texted Chris: "A mysterious piece of mail arrived today. You are prime suspect."

The other possibility – that it was authentic – was too overwhelming so she shoved it to the back of her mind. Her beginners were arriving. She dropped the card into her bag. As an afterthought, she took the envelope out of the trash and slipped it into the dark recesses with the card. She'd use this artifact in the future to prank Chris. She didn't yet know how or when, but she would prank her good.

Chapter 19

C hris was frantic with final details for two Grammy after-parties. In the midst of her long days, she noticed a text message from Lisette. Mysterious letter? Please, god, no more intrigue, she thought. She had called the FBI agent ex-boyfriend with a favor: Carl's trip log, specifically in and out of L.A. They were still on good terms and got together once in a while. He'd said he'd make a few calls. After the Grammys Sunday night, she would get back on the case. Meanwhile, on Friday night she had her Hangout with Lisette. It was not going to be an easy conversation, the hardest since she shared her cancer diagnosis. She scripted talking points so she didn't forget any important details.

Introduction:
- Are you alone? Is Maria out? Is Carl out of town? (What to do if not? Reschedule?)
- I have something shocking to tell you about C
- C is spending time with E
- I tailed him/did some research
- This is what I know:
  - Remember when I thought I saw C at LAX? It was C.
  - Tailed him to E's house
  - How I know it's her house, title search, was on market 2 years ago, no longer for sale

Questions:
- Did she know they were visiting?

- If not, what does she make of it?
- Let her talk
- Digging Deeper (acknowledge how weird this is, talk some sense about being fully informed)
  - Two years ago – any changes then?
  - Changes since then?
  - Let her talk

Moving Forward
- This is serious
- Finances: Make sure L understands what's at stake. "It's important that you have a complete financial picture."
- Let her talk

Next Steps
- Locate tax records, accountant might blab to C
- FBI boy compiling travel timeline – does L keep track of C's travels?
- Game face
- We will figure this out

Chapter 20

I cannot believe this," Lisette said. First she had gasped. Pain and anger darkened her brimming eyes. She blinked and tears squirted down her face. She pushed her hair back and wiped her cheeks using her fingers like windshield wipers. Her hands were shaking, Chris noticed.

"I hate to be the one to bring this to you," Chris said, "but I figured if it was me, I'd want to know."

Lisette was still processing. "This is insane," she said. "You're telling me that for the past two years, Carl has been visiting Edie regularly in Mission Viejo when I thought he was traveling for business? I can't wrap my head around it. He never even mentions her. It's like she hasn't existed for us in 30 years."

"It looks like the visits started about two years ago," Chris said. "Around the time her house was on the market. Maybe he was helping her move? Maybe something involving their kids? Maybe she needed to raise some money?"

"Oh who the fuck knows," Lisette snapped. "If it had been above board he would have told me about it. Instead, he's been living some weird double life!"

"It's more common than you think," Chris said. "Most guys don't get caught unless they die suddenly."

"I feel like such a fool. I am so used to Carl being away for work that I never questioned it. Especially the last two years when he was supposedly stockpiling for retirement. Said he had to work extra hard for the bonus so he could sock it away."

"Lisette," Chris asked, "speaking of socking away, how much do you know about your joint finances?"

Chris checked her talking points.

"It's important that you have a complete financial picture," she said, checking that off her list and allowing "wait time" for Lisette to think and respond.

"Oh my god, Maria," Lisette suddenly wailed. "This is precisely what I never wanted to happen to her." She was sobbing in earnest now into her hands. She popped up from her seat, disappeared off camera and returned with a wad of tissues pressed to her nose.

"I don't know, this is surreal, I just don't know," Lisette gulped.

"Do you have any Xanax?" Chris asked, going off-script. "I'm not a doctor, but this seems like a reasonable situation for anti-anxiety medication."

Lisette paused and did deep breathing, trying to calm her pounding heart and full-body trembling. She suddenly missed her mother, causing a renewed flood of tears. Chris let her cry. As her jag subsided, Lisette applied the wad of tissues to her eyes like a compress. Finally she looked back up at the screen.

"What am I going to do?" she asked.

"That depends," Chris said. "Do you love him?"

"I don't know," Lisette admitted. "I haven't been in love with him for such a long time, but our life was happy enough, or so I thought."

"Do you think you can keep it together long enough to formulate a plan?" Chris asked.

"What kind of plan?" Lisette asked.

"To be determined," Chris explained. "We'll figure it out. At this point, you are in control. You know about Carl, but he doesn't know you know. That gives you a little breathing room to decide what you want to do. And how to protect your assets, find out whether the 'socking away' he's been doing is above-board or off-shore."

"I don't know if I can 'play dumb,'" Lisette said. "I could call our accountant, I guess."

"No, don't do that, Lisette. The accountant will tell Carl. That's who pays his fee."

"Then how am I supposed to find out anything?" Lisette whined, exasperated.

"Do you have copies of your tax returns?" Chris asked.

"Yes," Lisette said. "They're all in a drawer of a file cabinet, by year."

"Great," Chris said. "That's a start. What about quarterly statements for IRAs, 401Ks, that sort of thing?"

"I could look around, maybe ask Carl in a roundabout way, like 'How are we going to pay for Maria's college?' something like that."

"That's good," Chris agreed. "As long as you can be casual and not arouse suspicion."

"This is what I deserve," Lisette said, suddenly morose. "Carl left Edie for me. Now he's leaving me for Edie." She succumbed to a new round of sobbing.

"You do not 'deserve' this, Lisette," Chris said. "Carl is a sneaky little weasel and a fuckwad. That's why we have to out-weasel him. Do you think you can hold it together while we figure it out?"

"Probably," Lisette said. "I've been pretending for a while. I suppose I can pretend a while longer."

"We're buying time, Lisette. In the meantime, do not text or email anything about this. Strictly phone conversations. Nothing in writing."

"Speaking of writing, I thought this call was for your confession about the letter," Lisette said, making an ironic face on top of her blotchy, tear-stained situation.

"What letter?" Chris asked.

"That card from 'Shane Stewart' you sent me," Lisette said, lifting her fingers in quote marks when she said the name.

"I don't know what you are talking about," Chris said.

"Hold on, let me refresh your memory," Lisette said, slipping into a prosecutorial persona and bending down to pull the card from her giant bag, the cave of wonders. "This card," she said, holding it up to the camera like Exhibit A.

"Georgia O'Keeffe," Chris recognized correctly. "Show the inside."

Lisette opened the card and displayed the text. Chris read quickly.

"Lunch," she snorted. "I'll have a Shane Stewart sandwich, please."

"It's not funny, Chris," Lisette said sternly, feeling all of the pain and humiliation of their conversation boil up inside her. "You've got to stop with the pranks. I'm too humiliated to stand it. Be my friend."

"First and foremost, I am your friend," Chris said, ignoring her own suddenly hurt feelings and offering sincere, unequivocal support. "Got that? Friend, not fiend, though I admit I have brought a steaming pile of unpleasantness to you tonight. I did it because I am your friend. Secondly, I have nothing to do with that card. Dust it for prints if you want. It is not my work."

"Swear?" Lisette said, her bloodshot eyes wide with surprise.

"On a stack of albums," Chris vouched.

"Christ on a crutch. What a fucking shitstorm," Lisette said.

"You can say that again," said Chris. "And there's even more – Derek called me for a date."

"What? Derek?" Lisette stuttered, overwhelmed by yet another turn in a conversation that would loom as epic in their lore.

"Yes. We're going out next week if I am available," Chris said. "He wants to do something normal that people our age supposedly do. Far from the limelight."

"Okay, that's it," Lisette said. "I have to go soak my head. I'm on tilt."

"Call me tomorrow after you've had time to think. Promise," Chris said.

"Promise," Lisette said. She sighed.

"Chris, I know how hard it must have been for you to tell me about Carl, but thank you," she said. "I feel like I'm in a dream or an alternate universe. I will need you to confirm tomorrow that we had this conversation, that all this is really happening."

"Give yourself some time to process and call me tomorrow," Chris said. "I love you."

"And I you," Lisette said, smiling wanly at the screen as she closed the tab.

Chapter 21

Carl's bag was packed and parked at the front door.

"Bye, pop," his son Gerald said, gripping him in a man hug with two pats on the back. He had perfected it watching "The Sopranos". He'd learned a lot of father-son skills from TV. With all of his business travel, Carl was frequently absent when Gerald was growing up. After the divorce, he wasn't around at all. By then, Gerald was headed off to college and adulthood. He'd most keenly missed his father at milestone moments like graduation, and when his own kids were born. But mostly it was a sustained ache he got used to over time, like arthritis.

But his mom was great! (Which he reminded himself daily.) She had always been there for him and his sister Sophie. Now, seeing their parents getting along so well, both were astonished on one hand and tremendously relieved overall. Carl's connections in Big Pharma had been extremely helpful. Their mother was participating in a clinical trial of a new MS drug that looked "promising." But her re-connection with her ex-husband had been better medicine than anything formulated in a laboratory. Her depression, which came with her diagnosis, had lifted, she was working remotely from home part-time, keeping busy and connected. Two years ago, when she was first diagnosed, she had threatened to take her own life. That's when Gerald called Carl.

First Carl had shown up to straighten out Edie's finances. Then he kept showing up to straighten out unfinished business between the two of them.

Gerald had been watching "The Parent Trap" with his 8-year-old daughter the week before.

"It's like papa and grandma," she had said. Her school was big on "text-to-life connections."

He had told her not to get her hopes up. But kids get their hopes up. Even grownup kids. To himself, never out loud, Gerald had formed the words "cautiously optimistic." He had silently, gleefully crossed his fingers when he'd overheard his parents talking about selling the house and getting a smaller place without stairs, maybe in a gated community on a golf course. Despite fatigue, some tingling and numbness, and occasional leg spasms, Edie still loved to play. She swore it improved her balance.

Gerald didn't wish the pain of divorce on anyone, and he felt bad for his teenage stepsister, Maria, who he'd only seen in pictures. The divorce had been acrimonious, leaving no opportunity for any "blended family" action. She'd learn, as he had, that life with an absentee father isn't much different if he's gone for work or gone for good. And he didn't have any feelings at all about his father's second wife. None at all.

Lisette, meanwhile, was devoting all her energies to getting her game face arranged, practicing on Maria as she pretended her life wasn't an absolute mess. As she faced the fact that her marriage was a big fat lie, she had searched for a shred of truth to hang onto. Hadn't it been great at first? She was so young when Carl came into her life and swept her off her feet. They'd met at a party in New York after a performance of Les Sylphides. His company was one of the corporate underwriters of the run. She'd been in the corps, which except for one waltz was mostly a tableau vivant. It was her all-time favorite costume, though, classic white net skirt and a satin bodice with tiny, delicate wings on the back – she'd worn it on Halloween forever. They'd talked about Chopin. After the next performance, he was waiting for her outside the stage door with flowers, half frozen, the collar of his overcoat turned up, a sappy, hopeful look on his face.

He'd presented himself as a man of the world, an Ivy Leaguer, well read, a corporate success. He said he felt strangled by his marriage. He had "outgrown" it, he said. He needed someone more interesting, more adventurous. He was as impressed with her success in classical ballet as he was amused by her devotion to rock music. He was a skilled and knowledgeable lover who cared about her pleasure and satisfaction. They had steamy trysts at hotels. Once they became so overheated while driving in a car they had to pull off the road to have a go then and there. The affair lasted three years.

Within weeks of Carl's divorce, they were married by a judge in Chicago on a Monday afternoon.

The first 10 years had been pretty good. Maria was born on their 10th anniversary, and the second decade of their marriage seemed like a happy blur centered on their daughter. Lisette had started working part-time at the conservatory when Maria was 5. The past seven years had been even busier with Lisette taking on more classes and Maria's life full with school, friends, sports and other activities.

When had she fallen out of love? She couldn't say exactly. It just sort of rubbed off over time as Carl spent more time traveling for work and Lisette and Maria formed their own unit. He started to be extraneous. And when he was home, he acted like a cranky old man more and more often. Carl seemed to realize it and had started to talk about retiring. Then came the big work surge two years ago, a final campaign to solidify their financial security.

Lisette sighed. She had gone through the timetable countless times over the weekend looking for clues about what and when and why. She felt empty and sad. She'd had a splitting grief headache. She stayed in bed late, then flopped from couch to bed and back again. She wished she felt more righteous indignation, more anger, more like a wronged victim. But in the final assessment, she decided simply that love fades. Work and kids and friends and vacations – all fill the calendar and conspire to keep us pushing forward with a sense of purpose so we don't have to face that sad fact. Love fades into a Newtonian law. Now Carl had provided a force to change their course – or stop it in its tracks.

How would she ever endure the waiting period until confronting Carl, pretending that business was as usual, but knowing that the unraveling had already begun? What would help her put on that game face during the fact-finding? He would be home in 24 hours. Everything had changed, how would she feign sameness? She desperately needed something to look forward to, some reward that would help her bear up, help balance out her anger and humiliation.

Peeling herself off the bed once more, she walked downstairs to her laptop. She opened her email and clicked "compose."

"Thank you for your note. I would be delighted to have lunch." She signed it "Lisette" and included her cell phone number. She clicked "send."

Chapter 22

Derek called Chris late Monday afternoon. Their paths had not crossed the night before, but both had late nights. Their respective parties had continued past sunup.

"I hate staying up until dawn," Chris said. "I used to love it. I feel like 10 pounds of shit in a 5-pound bag."

"I'm a bit crispy around the edges myself," Derek admitted. "But are you up for having a go at normal and appropriate adult activity tonight? Maybe a bite to eat? I promise to have you home by 10."

Chris's stomach rumbled.

"I could eat," she admitted.

She suggested an Italian restaurant with a wood-fired oven that produced the best chicken Chris had ever tasted outside of her grandmother's kitchen.

"I have the car," Derek said. "I'll come 'round for you."

By "have the car," Derek meant he had a driver, Chris realized as he arrived. Nothing ostentatious, not a stretch, but a tasteful Town Car. She approved. Every limo in L.A. was resting after last night, she suspected. The awards show had been the usual spectacle, but a mere warm-up for the parties afterward. This morning the city had been one big zombie movie set littered with the walking dead. Chris's workers found two award winners, nude and starting to sunburn, passed out in lounge chairs by the pool at one of party venues.

Sitting across the table, breathing in all the wonderful homey aromas of garlic and roasting meat, Chris studied Derek's face. He had pale blue eyes that were crinkly around the edges, flowing into deeper laugh lines that framed his cheekbones. He had wild eyebrows, a hawkish nose and a fine square chin with a dimple she hadn't noticed the first time they met.

"Did you have a beard last time I saw you?" she asked.

"Not a beard so much as being in need of a shave," he said.

"You shaved for our adult date?" she asked.

"Of course," he said with an antic grin. For an Englishman, his teeth were pretty good, Chris noticed. Not perfect like American orthodontic smiles – his two front teeth had a slight overlap, which she found charming. Chris was a sucker for imperfection.

The wine arrived. Derek had ordered an old Brunello. Chris preferred white, but decided to let Derek take the lead. She was curious to learn more about him and it was a relief to take a break from the endless decision-making of the past weeks and just sit back. Part of it was her PI training. You want to learn about people? Give them space to talk. They will. She was surprised how comfortable she felt with Derek. She had no expectations.

"Delicioso," he told the waiter. "Grazie."

"So tell me," Derek said, "when did you swear off dating?"

"I didn't swear it off as much as I stopped doing it," Chris said. "There was no one thing, no tragic love affair or creepy stalker experience. It just became unimportant to me. I have other priorities, my work, my friends. Aren't those dates?"

"I know what you mean," Derek said. "But I see those constant ads on the telly for online match-making for 'older' people, and I wonder if there's something wrong with me, if I'm becoming a hermit or something. The whole notion of going online and searching for a stranger with the potential to complete my life seems terribly sad somehow. Look at us. We managed to meet each other just going about our daily business. And here we are now, together, and it's quite lovely!"

Chris raised her glass in agreement. They looked each other in the eye as they clinked glasses.

"So, Derek, how long have you managed the Disgracefuls?" she asked.

"Christ, forever," he said. "I wasn't their first manager, I came aboard after the band's rehab. I've never been a druggie, and their original manager needed rehab more than the lads. The record company figured they needed someone who would keep them on the straight and narrow. I actually started out managing European tours for symphony orchestras. I did a one-year

MBA in music management, focusing on publishing, which was important as the market changed and technology suddenly had people hijacking copyrighted material right and left – along with the artists' royalties. I think that's why they hired me, mostly, plus the fact I can pass a pee test."

They didn't share a lot of personal background beyond neither had been married, neither had children or pets. Both had grown up in industrial cities, Detroit and Birmingham. Chris explained she actually grew up in Birmingham, too, it was the name of her posh suburb of Detroit.

Over their second glass of Brunello, they played a game called "You Were There," trying to match up Disgracefuls concerts they both might have been at, coming up with three possibilities. Over dinner, Chris told the story of her roundabout route to party planning. Derek's eyebrows shot up when Chris shared her PI background.

"You carry a gun?" he whispered, leaning confidentially toward her as if telling a terrible secret and eyeing her purse with alarm.

"Yes, well, no, not at this moment," Chris assured him. "But I do own one and I know how to use it. It's locked in a safe."

"You Americans and your guns," Derek said. "You scare the living shit out of the rest of the free world."

"Relax. I'm not doing any private eye stuff at the moment – at least not officially," Chris said. She admitted she had recently tailed "the husband of a friend" to his ex-wife's house. "But that was a favor, not a job."

"Some favor," Derek said. "How'd she take it?"

"It's complicated," Chris said.

"That's putting it mildly," Derek said. "Say, if you ever need a partner for a stakeout, I've always fancied that sort of intrigue. I'd come along if you liked. Or say you needed an unknown face to snoop around, ask questions. I'm your man."

"Thank you, Derek," Chris smiled, pleased that he was interested enough to offer.

"But leave the you-know-what at home," he stage whispered, laying his hand on the table in the shape of a pistol and rolling his eyes toward it. Chris couldn't stifle a giggle.

Late that night, Derek would search for past articles Chris had written for the newspaper. He was horrified at some of the heinous crimes she had covered. But his initial opinion of her as a pretty party planner was altered significantly. He now considered her armed and dangerous.

Chris made sure the Brunello didn't loosen her lips to the point she told her cancer story. She had decided if she and Derek were ever naked together, he'd see the scar and that would be when he'd learn what a tough woman she really was.

It wouldn't be that night. Derek had her home by 10, as promised, giving her a quick goodnight kiss at the entrance to her building and sending her along to get her rest.

It was a normal, grown-up dinner date. It felt pretty great.

Chapter 23

It worked – good god, man, you are a genius!" Shane shouted into the phone.

The ring tone had awakened Derek.

"What do you mean?" he asked groggily.

"I heard from Lisette!" Shane crowed. "She emailed me and agreed to lunch!"

"Fantastic," Derek said, suddenly awake and remembering his dinner with Chris the night before.

"Seriously, man, I owe you,'" Shane continued. "I'd about given up hope of hearing from her. But there it was when I checked my email this morning."

"Ladies love a hand-written note," Derek said. "What can I say?"

"I need to get to Chicago," Shane said.

"Not this week you don't," Derek corrected him. "We have music to create, session time booked. The soonest you could break away is next week, and just for the day, you'll have to come right back. Did she say when she is available?"

"No, just that she 'would be delighted to have lunch'. And her phone number."

"Ah, so you got her number," Derrick said approvingly. "That's progress. Congratulations."

"I feel like I'm in high school," Shane admitted. "I'm geezed!"

"That's great, mate," Derek said. "Really great."

"What's my next move?" Shane asked.

Derek smiled at the absurdity of giving advice to a man who had bedded women all over the globe. This was new territory for them both, he supposed. He wished the best for Shane. He understood the ridiculousness of Shane's life. Usually, all he had to do was point out a face in the crowd. The rest was a given, an old script well-rehearsed. Some young lovely would leave in the wee hours of the morning with a tale she was bursting to tell. Shane would go to sleep without a shred of responsibility for even remembering her name. It was a bad habit, an arrangement that, over time, diminished a man's ability to feel, to connect. A permanent state of adolescent anomie. Derek had observed over the years how band life retarded an artist's emotional growth. When fans worship you, you are in a protective bubble of adulation, you are always on the receiving end of compliments and gifts and positive reinforcement. They were rarely in the position of giving. They never had to put effort into making or keeping friends because everyone in their sphere so desperately wanted to be their friend.

Derek took hope in Shane's unexpected obsession with Lisette. It was the sort of emotional storm that created fertile ground for making great music. It wasn't lost on Derek that the Disgracefuls leaned heavily on their established songbook. Fans come to hear their favorites – you gotta play what got you there. But something fresh, unexpected even, would surprise the industry. And be potentially profitable.

"Have you been writing?" he asked. "Not emails and letters, I mean, music."

"I'm playing with a few ideas," Shane said.

"Well that's your next move, my friend. Write her a song. Channel all this exuberance into something truly great. Experience your emotions, suss them out. Take a few days to be a songwriter. Then and only then are you allowed to respond to her. And when you do, it will be to arrange this innocent lunch according to *her* availability. Be a gentleman. Don't talk about your schedule. Accommodate hers. Allow some romance into your life, Shane. Give. It'll do you good."

"I get you," Shane said. "Feelings."

"Precisely," Derek replied.

"By the way," he added, "I went out with Chris last night."

"The party planner friend?" Shane asked. "Now I really feel like I'm in high school. What's next? A double date? How did that go?"

"It was fantastic," Derek reported. "We went to dinner, we had spectacular wine and lively conversation, and some amazing wood-fire-roasted chicken that I might need to have again tonight. Fucking spectacular, I can't stop thinking about it. It was like bloody crack or something. Let's send Jake around to pick some up…"

Derek regained his train of thought.

"And, get this, Shane: The 'party planner' is also a former journalist and a private investigator. She's quite fascinating and a bit scary – she has a gun…"

"What the fuck?" Shane asked.

"No, she's not weird about it. Keeps it locked in a safe except for potentially dangerous situations."

"That's comforting," Shane said.

"We figured out that we were both at three particular Disgracefuls concerts, same place and time," Derek said. "It was interesting to think about. There we were at the same moment. Here we were now. Interesting, right? Oh, and I might go on a stakeout with her."

"A stakeout?"

"Yeah. Like if she needs somebody no one recognizes."

"You are insane." Shane said. "How could such a fabulous chick end up having dinner with the likes of you?"

"Dunno," Derek said. "She's quite fabulous."

"Did you score?" Shane asked, high schooler talk.

"No, you dim twit," Derek said sharply. More calmly, he explained, as if to a child, "We were both out until dawn the night before, man. We were beat, depleted. We had a relaxed kind of communion over Brunello and comfort food. I had her home at 10, as I said I would. It was pretty great."

Neither spoke for a few seconds.

"I think I love her," Derek said.

Chapter 24

By the time Carl walked through the door, Lisette had quite a bit of practice putting on her game face, was an expert in fact. As she honestly thought about their marriage over the weekend, she was forced to admit that it had been a very long time since she was truly happy upon Carl's return. She had developed a snarky little habit of saying to herself "Ugh" or "Damn" when his car pulled into their driveway, then plastering a false smile on her face and feigning delight. Being brutally honest, she admitted to dark fantasies – a plane crash, a virulent tropical disease, some other easy out with no villain, only victims. She was a conniving little bitch, and a coward, she decided. But now she had passed some threshold. She was playing the same game but the time clock was ticking down. The end was near, and now that all the tears and anger of the past few days were spent, she felt relief. The game would end soon, and Carl would be the bad guy. She felt prepared and almost calm. A bit entitled with the upper hand, perhaps. She also felt powerful and dangerous, like a shiny scalpel, capable of doing much damage but also capable of healing in skilled hands. She wondered if she might be a psychopath.

Chris had told her it was all right not to have all the answers right away. It was a process, she said, and things unfold and become clear along the way. Lisette had been torturing herself with the hardest and most immediate questions: Will Maria be all right? Would they have to sell the house? Where would they live? Would there be a custody agreement? Chris had told her not to get ahead of herself. She figured it would be only a matter of weeks before they had the goods on Carl and an idea of what "half of everything" would look like. They continued to talk on the phone only. No emails, no texts related to "the situation."

"Lisette," Chris told her, "you are such a perfectionist and you want to know all the answers beforehand and be the one in control. You have all the important answers already. Just try to hide what you know as well as you can for a little while longer. Then we'll let the cat out of the bag. I was thinking we could confront Carl in California, at Edie's house, old school private eye style. There'll be no denying the facts that way, no weaseling out."

"Hello darling, welcome home," Lisette greeted her husband, the weasel. "How was your trip?"

"Endless!" he responded jocularly. "That flight gets longer every time."

"Hi, Dad," Maria said, bouncing into the room. Literally bouncing – a volleyball. She held the ball under one arm and hugged her father with the other. Watching them, Lisette felt a crack in her façade. She swallowed the lump in her throat. It tasted like regret.

Buttoning down her composure, Lisette asked who was hungry. It was already dark outside. She had made a big Cobb salad and picked up butternut squash soup and black bread at the expensive deli. Carl fixed himself a bourbon and poured Lisette a glass of wine.

They gathered at the table while the soup heated on the stove. Lisette dressed the salad with olive oil and vinegar. As she tossed it she noted the bacon, bleu cheese, and sliced egg, vaguely wondering if she should serve it with a side of nitroglycerine. She had truly crossed over to the dark side, thinking a massive coronary would neatly solve all her problems. Possible on the psychopath, she noted. Lack of empathy? Actually, she did feel sorry for Carl, who would soon be on the receiving end of a huge blast of whup-ass. And Maria, of course, she needed to be protected as much as possible.

She kept up a conversation about trivial bits and pieces of their shared life: Maria had a game Thursday, could Carl go? A co-worker had given birth to a baby boy – he had a lot of hair! The lawn man noticed something wrong with a gutter. The mayoral election was the next day, let's vote. Misha caught a mouse and carried it so carefully in his mouth that when he spit it out it ran off, wet but unharmed. Could you please give the soup a stir?

Lisette congratulated herself internally. She thought she was doing very well, considering. Carl opened three drawers, finally found a spoon, and stirred the soup.

She surveyed the scene and wondered: Are the habits of a long marriage transferrable? What am I going to do with my wifely skills? I won't have a household to run any more. I will be alone. A middle-aged woman, a child off to college, a mouse-catching dog my sole companion.

Carl was looking at her expectantly. Had he asked a question?

"Sorry, what?" she said stupidly.

"Is something burning?" he repeated.

"Oh! The bread!" Lisette remembered, too late. She plunged her hands into oven mitts and grabbed the smoking loaf, now hard as a brick, quickly crossed the kitchen, and threw it into the backyard.

"Don't you eat that, Misha," she warned the dog, who, though tempted, turned back and came inside. He probably would eat it, but later, after it cooled. They both knew it. Theirs was an honest relationship.

Lisette had thought through the sex thing. She told Carl she was so sorry but she had a yeast infection and was temporarily off the market.

She couldn't bear the thought of it.

She hadn't heard back from Shane. Ah, well, that was probably for the best, though it was exciting to be asked. Maybe she'd hear from him next time the Disgracefuls were in town. Who knows? He had her number. One shitstorm at a time, please.

Chapter 25

Shane still wrote by hand with pencil and paper. He jotted ideas in a scratched and bent spiral notebook with curling corners. About 20 similar notebooks, some yellowed and crumbling, were in a box in a storage space. He considered them his "archives" and planned to donate them to the Rock & Roll Hall of Fame when the Disgracefuls were inducted. Rumor had it they were sure to be nominated this year.

His current notebook had unicorns and a rainbow on the cover. Tiffany had picked it up for him at a drugstore in Kansas City. She had drawn hundreds of hearts inside the cover before turning it over to him. He felt confident enough about two song ideas to bring them to his bandmates. The real magic happened through collaboration. They had created enough music together over the years to know how to be first ears for each other and how to offer their own suggestions, about structure, wordplay, tempo, guitar solos, and such. Many times different members had walked in with a catchy line or two that, once the others got a taste, turned into a hit.

Shane needed their input to move his Arrhythmia concept from the page to the stage. His other offering was a ballad with an unusual, aching chord progression that also might work as a blues tune, (and be easier to sing). He'd see what the guys thought.

With the band in L.A. for a couple of weeks, Chris heard from Derek daily, mostly text messages in short bursts: "That chicken was like crack!" "Had restaurant send over five chickens!" "Band headed back to rehab for roast chicken addiction." "Day 2 in studio. Regressing rapidly to infantile state." "Remedy: grownup get-together."

Chris's co-workers noticed her looking at her phone and smiling. They were used to her responding to the "ping" of a text message with a scowl. Chris was flattered and intrigued by Derek's attention. She kept a lid on it when she spoke with Lisette, mindful of her friend's tenuous situation and mental state. She wished she could just be giddy with Lisette, but there were too many emotional subplots in this scenario. It seemed wrong to be silly happy about her budding relationship while Lisette was suffering extreme stress about the imminent end of hers. Chris, at her age, found it unseemly to admit she kinda had a "boyfriend." Though it did make her giggle.

They had another dinner date at an English pub Chris thought Derek would enjoy. He had to get back to the studio after, so there was no awkward decision about whether Chris would invite him up. They sat close in the back seat and held hands on the way. Chris was aware that she was experiencing sexual desire for the first time since her cancer treatment. She had worried she'd permanently lost the inclination, and to feel that long lost yearning for intimacy both took her aback and gave her confidence. It would happen, this she knew, and she told him as much with the long, wet kiss she planted on him before getting out of the car and waving goodbye.

She didn't drop around the studio, though she would have liked to. She and Lisette had always loved hanging out during the recording process. Many of their friends in bands had made demos, even if they never made the big time. Musicians themselves, the girls enjoyed rather than endured the tedium of getting the right bass drum sound. They had a high tolerance for the minutia and repetition of song making. They'd been the "Fab Two," of course. But the recording process more closely paralleled their own adult work and art. How many times had Lisette repeated the barre exercises? How many times had Chris asked the same questions of witnesses, experts, cops, and criminals? Each fragment was examined, reworked, and perfected until the song, or the dance, or the story, was finally finished, and "finished" required an innate knowing that the intended result had been achieved, and letting go. Chris loved a convention from her early days in journalism: When you got to the end of your story, you typed

- 30 -

She still ended personal letters and emails to old journalist friends with that obsolete close. Even though it signified "the end," she wanted "- 30 -" to be fondly remembered. She felt a responsibility to keep it in the lexicon.

Maybe that was true for Lisette and Carl, too. Chris hoped they could get through their breakup with at least a few fond remembrances intact. After heartbreak, there's something noble about still being able to be kind to each other. Fond memories allowed that to happen.

Derek walked into a loud argument returning from dinner at the pub. Chris's kiss had seared him to his core. It took all his self-control not to turn the car around and shout her name from the street.

"It doesn't rhyme with anything! It's impossible," Rob, the bass player, was complaining.

"What if we just use it in the chorus?" Shane asked. "Let the story establish itself in the verse, then just blast 'arrhythmia' over and over in the chorus. Catchy!"

"It's not something I want to catch," Rob cracked. "We're lucky we don't all have it after the Eight Ball '80s."

"I can't even spell the fucking word," said the drummer, "and I think I do have it."

Everyone burst out laughing. The drummer was a notorious hypochondriac. He was constantly worried that one or all of his internal organs were failing. He wore surgical masks on airplanes and wiped himself down with antibacterial wipes after every cringing meet-and-greet. His band mates called him Howard Hughes to his face.

Shane wanted to humor the drummer. A relentless driving beat would be critical to the song.

"At least lay down the track before you keel over," he implored.

"You think I'm kidding," the drummer replied. "But you'd best keep EMS on speed dial while we work this out."

Groans.

"What else do you have, Shane?" Derek asked, knowing that the ballad was a work in progress, and thinking that if they didn't set aside "Arrhythmia" for the time being that the night would devolve into fond tales of cocaine abuse that would tempt their recovery, always a risk.

Shane picked up an acoustic guitar and consulted his spiral notebook. "It's in D." He strummed a few hesitant minor chords, then started singing along, some words, some la-la-la filling out the lyrics that were thin indeed at present. The lead guitar player joined in, riffing along with the rhythm guitar. Even unfinished, the song cast a spell. It mined a spectrum of emotions, from despair to plaintive, then on to hopeful, then back to despair, ultimately finishing with a lift.

When he finished, all were silent as stones.

"That's not like anything we've done before," Rob finally said.

"It makes me want to cry," said the keyboardist. "That minor sharp to minor seventh gave me fucking arrhythmia. Who's got nitro?"

"Fuck me," said the lead guitar. "What's it called?"

"Don't know yet," Shane said. "It's very much a work in progress."

"What's it about?" asked Rob.

"Yearning," Shane said. "A woman. Home."

"Damn," said the drummer. Hesitantly, he added, "All I brought was a novelty song, I call it 'Hammered for the Holidays.' It sounds like Merle Haggard, but I bet it would make us a shitload of money forever!"

Chapter 26

Priya welcomed her father, smiling broadly. She looked so much like Shane they could have been fraternal twins. Priya, so over the moon to be solidly pregnant, wore a flowing Indian kaftan.

"Look!" she said, turning sideways and cinching the fabric to her body to show her tiny baby bump.

"May I?" Shane asked.

Priya nodded and Shane placed his hands on the bump. Old hands, not quite gnarled but on their way, laid themselves protectively over a developing fetus the size of a jumbo shrimp. Eyes and a heartbeat and fingers and toes, tiny curls of ears. Shane had been an ardent and doting father-to-be. He'd read all the books and was an able coach through the births of both his daughters. He was a sap for babies.

"Shane!" Daniel, Priya's husband, greeted him, emerging from the kitchen. "Isn't this exciting?"

"Congratulations, dad," Shane said, removing his hands from Priya's bump and offering one in a hearty handshake that turned into a hug. Shane felt tears prickling in the corners of his eyes.

"So happy for you," he said huskily.

He and Jill had been kids themselves when they had Priya. A couple years out of college, the band just taking off, it was an inconvenient event. But Shane had been there for Jill. By sheer luck, the band had two days off when the call came.

"The birth spasm has begun," Jill had announced in a Conehead voice over the phone. Shane was on the next plane, arriving for the hard labor.

Priya arrived with a lusty cry and a head full of hair. She was perfect.

Growing up, he told her the story every year on her birthday. Now she was 37. He supposed his early parenthood and her late parenthood evened things out.

"Promise me, if you know whether it's a boy or girl, please don't tell me," he begged.

Suki had been so sure Autumn was a boy she only bought boy baby clothes. When Autumn was born, they looked at their tiny squirming bundle and asked, "Who are you?" They had no prenatal testing for the gender of their baby, but constructed their own whimsical preconceptions, interpreted cravings and feelings, consulted ancient great-aunts who prided themselves on their prediction records. It took them two days to name her. It was like the universe had delivered a stern rebuke about presumptions. Fortunately, Autumn rocked the blue airplane and bulldozer baby clothes. They would not have been surprised if she grew up to work in the building trades.

Daniel had marinated a massive salmon filet in ginger, orange juice, red pepper flakes, and soy sauce, and cooked it outdoors over mesquite charcoal until it was crispy around the edges. There was saffron rice, spinach salad, and haricots verts. Shane was hungry. The road was one thing, recording quite another. His brain felt tired and stimulated at the same time from the band's work that day. The creative process had its own special tension.

"This looks amazing," he said, grateful beyond words for a home-cooked meal. He'd been on a steady diet of chicken that Derek kept ordering from some restaurant. It was very good, but every night, really?

"I eat more chicken any man ever seen, yeah yeah," he'd sung to Derek the last time he arrived with two huge carryout bags. The band responded by smoothly picking up "Back Door Man" and rocking it to the bitter end. So ended the chicken delivery.

"How are you feeling about being a granddad?" Priya asked, between bites. She was devouring the salmon like someone who'd been lost in the wilderness.

"This is just between us," Shane started, pausing to meet their eyes with a "no bullshit" warning. Priya and Daniel nodded solemn agreement and chewed. "It has affected me profoundly. It's like you two have presented me with this amazing gift, a generational milestone, which I embrace with all my heart. That means I need to acknowledge and accept my age, and my standing in the family. I want to be worthy of being the patriarch, 'a man in full.' I feel myself changing. And – this is top secret – I have a serious crush on a woman – a woman closer to my own age."

"The ballerina?" asked Priya.

Shane nearly choked on a leaf of spinach.

"Autumn told me," Priya said, refreshing his water glass, "last fall. She said you were gobsmacked by an encounter at a bookstore with a stunning woman of an appropriate age. You started wearing your hair like hers, with the streak."

Shane burst out laughing. Though his girls were stepsisters 13 years apart in age, their relationship was close. They were in constant communication and their father encouraged them to spend time together by underwriting unlimited air travel between Los Angeles and New York.

"You girls are terrible gossips," he chastised Priya.

"What's her name?" Priya inquired.

"Lisette," Shane responded, his eyes misting over dreamily. Snapping out of his reverie, he added, "I've met her three times, briefly, including the chance encounter at the bookstore. But I sent her a card and she agreed to have lunch with me in Chicago, where she lives, and hopefully that will take place soon. Keep your fingers crossed for me!"

Priya and Daniel were looking at Shane as if he'd grown a third eye.

"You sent her a card? Like a greeting card?" Priya asked. "Dad, who are you?"

"As I said, I'm changing," Shane said. "It's good, right? Took me nearly an hour to pick out the right card."

"That's quite…amazing," Priya said, struggling to imagine her father inspecting card after card. Daniel nodded in agreement. He and Priya had been together for 10 years, and Daniel had seen Shane's love parade of women come and go. Starlets, singers, and most recently Tiffany, his "assistant." They kept track of Shane's romantic life by flipping through the tabloids in the grocery store checkout. Having Shane as his father-in-law had been surreal and intimidating at first, but Shane and Daniel had bonded over their mutual love for Priya. Her happiness was foremost to both of them. And now, blessedly, a baby. They were in it for keeps. Daniel was an architectural renderer who worked in a studio they built in their backyard. Born in Haiti, fluent in French and Creole, he added a bit of color to their white family. Daniel figured that adding a dancer to the mix of artists and musicians in the family would foster even greater diversity.

"When do we get to meet her?" Priya asked, noting to herself that her father had removed the beads and shells from his hair.

"Let's not get ahead of ourselves," Shane cautioned, sounding like Derek. "We haven't even had a proper date yet."

"How did you meet?" Daniel asked.

"It was classic," Shane said, launching into the story of the wardrobe crisis in Chicago. Priya decided she liked Lisette already. Learning of Maria through hearing the first-aid tent drama, her mind raced ahead to the possibility of a second stepsister. She quickly reeled herself in. No sense getting ahead of themselves.

Chapter 27

Something was going on. Maria could feel it. Her mom's face looked… frozen. Had she gotten Botox? There was a tension around her Maria couldn't identify. She'd first noticed it after her mom's trip to L.A., which made her worry that Aunt Chris was sick again. Her parents were constantly protecting her from one thing or another. She wasn't a baby.

Concern about Chris led her to snoop in her mother's phone, but Maria found no incriminating text messages or phone calls. But walking past her mother's laptop, open on the kitchen counter while Lisette was in the shower, she sleuthed further in email. She found what she was looking for in "sent mail." A single email. Her mother was communicating with Shane Stewart! Maria's heart pounded as she opened it. The message was brief:

"Thank you for your note. I would be delighted to have lunch."

Lisette had sent it a week before. There had been no response, as far as Maria could determine. With shaking hands, she clicked back to Lisette's inbox and minimized the screen, leaving the laptop as she had found it.

After the concert and again after the chance meeting in the bookstore, Maria had researched Shane. She knew he'd been married twice, and had a daughter from each marriage. Autumn, whom she'd met, was the younger one. Her older sister with the strange name was the daughter of Shane and his college sweetheart.

Through an article from a U.K. magazine titled "On the rocks?" Maria had attached a name to the young blonde with the spikes on her dress. Tiffany had been Shane's girlfriend until last fall. She was about the same age as Autumn, and the article hinted that was the reason for the breakup, that Shane's daughters didn't approve. The younger woman scenario didn't surprise Maria. It came with the territory, she thought, didn't old rock stars always pair up with younger women? Mick Jagger was over 70 and had a new baby! The supermodel Svetlana, barely out of her teens, had posted a video of Shane sleeping on Instagram. Maria had seen it in her @shanestewart feed just once before the video suddenly disappeared.

In conversations with her girlfriends after the concert, every single one said that, given the opportunity, she'd sleep with him. Maria was the only one who said she wouldn't, and one reason was because of the way she'd seen him look at Lisette. She didn't give that as her explanation, though. She just said "Ew."

Maria was not very worldly in the ways of love. She'd had crushes, but never a steady boyfriend. What she knew about sex was mainly from movies, novels, friends, and social media. Her friends tended to run as a pack, coupling up for prom dates and such, and that was fine with her. She thought she might be gay, but no opportunities for exploring that option had presented themselves. With college on the horizon, she back-burnered that huge question for the time being. Still, she wondered. Was she this way because her parents were overprotective? Had her mother's neurotic "worst case scenario" talks, intended to raise her personal safety IQ, backfired and made her afraid of intimacy? Had her parents' marriage, which appeared to Maria to be a lot of "going through the motions" and not much joy, made her wonder what was the point? Had she shut down a part of herself after that creepy incident with the tennis coach who tried to feel her up when he was supposed to be improving her backhand? Now this!

Maria's initial shock quickly turned to anger. Was her "perfect" mother cheating on her father? Was she planning to? Was Shane Stewart a home-wrecker? Half her friends' parents were divorced, but that did not make her feel any less fearful. And on top of the fear and outrage, she felt guilty about snooping. She'd have to admit to it if she confronted her mother.

In a few days, Maria and Lisette were heading to L.A. for a quickie college tour. She'd ask Chris. Chris would know. And Chris would never lie to Maria.

Chris, meanwhile, had heard back from her law enforcement contacts about Carl's flight itineraries and financial dealings. The trip log made it clear that Carl had been padding his business trips with stops in L.A., sometimes before heading south, sometimes on the way back, and on two occasions, both before and after. And, it looked like he would be in L.A. Sunday night before traveling to Mexico City. Chris liked the idea of confronting Carl at Edie's house. It was harsh, but Chris thought it would cut through bullshit faster than any other method. It might also save a lot of money on lawyers. When the truth was out, Carl might be willing to mediate a quick settlement.

The financials had been pretty straightforward. Carl had diverted $250,000 from a retirement fund two years ago to get Edie out from under water on her mortgage. There didn't seem to be any other major siphoning off of assets into secret accounts. Lisette would be all right financially. She had the cottage, after all, where she'd always said she'd live if she had the choice. She'd told Chris repeatedly over the years as she scrimped and saved her teaching money to fix it up that they never need worry about having a roof over their heads when they were old and gray and hump-backed. They'd be happy as clams there. They'd be just fine.

Now all Chris needed to do was convince Lisette to join her Sunday night for what she'd started referring to as "the raid" – just to herself, of course. It was exactly the sort of thing that Lisette loathed most: a big fat confrontation. Chris thought she might ask Derek to come along for back-up.

Chapter 28

Lisette and Maria didn't talk much on the four-hour flight. Maria passed the time on her laptop, researching various programs and viewing idyllic pictures and videos of campus life at UCLA.

When they said goodbye to Carl, Lisette felt sick with the knowledge that he'd be traveling right behind them in 24 hours on one of his secret missions. Not so secret now, she thought. Her stomach lurched. She pretended to read a novel on her Kindle but her mind churned along with her stomach as she tortured herself with a thousand questions.

How could he have pulled it off for so long? She felt like a fool. Was she to blame? Was the cause of Carl's secret life her disinvestment in the marriage over time? Why hadn't she picked up on it? Was it a marriage of convenience for both of them? When had the love gone out of it? Are all marriages merely a marathon? Is any marriage truly happy over the long run of decades? When does it become a matter of one merely outlasting the other, wondering every day which one would die first, like in Don DeLillo? She had to hand it to Carl: He'd been a smooth operator in his deceit. He'd had practice – they'd both had practice – with their affair, she admitted. They'd both deceived Edie. Isn't turnabout fair play?

She was exhausted when the plane finally landed. To change her mind and turn back now was not an option, it would only prolong the agony. Best get this over with. Chris was picking them up, same place as last time. She couldn't wait for the comfort of her friendship, the warm cocoon of trust and support that never wavered.

"Hello my loves!" Chris exclaimed, jumping out of the driver's seat to wrap her arms around Maria, then Lisette. "Look at you!" she said, hugging Maria a second time. "My sweet, sweet girl!"

"Fact 1: I could get used to this weather," Maria announced, peeling off her jacket and changing her boots for sneakers in the back seat. "Fact 2: I might be interested in their film program."

Lisette wondered where that idea came from. Oh, right, the research on the plane. Maria had never expressed any interest in movies other than what she wanted to see any given weekend.

"What about journalism?" Chris asked. "The industry is desperate for young people who know technology and can parachute into a story and cover it by tweets, pictures, and video. I can totally see you doing that."

"Maybe," Maria said. "I'll check it out."

Chris dropped them off at the campus in time for the afternoon tour and they arranged to meet up in three hours. While Lisette and Maria did the college thing, Chris dashed home to load in a few essentials, race around with the vacuum cleaner, and make up beds. One guest would be on the couch. The other would share Chris's queen-size bed. Chris would try to wrangle Lisette as her bunkie. Tonight was her only opportunity to convince Lisette to come on the raid. Carl would arrive early the following afternoon. Prime time for the mission was early evening. The only holes in the plan were if Lisette came along, what would they do about Maria during the time it would take to get to Mission Viejo, confront Carl, and get back to L.A.? The other hole, and it was a big one, was if Carl wasn't there.

Chris had asked Derek to come along.

"Derek, do you know how to be intimidating?"

"Fuck yeah, how do you think a record deal gets signed?"

"Were you serious when you said you'd go on a stakeout with me?"

"I'm intrigued. Tell me more. Will there be danger? Are we in a Crips/Bloods situation?"

"No, nothing like that. Remember the friend I told you about whose husband is shacking with his ex-wife on the sly?"

"Yes."

"Sunday night, we're going to catch him in the act and confront him."

"Oh my. That's rather harsh."

"Is this something you could possibly be in on as backup?"

"What exactly does it involve? You won't bring that gun of yours, will you? I can't be responsible for a weapon – I might shoot off my nuts by accident. Happens all the time to those thugs running 'round with pistols in their waistbands."

"Derek, stop. It's not that kind of confrontation. No pistols in waistbands, no street fight. It's more emotional than physical."

"Chris, darling, I desperately desire both emotional and physical intrigue with you," Derek said, his voice dropping as he remembered that delicious, scorching kiss.

"Does that mean you'll come along? I mostly need you to stand outside looking intimidating."

"I'll do it." That kiss was talking.

"One more detail: It's Lisette's husband."

"Lisette?! Who the fuck would cheat on her? The lout! The pecker!"

"I know, right? Will you help us out?"

"Bloody right I will." Now his courage was up. He was flexing his arm muscles unconsciously and rolling his shoulders like a prize fighter.

"I will text you an address and time. You will meet us there. It's an hour away."

"Roger that. I'll get the car. Should we synchronize our watches?"

"Not necessary. I will text you when we arrive. Once we are there, you will take the position outside. Just stand by the car with your arms folded, looking badass. I will signal you if we need you to come inside. It's strictly an 'as needed' situation."

"I'll do it! We're in the studio Sunday, but I can break away. I'll say I've gone for chicken."

Chapter 29

"Aunt Chris," Maria said, "I think something is going on with my parents."

Lisette was in the shower. They'd had dinner, takeout burgers that would sustain a small village. The two of them were full of meat as they lounged about, digesting. Maria was on the couch, Chris on the floor by Maria's feet.

"What do you mean, sweetheart?" Chris asked.

"I think my mom is about to run off with Shane Stewart," Maria blurted, bursting into tears.

"Good lord! What makes you think that?"

"I saw an email. They were having lunch," Maria confessed, tears steaming, adding knowingly, "if that's what you call it."

"No, I'm positive it's just lunch," Chris assured her. "And that's not even for sure. He likes your mom. Who doesn't? She's terrific. It's good to keep making new friends throughout our lives. That's all it's about so far."

"Then why didn't she tell me?" Maria said, her suspicions sticking fast.

"Sweetie, there's nothing to tell," Chris said.

"That's hard to believe," Maria sniffed, chin trembling and fresh tears of frustration brimming in her gray eyes. "Mom and Dad both try to protect me from so much stuff. I'm practically an adult! I'm going to be leaving home in just a few months! I need to know what's going on!"

Lisette, light as a cat on her feet, stood in the doorway. The other two had not heard her approach.

"What's going on?" she asked, blotting her hair with a towel.

"Maria?" Chris said, giving her the opportunity to speak for herself.

Chris wanted Maria to grow up to be a strong woman. It might as well start here and now, she figured. The girl had just said she was tired of being protected and that secrets were eating her up. "Why don't you tell your mom. I can step out if you'd like."

"No, Chris, stay," Maria ordered. She took a deep breath.

"God, she's so like Lisette," Chris thought.

"Mom," Maria said, "You need to tell me what's going on. Everything. No protecting me. I can handle it."

"Oh god," Lisette exhaled, shutting her eyes. "Chris, did you?"

Chris shook her head.

"I figured it out myself, mom," Maria said. "You've been acting so weird. Like a pod person."

"I'm so sorry, sweetheart," Lisette said, concern on her face. "We had to keep it secret until we knew for sure what your father was up to. Now we are certain that he's been, um, visiting with Edie, his first wife. For quite some time. Regularly."

Maria's eyes went huge with surprise.

"What! Dad?" she squeaked. "Dad's cheating?"

"I'm afraid so, precious, I'm so sorry," Lisette said, crouching by Maria and sweeping her into a hug.

"But what about you?" Maria demanded, pulling away. "You and Shane Stewart!"

"What?" Lisette asked, stunned. "There's nothing going on between me and Shane Stewart."

"I saw the email, Mom, about 'lunch'," Maria said, shaking with anger now, raising her fingers in quote marks around "lunch," uttering the word with utmost 17-year-old sarcasm. More lies.

"Tell her, Lisette," Chris interjected. "Might as well pull the pin, put it all on the table."

"Yeah, mom," Maria said. "Tell me the truth. Everything."

"Okay, okay," Lisette grimaced, squirming from the discord, shaking from the unexpected confrontation, hating so much that she'd dropped in Maria's esteem.

"When I visited Aunt Chris a few weeks ago, we went to a Disgracefuls concert," she admitted. "Not just the concert, we went to the meet-and-greet before the show and talked to Shane."

"Jesus Christ," Maria exploded. "What are you, Mom, some kind of secret groupie! What about after the show? What else happened, Mom?"

"Well, Shane invited us back afterward, but when we got there, he was involved with a young woman and we didn't want to butt in. So we left."

"You left?"

"Yes," Chris said emphatically. "I was there. We left."

"What about the note and the lunch, then?" Maria demanded.

Chris had a fleeting thought that Maria might have a future as a detective.

"Shane sent me a card saying he'd like to take me to lunch," Lisette said, repeating "lunch" with emphasis. "I thought that would be interesting. So I agreed. And that's where it stands. I haven't heard anything further."

"What else does he want?" Maria asked.

"Lunch is all that I agreed to," Lisette answered. "That's the truth."

"Sometimes famous people just crave normalcy," Chris explained. "They want to make friends outside the usual circle of butt-kissers and fans. Over the long run, their lives can get lonely and weird. And your mother, by the way, is an interesting woman who can hold her own in any situation. Why shouldn't she have lunch with Shane Stewart?"

"What a shitstorm," Maria said, throwing up her hands.

The two older women burst out laughing. Maria's unexpected profanity broke the tension.

"You can say that again, baby blue," Chris said.

"Maria, this isn't how I wanted to tell you, and I'm sure it's not how your father would want this handled. He doesn't know yet that we know about his, um, his situation," Lisette said.

"When are you planning to tell him?" Maria asked.

"Tomorrow night," Chris said. "I am planning to knock on Edie's door and inform them."

"Where does she live?" Maria continued her line of questioning.

"About an hour from here," Chris said.

Maria was quiet.

"Look, as long as we're all spilling our guts, I've got something to share," Chris said. "I've been seeing Derek, the Disgracefuls' manager. We went out to dinner two times. ONLY dinner. I really like him. He's kind of turning into my boyfriend, at least I hope so. He texts me constantly. There. Now everything's out."

"Derek's nice," Maria said. "I remember him."

"When were you planning to tell me?" Lisette asked Chris.

"Soon," Chris said, "after we got through the nastiness. I just didn't want to be all ga-ga while you're all boo hoo."

Maria turned to Lisette.

"Are you and dad going to get a divorce?" she asked.

"I'm afraid so, honey," Lisette said sadly. "Afraid so."

Maria sighed, crumpled, and sniffed, a trickle of tears slowly rolling down her face. Lisette sighed. She had to admit, even though she was completely wrung out, she felt like some of the weight had been lifted off her shoulders. The more she thought about how Carl's actions had hurt Maria, she felt her sadness and stress come together in a raging river of pissed off.

"Maria," she said, "thank you for forcing all this into the open. You are so much braver than I am. I hope you understand that you are the most important person in my life. I'm sorry I disappointed you. And I'm sorry Dad disappointed both of us."

"Am I still going to college?" Maria asked.

"Of course!" Chris and Lisette answered together.

"It's going to be all right, you guys," Chris added, pulling the three of them together in a group hug. "It sucks now, it hurts like hell, but it'll be all right."

Maria lay awake late into the night, weeping intermittently, thinking about how her life had imploded in one day. Why had Dad gone back to his old wife, she wondered. Mom does everything for us. What would happen tomorrow when Chris visited him? Mom and I should be there, she thought. She needed to hear Carl's side of the story.

Chapter 30

I'm going on a chicken run," Derek announced, standing and stretching dramatically, trying to project an image of intense boredom. The band members ignored him. They were in various poses of standing or sitting around the studio. They'd been debating the microphone setup on the drum kit for hours, trying to achieve a Bonham-esque cymbal sound. It was delicious torture for the musicians, who suffered from varying degrees of hearing loss. They were striving to detect nuances that may or may not have been evident. It was purely subjective. It had been easier to reach consensus in their drug days, either because their hearing was better or they were in a hurry to get back to getting high.

Derek was far from bored. He was actually wound tight with nerves about the mission. He kept mixing up the signal Chris would give if she needed him. Was he supposed to charge in if she opened the curtains or closed them? What had seemed so appealing about going along as "back-up"?

"All right, then," he said, sliding his arms into his jacket and leaving the studio. The car idled outside, Jake behind the wheel. Derek reached into the inside pocket of his jacket, pulled out a piece of paper with the address of the sting operation and handed it to Jake. They were pulling out of the parking lot when Jake suddenly braked hard. Shane's face appeared in Derek's window. He motioned to let him in the car.

"Bloody hell," Derek muttered, rolling down the window instead.

"Open up, man," Shane said. "I'll ride along."

"That's not a good idea," Derek said.

"Why not?" Shane asked.

"The boys need your ear, you should stay," Derek said. He was a terrible liar.

"Those wankers will be in the same place when we get back," Shane said. "It's an exercise in futility. Now let me in."

"I can't," Derek said, breaking out in a sweat. "I'm on a secret mission."

"To get chicken? What, you don't want anyone else to know your chicken source?"

"No, man, it's extremely complicated."

"Open up."

"You can't come, Shane," Derek sputtered.

"Open the door."

"No, Shane, really. You can't come along."

"Open the door or I'll fire you."

Derek opened the door.

"Look, if you must know, I'm helping Chris with something."

"Are you slipping out for a tryst?" Shane asked, leering.

"Not at all," Derek said, immediately wishing he had gone with the tryst defense. "Bollocks."

"What is up with you, man?" Shane persisted. "Move over. I'd love to see Chris. Maybe get some info on Lisette."

"I'm helping Chris with a case, if you must know, a stakeout, and it could be dangerous. You can't come along."

"Are you serious? That sounds a thousand times more interesting than what's happening in there," he said, nodding towards the building. He was halfway into the car.

"Fuck," Derek said, sweating in earnest, a trickle running down his temple. "You have to promise me you'll stay in the car at all times. Not even a finger outside of the car. Not a hair."

"I will behave," Shane promised. Unlike Derek, he was a great liar.

As the car drove off into the twilight, Shane kept on Derek, needling him for details about his relationship with Chris, eventually circling back to the case they were about to involve themselves in. Derek was no James Bond. By the time they'd crossed into Orange County, he'd spilled the beans that Chris's case involved "a friend's" husband. By the time they took the Mission Viejo exit, Shane was briefed on the particulars of the husband cheating with his ex-wife. Derek did manage, however, not to reveal that the "friend" involved was Lisette, and he was feeling good about that, at least.

He figured he'd stand outside the car with his arms crossed while Chris went inside, wait until she came out, and they'd be on their way. No one would see Shane through the tinted windows. Easy. He had sweated through his shirt.

Chris, meanwhile, was tearing up the highway, making up lost time spent arguing with Lisette and Maria about who would come along. Lisette had been dead-set against allowing Maria to accompany them.

It was Maria who threw Lisette's own words back at her.

"You said it was best to have the truth come out," Maria argued, adamant and loud. "You said I was brave. If you mean it, let me come along. It's my family, too. Let me deal with my own life!"

In the end, Lisette had acquiesced. She was an emotional shell, a nervous wreck. She was on the edge. But Maria had taught her an important lesson the night before about the freedom that truth brings. In retrospect, she had been too fierce a protector of Maria, a tiger mom. Her daughter had practically told her that it was crippling her. It was time to loosen her grasp and stop "protecting" Maria. She folded. She caved. What a colossal mess, she was thinking as Chris's car drove south at a high rate of speed.

"Please slow down," she implored Chris as she worried about (in order of likelihood) getting rear-ended (whiplash), getting sideswiped or sideswiping another vehicle (leading to a rollover), and getting "pancaked" between semi trucks (certain death). She kept her thoughts to herself and worried next about what was available to throw up into. In her life, she had barfed into her hat on an "L" train early in her pregnancy and into her purse while riding an interminable elevator after a drunken holiday party. Might be the purse again, she thought, grimacing.

"We don't want to get there after our backup," Chris insisted. "A strange car stopped on a residential street can be a tip-off. People run out the back door. Nosy neighbors call the cops."

While Lisette was in misery, Maria felt strangely excited and free. She had grown the fuck up in the past 24 hours, she realized. She felt older, taller and stronger even. More important, she had taught the two women she admired most a few new things, she had shown them who she was. She had been brave, she had insisted on the truth, and she had pulled back the curtain on deceit, exposing different "truths" than she had assumed. That was her biggest takeaway, about wrong assumptions. And all day today, she had persisted with her mother and Chris, and she ultimately won. In the past 24 hours, she had taken giant steps into her adult life. If she could do this, face her father with the truth, she could do anything.

Chris came in hot on the driveway at 465 Briar Circle, riding the bumper of a Toyota Camry with Oregon plates, an obvious rental. Carl was here! From this point they needed to move fast. They'd passed the Town Car pulling into the circle. She texted Derek: "Going in, position car on street outside 465."

"Let's go," Chris said, bolting first out of the car. Maria sprang out next and Lisette brought up the rear, hands in her pockets, head down, a reluctant Pieta of humiliation.

Chris knocked four times with authority on the front door. The three women could barely hear the knock over the pounding of their hearts.

After a pause, they heard footsteps. The door opened, revealing a gray-haired woman in a lavender sweat suit. She looked at Chris, front and center, expectantly.

"Is Carl here?" Chris said.

A look of concern replaced the friendly face that had opened the door. She turned her gaze from Chris to Maria, and a flash of recognition caused her eyes to widen. Then she saw Lisette on the sidewalk behind them and her alarm intensified.

"Oh dear," she said.

Maria looked beyond Edie and noticed a walker in the front hallway.

"We don't want any trouble," Chris was saying. "We know he's here and we need to talk to him."

"Oh dear," Edie said again. But she opened the door and stepped back, allowing them in. In her head, Edie was thinking, "Here we go." She was the least surprised of anyone. Amazing, really, that the secret lasted as long as this. A confrontation was a small price for having the charade over at last. Rip off the Band-Aid. "Thy will be done," she prayed.

"Carl!" she called.

The house smelled like corned beef and cabbage. "60 Minutes" was on in a room nearby, they could hear the trademark stopwatch tick-tick-tick, then an advertisement for a Hepatitis C drug started.

They followed Edie's gaze to a doorway that was the source of the TV sound. Then Carl was standing in the doorway. Seeing them all there – Edie, Chris, Maria, and just the part of Lisette's hair behind them – he stopped in his tracks and grabbed his chest. His eyes widened.

"Oh god!" he choked.

"Dad!" Maria cried.

"Carl, sit down," Edie rushed to him, took his arm, and guided him to the staircase and into a sitting position on a step.

"Can you breathe? Are you having arrhythmia? Chest pains?" Edie asked.

"I'm calling an ambulance," Chris said, pulling her cell phone from a pocket.

"No!" Carl said. "Don't. I'm all right. Just give me a minute."

The four women stared at him. He was ashen and trembling. His mouth turned down. He suddenly looked very old. Elbows on his knees, he put his head in his hands. Seconds passed before he looked up.

"Well this is a surprise," he said at last.

"No shit," Maria said.

"Maria!" Carl reprimanded.

"No, Dad, you have some explaining to do," Maria confronted him.

"Let's all just calm down," Edie said. Her legs were spasming. She would be the next one down.

Carl had not met Lisette's downcast eyes. Maria looked at Chris.

"Look, Carl," Chris said, "your secret is out. It's time for some truth-telling. Why don't you and Maria and Lisette go have a little chat. Edie and I will wait in the kitchen. Are you sure you don't need 911? I don't want you having a grabber before they get some answers from you."

"Thank you for your concern, Chris," Carl said bitterly. He had always been jealous of what he perceived as her hold over Lisette. "Come, this way," he said, rising slowly and indicating the TV room. "Lisette…" he shrugged with his hands out, looking as old as the mummies at the Field Museum. She did not look up.

The three of them went into the room. Carl shut the door.

"Do you own any weapons?" Chris asked Edie.

"No! Of course not!" Edie answered, horrified.

"Sure about that?" Chris pushed. She was digging this.

The two women went into the kitchen. The source of the gaseous fumes was simmering on the stove. Chris noticed that Edie had set two clean plates and silverware on the counter next to the bubbling pot.

"Sorry to interrupt your dinner," Chris said.

"Would you like tea?" Edie asked.

"No thank you," Chris replied.

"Let's sit," Edie said. Her legs were killing her.

"So tell me all about it, Edie," Chris said when both had settled into seats across from each other in the little breakfast nook.

Edie told Chris the story from her point of view. MS, money troubles, Carl riding to the rescue. How over time they sort of "got back together." That they were thinking of downsizing for Carl's retirement...

"Sounds like you have it all planned out," Chris said. "What about Lisette? What about Maria?"

"They are not my concern," Edie said coldly. "That's Carl's business."

Chris looked at her, disbelieving.

"So, what goes around comes around?" Chris asked.

"Something like that," Edie said.

"What a cold bitch," Chris thought to herself.

The only voice they heard coming from the TV room was Maria's. Her volume slowly diminished and though they couldn't make out words, they heard Carl's deeper voice speaking for quite a while.

"When were you planning to tell us about all this?" Maria asked. Her voice trembled, but she was not crying.

"I'm truly sorry, Maria. I should have been honest," he admitted. "I just got in so deep at some point I couldn't face the two of you, or myself for that matter."

"That's too easy, Dad," Maria chastised him. "Why? What does Edie have that we don't have?"

Maria sounded like the wronged wife. Lisette had yet to even speak. The confrontation-avoider stood back and let the drama play out between Carl and Maria.

"Maria, before I met your mother I was married to Edie for 20 years. We have two children together, now grandchildren. Our son Gerald called me when she needed help. She has MS. I had always felt guilty about doing wrong to Edie in the past. I saw helping her out now, all these years later, as a belated opportunity to do right by her. The more I helped out here, the more urgent it became to keep my secret. I was in too deep and couldn't figure out how to get out. The truth is, I didn't want to get out. I fell in love with Edie again."

Carl sighed.

"I'm so sorry, Maria," he said. "I love you so much. That's why I couldn't leave."

"Don't even go there, Dad," Maria said, her voice rising again. "Don't use love for an excuse for all these lies. Don't make this mess my fault. This is on you."

Lisette was in wonder. How was Maria able to do this? When did she get so wise? So fearless?

"Maria, there comes a time in a man's life when he just wants to be comfortable. Edie and I have history. We grew up together. We understand each other. We're both pushing 70. We have an opportunity to write our last chapter together, to set things right in the end."

God, Carl was insufferable, Lisette thought. What a fucking narcissist. She had heard enough. She looked straight at Carl, eyes blazing.

"Lisette, I'm so sorry," Carl said.

"Fuck off, Carl," she said, turning and leaving the room. She found Chris and Edie in the gas chamber, sitting in a breakfast nook.

"Chris, I think we're done here," she said, and headed for the front door. Leaving the house, she nearly ran smack into Derek.

"Everything all right in there?" he asked.

Lisette nodded, too emotionally drained to speak, and turned toward Chris's car.

"Lisette, is that you?" called a voice from behind Derek.

Shane was walking briskly up the sidewalk.

"Lisette, I didn't know you were in on this caper," Shane said, approaching. "Helping Chris with her detective work?"

As he drew closer, he saw Lisette's face and realized in an instant why he had no business here.

"Shane, what are you doing here?" Lisette asked. The world seemed to tumble around her as if she were rolling in a clothes dryer. "Am I fainting?" she wondered, gracefully crumpling onto the grass of the front lawn while her vision faded to black.

"Mom!" Maria cried, bolting from the house, Chris on her heels.

"Jesus Christ!" Chris barked. "Man down!"

As Chris and Maria worked to revive Lisette, patting her hands and talking to her as she groggily came to, Edie and Carl crowded through the front door and onto the porch. Derek positioned himself between the gray-haired couple and the scene on the lawn. He placed his feet apart and crossed his arms.

"That's far enough," he told them, scowling. He was so nervous he feared he might wet himself.

Lisette was trying to sit up, looking at the faces of concern looming over her. Maria and Chris were on either side. Shane was kneeling by her feet.

"How do you feel?" Chris asked. "Any shortness of breath, pressure in your chest, weakness in arms or legs?"

Her face looked normal, it isn't a stroke, Chris calculated, relieved.

"No, I think I just fainted," Lisette said.

"My god, aren't you Shane Stewart?" Edie piped from the porch. "What on earth are you doing here?"

Shane stood up, walked to Derek's side and looked Carl in the eyes.

"I think I might be in love with your wife," Shane said.

Carl gasped and grabbed his chest. Lisette swooned.

"That's it!" Chris announced, dialing 9-1-1.

Chapter 31

The ambulance siren brought neighbors out of their houses, clustering in small groups around their cul-de-sac. They all knew Edie and figured she was having a medical emergency related to her condition. Their concern was genuine.

"Isn't that Shane What's-His-Name, you know, the rock star?" one of the neighbors asked another. The celeb sighting started a buzz while the paramedics took Carl's blood pressure and listened to his heartbeat. Lisette refused treatment and sat in Chris's car.

Chris and Maria hovered and listened in on the paramedics. A teenager from two doors down jogged up to Shane and asked for a selfie. Derek wondered if he was supposed to tackle the kid.

"I can't believe you're here, in my neighborhood, on my circle," the kid gushed to Shane. "Oh, hey Mr. Anderson. You feeling all right?"

"I'd feel a lot better if you'd all go home," Carl snapped. The crowd quickly dispersed, but Derek noticed a lot of curtain action up and down the street. He faced the nosy neighbors with legs astride, arms crossed. For good measure, he took sunglasses out of his jacket pocket and put them on, then resumed his pose. Night had fallen. Chris glanced at him and shook her head.

Once Carl had been checked and cleared, and the paramedics had their pictures taken with Shane, Chris walked over to Derek and Shane, leaving Maria to say goodbye to her father.

"Nice work. You guys sure know how to blend in," she said. "This is going to be all over social media. Probably being posted as we speak. You should go."

"I want to respect Lisette's space right now," Shane said to Chris, looking beyond her. Lisette was sitting in the back seat of Chris's car with a hoodie up over her head. She looked like she was next in line for a perp walk. She'd nearly fainted a second time when Shane confronted Carl. "Do you think I could talk to her? Or should we leave without saying goodbye?"

"I'll tell her the 'respecting her space' part. Let's really do that. We'll be in touch when this dies down a little. It was pretty surreal. Let's all take a breath."

"And Derek," she said, wheeling on him. "You are fired! Never let me take you on backup again!"

"Thank god," Derek said. "That suits me fine. I'm no Cormoran Strike, that's for sure."

A week later, in bed, Derek and Chris would re-tell the story from their individual perspectives, giving full rein to the warped hilarity of their intervention.

"I was so sweaty!" Derek would say. "I was bloody terrified. At one point I thought I might piss myself."

"I was nearly unconscious from cabbage fumes," Chris would try to best him. "I think Edie was trying to off me via suffocation and bury me in a shallow grave under the hummingbird feeder."

"'I think I might be in love with your wife'," Derek would sit up to deliver the quote, jabbing his finger into the air like a Shakespearean actor. Shane hadn't jabbed, merely proclaimed. "Not quite Clapton, a little hedging there with 'I think, I might' as opposed to the bold declaration: 'I'm in love with your wife.' Nevertheless, it was an epic moment. Fucking epic!"

"Shane's lucky Carl didn't have him charged with seduction or adultery, like Frank Sinatra," Derek added.

"That was 1938, the charge doesn't even exist any more," Chris would say, snuggling close and continuing to erupt into giggles until she finally found her sleep, leaving Derek wondering, "How does she know these things?"

Lisette and Maria flew home to Chicago holding hands, reflective. They were whacked from the stunning discoveries. It had been a revelation on many levels. It had taken all they had. They'd regroup for a few days, then on to the final college tour, University of Michigan.

Chapter 32

The standard question is 'Can you see yourself here?' It's like a running gag – they say it on every tour!" Maria said. "But mom, I actually can see myself here. It's so familiar, but exciting. I love it."

She was under the spell of the maize and blue. They were walking through "The Diag," Maria was wearing her New York boots. It was late winter, a crust of snow invisibly and oh so slowly evaporating into the freezing air.

"Maria, be honest," Lisette said. "Is Ann Arbor so appealing because it's close and you're worried about me?"

"No, Mom, it just feels like home to me. I'm 'dug in' in Michigan from my whole life. I remember going to the art fair in Ann Arbor with you from when I was a little girl. And I can bring friends to the cottage. Mom, it's perfect. This is it. This is where I see myself for the next five years."

"Five?" Lisette croaked. She felt like lying down immediately. After nearly a year of college tours, they had a winner! And it was quite brilliant that they could meet at the cottage any weekend, maybe even spend entire summers, as Lisette and Chris had done.

So off went the final papers.

Lisette spent the following week or so in a lovely Carl-Free Zone. Perhaps they'd talk again. Perhaps her last words to her longtime husband would be "Fuck off, Carl."

She was not so much singed by heartbreak as she was frozen by long-standing emotional disengagement. She felt intense relief. The truth had set her free. She was thawing out.

She sat at her laptop staring at the screen, not really seeing it, replaying and analyzing the sting operation. She couldn't believe she fainted and came to with Shane telling Carl he was in love with her! Or might be, whatever. Maria had been magnificent. Lisette thought she had better start saving for law school. She'd been thinking about Carl's soliloquy about "last chapters," about setting things right. There is so much guilt to love sometimes. People like to portray it as sacrifice, as a noble act of selflessness. But is it? Who are we loyal to in the end? What does it say about us?

"About that lunch" was the subject line in Shane's email. Its appearance with a "ping" caused Lisette's stomach to execute a complete flip.

Dear Lisette,

I did not realize until I saw your face that you were involved in Chris's case in Orange County. I apologize for intruding on a personal moment. I wish I could blame Derek, but I forced him to bring me along.

I further apologize for blurting out my feelings for you. I hope my impetuous behavior does not further complicate your situation, or make you think I am insane.

We should talk. Could we still have lunch? Please call! I will come to Chicago at your convenience. Hoping to hear from you,

Shane (cell phone #)

"Why not?" Lisette thought. Lawyers were finalizing a settlement, she and Carl were officially separated. After the scene in California, neither had the stomach for protracted drama over division of assets. So yes, she would have lunch with Shane – after consulting with Maria. No more secrets! She reread his email critically and decided he was articulate and thoughtful, even if his lovelorn bit was borderline crazy. They'd gotten along well in their brief meetings. Now they could start actually getting to know each other. Her stomach did another flip.

After Lisette had returned to Chicago, Chris had sent her the Rorschach photo from the meet-and-greet in L.A. Lisette called it up on her computer several times a day to convince herself that Shane Stewart was not a delusion, that she was not having some sort of psychotic break. Having a first-name relationship with someone so public, someone she had admired as a fan for decades, was just so weird! Lisette was not someone with famous friends. That part required getting used to, separating the man from the persona, establishing familiarity as just two people, a man and a woman, away from the fame. She had been too shut down after the confrontation to notice the paramedics and the neighbor boy asking for pictures with Shane. That thought never crossed her mind. She was thinking old school, like if the two of them were having lunch and someone interrupted asking for an autograph, well that would be a first for Lisette. It must be terribly flattering, she imagined. She didn't think about the downside: crazy stalkers, bathing suit photos making the tabloids' "Worst Beach Bodies" issues, social media with endless attacks on/defenses of the band.

The picture on her screen had not been made public. Chris had controlled that. She'd waited to share it with Lisette until about a week after the "intervention," as Chris now referred to the event. It sounded so much more humane than "raid" or "bust." It made it easier to talk about somehow, clinically appropriate.

Lisette studied the picture. She and Shane were standing face-to-face, their hands joined, arms out, looking at each other, smiling. They could have been dancing, but Lisette remembered the moment and knew they were standing still. Chris was in the background, grinning at them through her sunglasses. Their two dark heads with white streaks met in the middle. They were nearly the same height, thanks to Lisette's tall boots. It was a weird twin image, almost symmetrical, like a butterfly, though she was in black and he was wearing white. Lisette assumed that it was the only picture in existence of the two of them together. She was unaware that from their first meeting in the first-aid tent, people had snapped shots of the two of them together. They were saved on phones of everyday people, some in Chicago, some in California. Lisette was a terribly private person. Could she live with that?

She dialed his number. He answered after the third ring.

"Hi, Shane, it's Lisette," she said.

"Hi, Lisette," he said, Frenching it up with a dramatic long e and a buzzing z. "I am so happy to hear from you. I should be happy, right?"

"If happiness is lunch, then yes," she said.

"How are you? I mean, after the, uh, situation," he stuttered. "You doing all right?"

"Better every day," she said.

"It was crazy. Every time we meet it's crazy, right? Always some drama, or surprise," he said.

"You're right!" Lisette agreed. "I hadn't thought about it but you are right. Every time but the meet-and-greet."

"Ah, but there was drama that night," Shane corrected her. "I asked you to come back after the show, and when you got there, I was involved with my daughter Priya and missed you. She told me she was pregnant! It was one of those moments that blocked everything else out. Sorry."

"No, it's fine," Lisette said, thinking "It was his daughter!"

"How lovely, congratulations," she said. "When is the baby due?"

"Late August," Shane said. "She has a little bump."

"Aww," Lisette said, remembering Maria as a jumbo shrimp.

"When can I see you?" Shane asked. "What about this this lunch, Lisette?"

"I'm free on Fridays which is probably terrible for you," she said. "I have two months left in the semester."

"And what are you doing after that?" he asked.

"I'm going to Michigan!" Lisette said. "To the beach, to the sunshine and waves for the whole glorious summer! I'm so excited! It's something I've always wanted to do."

She paused and decided to say what she was thinking.

"I am suddenly in a position to do whatever I please," she said.

"What's in Michigan?" Shane asked.

"I have a tiny beach cottage there," Lisette explained. "It's my favorite place."

"Lake Michigan?" Shane asked. "The 'Sunset Coast?'"

"Yes, the 'Big Water' – and how do you know about the 'Sunset Coast'?"

"I grew up in Indiana," Shane confessed. "Terre Haute. We'd go up to Michigan in summer to get away, camping."

The only camping Lisette had ever done in Michigan was a weekend in the dunes when she was 21 with a drummer and his puppy. As a teenager, she'd gone along many years when Chris's family rented big, rambling houses on the lakeshore for a week or two of drinking, swimming, sailing, tennis, beach volleyball, sunsets, bonfires, and more drinking. And in college, of course, when she and Chris were waitressing and gigging as the "Fab Two," they shared a tiny furnished room above the restaurant.

"When was the last time you were there?" she asked.

"We go to Detroit pretty regularly, but it's probably been 40 years since I've been on the other side of the state."

"Well when you come to Chicago, we'll go to the lakefront and wave across the lake," Lisette said, getting them back on track.

"Great," Shane said.

Shane's Midwest roots took Lisette by surprise. She pictured him with that startling face (from the black-and-white picture Maria showed her in the book) in some John Mellencamp scenario, a teenager in a white undershirt, jeans, and boots, dirt under his nails, at a hamburger drive-in. In fact, Shane's father was an English professor at Indiana State University Terre Haute, "Home of Larry Bird." His mother was a legal secretary, a crackerjack, smart and knowledgeable enough to have been a state's attorney in a different era. It just wasn't her time. Even though Terre Haute was a small town, it would be impossible to track down Shane Stewart's parents without knowing he was christened Shane Stewart Lundelius.

"So, do you have any trips to Chicago coming up?" Lisette asked. She felt comfortable about moving things along. She was in charge! "Any shows or other business?"

"Not really, we're writing for a few weeks, in L.A.," Shane explained. "But I could bust out for a day and come see you, have lunch."

"Do you have someplace in mind you want to go?" Lisette asked.

"I don't," Shane said. Lisette could not see him hitting himself in the head with the heel of his hand. Shit! What a rube! He should have had a suggestion ready – he was a man of the world! "Do you have a favorite place?"

"That depends," Lisette said. "Do you have dietary restrictions, are you a vegan or a vegetarian, pescatarian, do you do dairy or eggs, any nut allergies? What do you like?"

Shane was thrown off by the pelting of questions and lost his train of thought completely and suffered sudden blurred vision at the words "What do you like?" He hit himself in the head again. Focus, man!

"No dietary restrictions whatsoever," he said. "I am, however, a bit worn out on chicken at the moment."

"I can imagine," Lisette laughed. Chris had told her about Derek's chicken jag.

"I have a favorite restaurant," Lisette said. "The food is always perfect, and the view is charming. There's a jazz trio that starts at 5, and it gets pretty packed after that."

"So the only question is when," Shane summarized.

"Why don't you see how the writing goes and let me know when a Friday or a weekend day pops up? You're the one who has to travel four hours both ways," Lisette said. "I could go to Michigan and back twice with the time you'll spend in the air."

"So, to be continued? I will let you know by Thursday if it will be this week, depending on how it's going in the studio, is that all right?" Shane asked.

"Sounds like a plan," Lisette confirmed, cringing that she used that worn-out phrase. She understood the dynamics and power of creative tension. To create art requires a delicate balance of struggle, anxiety, awareness, spark, doubt, redemption, perspective, gratification, and terror. There is a certain disequilibrium in the zone of proximal development that comes from striving, pushing the boundaries of one's imagination, pushing past accumulated knowledge to construct something new. The longer she could string out the lunch date, the more time Shane would have to channel that tortured anticipation and energy into the work. Any artist – or muse – knew that. Lisette counted muses as artists, too.

"Work hard. Make something beautiful," she said. "Don't stop on account of lunch, see it through. You can text me how it's going. Lunch can wait – there will always be Arctic char."

As they hung up with "talk to you soon," Shane raised his arms like a triumphant prize fighter and tumbled head first into long-ago memories of the Michigan dunes, the sparkle of the sun on the water, the splash of the waves, the cries of the gulls, the lake turning into a pool of pink under a fiery sunset. Meteor showers against the black sky. Sandy beds and the smell of Coppertone.

He picked up his notebook and jotted down the images. Underneath he wrote "Tip your face to the sun. Let me be your only one…" His ballad was growing lyrics. He kept writing, "Walking on the shore, you and me forevermore…"

He texted Lisette: Send me a list of 5 things you love about Michigan.

"Maria!" Lisette called. She brought Maria up to speed, telling her everything, then asked, "What do you think?"

"I think you are a genius," Maria grinned. "You gotta give people space."

Maria had been floating on a cloud of excitement about her college decision. About a dozen of her classmates were headed to U of M, and others had been accepted to various smaller universities in Michigan, thanks to an in-state tuition agreement with Illinois.

Since the intervention, followed closely by her college decision, Maria had a new swagger. She was a short-timer. She was already acting like an emancipated adult home for a visit. The power structure had shifted. Lisette was constantly reminding herself to loosen the reins, and it wasn't easy. Fortunately, they had a lot of decisions to make, and it gave them neutral ground on which to work out their new partnership. The biggest question was where would they live?

Maria would be 18 in May, so she was not bound by any custody agreement. It would be up to Maria and Carl to work out holidays and visits. They were in touch by phone and text messages. Lisette was relieved to relinquish control of these emotional chores, details she had managed for so many years. She vaguely wondered whether Carl would stick with his Thanksgiving in New York City tradition and if and how he was planning to integrate Maria into his new/old family. His guilt made his phone calls with Maria awkward. His graduation gift to Maria was a trip to Europe.

Lisette and Maria didn't really need their big house with its big yard. Misha had settled into dog middle age. He preferred walks with his humans to chasing squirrels alone outdoors. Lisette worried about making too many changes at once. But it was Maria who showed her an article in the Homes section about a new lofts conversion in a former school. "It's near the conservatory," she said, handing the newspaper to her mother. "You should think about downsizing."

"I love the concept," Lisette said. The thought of moving paralyzed her when she thought of all of their closets full of things, the basement, the garage. "What if I wasn't teaching at the conservatory?" she thought. She wanted to consider every scenario.

"We should both think about downsizing," Lisette said. "As you pack for school, let's do a full inventory and get rid of all of our accumulated junk. I don't want to move too fast, and we can take the whole summer to explore our options." She started a new pile on her desk, anchored by the article, soon to be buried under lists titled "Get Rid Of," "Keep," "Take to School," and "Take to Cottage." They were moving on.

Chapter 33

When Derek had seen the scar, a look of concern crossed his face. He slowly raised his eyes to meet Chris's.

"When?" Derek asked.

"Three years ago," Chris said. "Lumpectomy, chemo, radiation. A lost year."

"I'm so sorry," Derek said. "Does it hurt?" he asked, lightly tracing the scar with his finger.

"Not at all," Chris answered. "Does it freak you out?"

"Love, you don't get to be our age and not have danced with death," he said. "Why just a few weeks ago we faced two possible heart attacks and a fainting spell that might have been a subdural hematoma. Every day's a gift, right?"

"Derek, you sound like one of those platitudes on Facebook," Chris jibed him. "Just so you know, I had clean margins and lymph nodes. I have a clean bill of health. I'm good to go."

"And I am very, very happy about that," Derek said, pulling her close and kissing her neck.

The thought of her suffering sent a pain so sharp through his heart that he banished it forever, then and there. Sent it packing. He'd lost his mother to breast cancer. Surely his dues had been paid.

Derek was definitely in love with Chris. The thought of going on the road again with the band troubled him. He was happy staying in one place for a while, especially if that place was where Chris was.

Lisette, meanwhile, was doing a Chris thing: making a list. Hmmm.

Five things I love about Michigan. Only five? Lisette made a list:

The golden light

The silky air

The sound of the waves

The trees in fall

The ever-changing sky

She could go on and on about the eternal days of June and July, when the sun didn't drop into the water until 9:30, and the stunning afterglow lingered, slowly ebbing, until nearly 11.

The exercise fueled Lisette's eagerness to be there – she wanted to jump into the car and go right now! "Soon," she told herself. "Soon."

She had plenty to keep her busy in Chicago until the semester ended. The observation days and recital would be here before she knew it!

Word was out at the conservatory. Maddie had brought a basket of muffins with a sweet note. Evelyn had lingered after senior ballet, stretching on the barre until the others cleared out.

"I'm sorry to hear about your divorce, we all are," she said. "I just wanted to acknowledge, Lisette, and let you know that we are here for you."

"Thanks, Evelyn," Lisette said, feeling the color rise in her face.

Evelyn hesitated, then blurted out, "And if that Shane Stewart has anything to do with it, well, my mother always said, 'Trade up!' Life is meant to be exciting. You go girl!" And with that, Evelyn executed four *glissades* on her way to the doorway, spider-like on her spindly legs, ending with a wobbly *pirouette* and a wave over her shoulder.

The ladies often stopped for tea or martinis after class. Tonight it was martinis. As they discussed Lisette's divorce, nearly every one had a sob story. Maddie was the leadoff batter.

"We were watching a movie at home and he responded to a text. It was from a woman at work asking 'Whatcha doin?' And he replied 'Nothing.' I read the texts when he went to the bathroom (which these days is about every 20 minutes)." The others nodded knowingly. "When he came back in the room I let him have it! First of all, why was he getting late-night texts from a woman at work? Secondly, we weren't doing 'nothing.' I asked him, 'Am I nothing?' He was on my shit list for weeks. But one good thing about texting and Facebook and all the social media, it's pretty hard to get away with fooling around. You don't need CSI to connect the dots any more."

Shira followed with her own texting story.

"My husband was just home from the hospital and I sent 'thank you' texts with a picture of him back at home to all the people who had sent 'get well' cards. Almost instantly, a woman who lives down the block texted back – to my phone, mind you – 'You certainly look a whole lot better than the hospital pic! Love you massively and seriously hope you heal quickly' – then this cloud of red and pink heart emojis! I would have wrung his neck if it hadn't been in a brace! I wanted to murder!"

"Him or her?" asked Evelyn.

"Both!" Shira said emphatically.

"Did you let her know it was your phone?" asked Evelyn.

"I did," Shira said. "I texted back 'Um, this is Shira, but I'll pass your message along.' The fact that she didn't know the number was some consolation that they weren't in regular contact. But I was pissed. And when I'm upset, I clean. I vacuumed for a solid hour. Vigorously."

"Did she apologize?" Evelyn asked.

"Never," Shira said. "What a troll. But I have to admit, with all his health problems, I was tempted to tell her to come get him! Let her take care of his sickly ass."

"Hear hear!" crowed Evelyn. Turning somber, she lowered her voice.

"I was married to my Teddy for 32 years. I raised our two boys and thought we had a perfect life, or as near perfect as marriage can be, right? Every marriage has its ups and downs. Then one day he tells me he has a girlfriend and he wants a divorce! They'd been fooling around for more than a year! I was so ashamed, and I was suddenly broke. I went to Andre to try to sell my furs on consignment. He asked me if I'd joined PETA! When I told him the story, he offered me a job! He said, 'Mrs. Proctor, you've been a good customer all these years. You send me a lot of business. You are a beautiful lady, a fine lady, you have impeccable taste. You need work, you come work for me.' I was an over-50 housewife, abandoned, lost, desperate. Divorce is when you learn who your friends are."

"Evelyn, I had no idea," Maddie said, wiping a tear.

"It was horrible," Evelyn admitted. "But you know what was the hardest thing?"

The women, all 10-20 years younger than Evelyn, looked at her expectantly.

"Pulling myself back from the brink of bitterness," Evelyn said. "You can fake happiness, but bitterness is like measles – you can see it a mile away. I was 51. That might sound old to some of you but I still had my period! I was hurt and angry. I felt defeated. I could see disappointment and bitterness starting to take over my face – the worry and concern, the set of my mouth, the frown lines between my brows. I could taste the bile. And in the midst of this darkness, my pride kicked in. I simply refused to let Teddy ruin my looks or my outlook on life! Bitterness is ugly and malignant. I cast it off and that was my saving grace."

"I know what you mean," Shira said. "I've been in a perpetual state of annoyance for years. It's not helping my looks or my outlook."

"Well I'll tell you one more thing: I've had quite a few lovers in the meantime and every one came back for more," Evelyn whispered confidentially. "If you have the right lubricant, Viagra, and ballet class, you can have great sex for the rest of your life! I told Lisette to 'trade up' from that pompous ass Carl. I hope she runs off with that rock star, you know, that babe who sent the flowers?"

"That would be rich," Maddie said. The others nodded their assent. "That would be fucking brilliant," Maddie underscored.

Lisette had left it up to the seniors to decide whether they wanted to perform in the recital, and they had voted unanimously to take part. They also wanted their recital number be their dance that used the Disgracefuls' song. It might fit into the program after the jazz dancers, right before intermission, Lisette thought. She knew they were rallying for her sake, and loved them for it. It takes a special kind of nerve to perform in public, and they were choosing to be fearless and let it rip. Lisette knew it would be the hit of the show.

She was starting to wonder if it might be her "swan song." With everything that was going on, would she be back in the fall? Other teachers were handling the reduced schedule of summer classes.

"Stop overthinking," she commanded herself. She repeated to herself what had become her mantra: "Let go, let whatever's next unfold in its own time. Trust."

Giving up control was a new mindset for her. The more she practiced, the more she appreciated it. She might even revert to liking being out of control. She'd been buttoned down for far too long.

Chapter 34

W here's Rob?" Shane asked. The bass player had been late regularly during their stay in L.A. He was a no-show Friday, which pissed Shane off because he could have had lunch in Chicago, but decided to stick with the writing and recording. It was going well.

The ballad had written itself. Shane had not accessed that pure zone of conception for a long time. It was almost creepy, Ouija board stuff. The words just showed up. He thought he might be delusional – or bipolar even – the way the process claimed him as an artist, rather than the artist controlling the process. Had he experienced a creative breakthrough? Was he losing his mind?

"Rob must be tangled up with being at home, the grandkids," Shane thought. Rob's family had lived in L.A for 30 years. When the band was there, Rob slept in his own bed with his wife, the mother of their children. Those kids and their kids were nearby, it was a homey set-up, hard to disengage from. Swimming pool, hot tub, beach, outdoor kitchen, a potager and raised beds of organic vegetables. They were dug in, literally. It was a lifestyle Shane envied, the togetherness, the continuity, casual drop-ins from the people who really matter. It was also an elegant lifestyle, involving continual revisions to the landscape and interior design, acquisitions of fine art, as well as constant upgrades in technology. Rob's family life was a 21st Century hippie version of "The Beverly Hillbillies."

That's where Rob was, at home, trying and failing to master the Fire Stick. He wasn't frolicking in the pool or basting in the hot tub. He was sitting in the basement entertainment center fiddling with the Fire Stick for hours on end.

For years, Rob had dealt with chronic pain. At first he thought he'd injured his shoulder, that's where the pain first showed up, a dull ache that turned into a burn. Within a week, it spread down his right arm, a painful tingling that went all the way to his fingertips. An MRI showed two herniated discs in his neck. He'd been shocked – he had no idea how he'd injured himself and why a neck injury was wrecking his arm. A bass player needs two functioning arms. Rob had come to dread live performances. Wearing a guitar strap was the worst pain trigger. Lately he'd had weakness and trembling in his right arm. His doctor ordered a new MRI, which revealed arthritis and stenosis were further stressing the damaged discs.

A neurosurgeon recommended surgery, but Rob had a wild, irrational fear of hospitals in general and operations in particular. Instead, he'd been managing his pain with heat, massage, electrical impulses, acupuncture, and opioids. How did a former junkie get opioids? Baby, please. Even with the hydrocodone, interspersed with Tramadol, he'd paced the house at night with his right arm raised over his head, seeking relief from the searing agony of nerve pain.

That's when another doctor prescribed Fentanyl. About 12 hours after applying the first patch of the pain blocker, Rob felt blessed relief. He knew junkies somehow extracted the drug from the 3-day patches and either snorted or injected the distilled Fentanyl, but Rob wasn't interested in another stint in rehab. He vowed to follow the doctor's orders and the prescribed dosage, which mostly pushed the pain to the background. The hope was that the aggravation would lessen over a week or two and he'd be able to get off the patch. Even with the patch, the days in the studio were grueling for him and causing "breakthrough pain," for which he'd pop a Vicodin or a couple of Tramadols.

"You're awfully quiet," the drummer noticed.

"The neck's been bothering me," he'd explained. That much was evident. His head was starting to jut forward like a turtle's. The drugs made him feel detached, like he was riding in the back seat, observing life through a window. He hadn't added much to the collaboration. He avoided meeting his bandmates' eyes because he knew his own were glassy from the narcotics. The others would pick up on it. It made him paranoid.

He preferred to be alone with the Fire Stick, burning away the hours figuring out how to access movies. Sometimes it worked, sometimes it didn't. He'd watched countless how-to videos on YouTube. It had become an obsession. Occasionally his family would hear "Son of a bitch!" or "God-damn it!" from below. If anyone suspected Rob was slipping into darkness, no one said anything.

"I'll give him a call," Derek said. He'd noticed Rob's personality change. He accepted the "bum neck" excuse, but also noticed his pin-dot pupils. It was his job as manager to be on top of it.

The whole band had done rehab together. Three faced the fact that they were addicts and/or alcoholics, and they had worked the Steps religiously for more than 20 years. Drummers get a bad rap, but the Disgracefuls' drummer was clean as a whistle, always had been. He did rehab with his bandmates to show solidarity. Shane was a social drinker, wine only, no spirits, who also enjoyed high-quality cannabis in the right situation. In their early years pills held an attraction for him, but never needles. He'd sworn off pills after a humiliating experience on stage – an "I've fallen and I can't get up" disaster in front of 30,000 people. After that, he never took the stage again in any condition other than stone cold sober. The rehab experience had shown him he was vulnerable, everyone is, and he practiced moderation but not abstinence. That's what worked for him. He realized that he was chairman of the board of a corporation. There was no room for fuckups at the board table. No DUIs, no nosedives, no terrible things for his girls to hear about at school. He had to keep it together.

"Rob, where are you, man?" Derek asked Rob's voicemail. "We've got the drums right and you're up next. Call me! I'm sending Jake to pick you up."

Derek rode along, thinking they'd pick up chicken on the way back to the studio. By now he was on a first-name basis with the maître d', the chef, and the general manager. He blew in a phone call and ordered four chickens. He hadn't ordered for the band since "Back Door Man," and now that he remembered the moment, that song was stuck in his head. It teased his brain in disjointed snatches all the way to Rob's. The town car pulled into the gated drive and stopped at the portico of the Greek Revival mansion. Rob's wife, Lynn, was watering the urns of tropical plants on the front porch, enormous elephant ears, palms, cannas, and caladium.

"Don't you have someone to do that for you?" Derek joshed her in greeting.

"I like to get my hands dirty," she said, giving Derek a hug. "Remember, I'm just a farm girl from Nebraska. This here's exotic stuff."

"Do you have any chard at the moment?" Derek asked. Lynn's kitchen garden, her potager, was a wonder. It was her pride and joy and she enjoyed sharing its bounty as much as Derek enjoyed its fresh organic produce.

"Yes, I'll pick some for you. I also have kale, a few peppers and some cherry tomatoes – I'll make up a nice bag of salad for you boys," she said as they walked up the front steps, through the foyer and into the kitchen. "Rob's in the basement."

Derek descended. Rob was unshaven, riveted to the giant TV screen with a small black remote in his hand. The screen was blue, with a white spinning wheel.

"Rob," Derek said. "What are you doing, man?"

"Goddamned Fire Stick," Rob said, still staring at the spinning wheel.

"Rob, look at me," Derek insisted, standing in front of the screen. "It's time to step away from the Fire Stick and go to work. You look like shit, by the way."

Rob finally met Derek's eyes.

"I know man, my neck's been killing me," he complained.

"What's all this?" Derek asked, pointing to a pile of ointments, a heating pad, a foam neck support, and a vial of pills. He picked up the vial, noting the dosage, the date, the doctor's name and the number of pills prescribed, and the number left in the bottle. "Tramadol?" he asked.

"It's from the doctor," Rob said. "I'm hurt."

"Does the doctor know your history?" Derek asked. "I know it's not heroin, but you need to be careful with this shit."

"I'm aware of that," Rob said, defensive. The other prescriptions were stashed in a bathroom drawer behind linens. He had a couple of loose Oxys and Vicodins in his pants pocket "just in case." He was on his fourth Fentanyl patch in week two of that nasty business. At least the pain was not unbearable with that, he told himself. Without it his neck felt like it was filled with shards of broken glass. He was enjoying his legal high, but he'd deny it, even act put-upon that he was in so much pain he "needed" to take opioids. Poor Rob!

"Come on," Derek said, taking the Fire Stick from Rob's hand and turning off the TV. "We're recording drums and bass today, and we're late. Go wash up and let's go."

Like a reluctant child, Rob dramatically forced himself off the couch.

"Slave driver," he muttered, but he walked to the stairs. Derek chatted with Lynn as she washed the dirt from the vegetables, shook the water off the leaves of chard and kale, and packed him a giant Ziploc of salad fixings. Derek shoved a leaf of chard into his mouth.

"Delicious," he proclaimed, chewing.

"What's going on with Rob?" he asked Lynn. "I mean with the neck pain?"

"Well, his neck is all jacked up," she said, counting on her fingers, "he's been to a bunch of doctors (2) and (3) doesn't want to have surgery, so they're (4) treating the pain and (5) he's been doing physical therapy."

"What did the doctor say about the opioids, I mean with Rob's history?" Derek asked. "Were there concerns?"

"Of course, but he was in agony! It is a legitimate treatment and he swore he'd stick to the prescribed dosage. We talked about it," she explained.

"Okay, that's good," Derek said. "Let's both keep on top of this. I'm concerned."

"I hear you," Lynn said. "I will on my end."

"Let's keep in touch," Derek said, sweeping his finger across his phone to make sure he had Lynn's cell. He found it, and read the number off to her, double-checking. In graduate school they teach you to attend to such details like a mofo.

Rob came downstairs in a clean shirt. He had combed his hair and washed his face. He couldn't wash the glassy sheen off his eyes, though. Derek would be watching him like a hawk, and would be calling the Tramadol doctor first chance he had. No Elvis endings on his watch, he vowed.

The recording studio erupted into chaos at the arrival of Rob, Derek, and four fire-roasted chickens. Rather than rush Rob right into the studio with the drummer, Derek allowed some time for the guys to rib each other, for Rob to explain himself, and for everyone to have some chicken and salad, elaborately tossed by Derek, in the studio kitchen. Lynn had even included a Tupperware container of ginger vinaigrette that complemented the chicken. Everyone got their nutrition on. Afterward, Derek did a temperature check. It was another trait that made him a successful manager: He knew how to create conditions for thoughtful cohesion.

"Everybody feeling good?" he asked the group, sitting on bar stools around a high counter, plates empty. They nodded and said "Thanks, man" and "'Preciate it" to Derek. "All right then, let's get to it."

After everyone had washed their hands, they got to work, tuning up, riffing. Rob was able to play sitting down with his guitar on his lap without the meddlesome guitar strap and heavy guitar weighing down on his neck. The band wanted him to be comfortable. They needed his heavy signature sound at the bottom. His bass line was the anchor of the Disgracefuls' iconic brand – not flashy, but solid and steady. Drums and bass recorded together first, then the other guitars would layer over that foundation. The drummer and Rob would hear the others in their headphones, but guitars would actually record later. Vocals came last. Derek gave Rob a little pep talk.

"Get your focus on, give it everything you've got, and once we get this down, you are free to go back to your Fire Stick," Derek told Rob. He knew how to motivate a junkie. You dangle things upside down. A million musicians would die to be in Rob's place in terms of the fame, fortune, and artistry. But to Rob it was his job, and he took it for granted. And yes, he was coping with a medical event. He felt frail. And yes, he was old, the oldest member of the band. And he was tired of the road and just wanted to stay home with his creature comforts, his groovy wife, his above-average grandchildren, and the Fire Stick's spinning wheel. Was that too much to ask?

"Get your focus on," Derek was saying.

The drummer counted off. Rob reached deep inside and started to play. As if a switch was thrown, he did that "ten thousand times" thing. Even on auto-pilot, he played masterfully.

"Rob's a motherfucker," said the engineer.

Derek agreed.

Chapter 35

Lisette stood in her closet trying to decide what to wear on her lunch date with Shane. It was finally Friday! He was stopping in Chicago for six hours, then on to New York to see Autumn for a day, then back to L.A. on Sunday. He was coming straight from the airport to the restaurant, then back to the airport. He could get deep vein thrombosis from all that air travel! She would remind him to get up and walk the aisle and to drink lots of water.

She settled on a black dress embroidered with green ferns, and her black New York boots. She chose her pink cashmere coat with a fox collar dyed to match. Simple diamond earrings, in a European drop setting, gold. She took a selfie in the mirror and sent it to Maria for confirmation. Maria texted back "Bombshell!"

At 12:30 she put on her pink lipstick while Misha was outside doing his business, then set off for downtown. She expected the traffic from the airport to be brutal on a Friday, so she'd probably arrive first. That was fine. She'd be in control.

But to her surprise, as soon as she walked in the door, a tall, handsome man with a well-known face hopped up from the bar and greeted her.

"Lisette!" Shane said. "Let me look at you."

He took her hand, raised it up high, and turned her around. She knew this move well and executed it gracefully, coming to rest in front of him, standing tall. Their eyes locked.

"Hi," she said.

"Your table is ready," said the hostess, bustling with efficiency the second she saw Shane Fucking Stewart walk through the door. She had already alerted the kitchen, the manager, and several friends, including one who wrote a gossip blog. She had hidden behind a partition and snapped a few pictures while he waited.

Shane could not keep his eyes off Lisette. He swept his arm, indicating "after you," encouraging her to walk ahead of him, just to ogle her from behind. He was light-headed from watching her ass when they reached a corner table with a sweeping floor-to-ceiling view of Michigan Avenue in early spring. Tulips were everywhere!

"This is lovely, thank you," Lisette said, dismissing the hostess. She slipped out of her coat and threw it over an extra chair. Shane did the same. Their coats were embracing in the next chair. It was weird and obvious and lascivious. Shane was grateful to sit.

This was their fifth meeting, but their first time alone. They looked expectantly at each other, then both spoke at the same instant: "It's so great to see you!" They burst into nervous laughter.

"Let's take a breath," Shane suggested. They took a breath, a waiter arrived with water and menus. Neither looked at the menus. It helped that they had exchanged texts and emails, but here they were, face-to-face. What to say?

"How have you been, really?" Shane asked.

"Mostly good," Lisette smiled, then frowned, "sometimes scattered, angry, feeling up in the air."

"A lot of changes," Shane observed. "How about Maria choosing Michigan!"

"She's pretty pumped up," Lisette said. "I was worried she picked Michigan because it's close and she was worried about me, but she insists that's not the case. Do you still worry about your girls?"

"Every day," Shane admitted. "I never expected to be actively parenting at this stage. Priya's 37 and Autumn's 24, but I am constantly checking on them. Our generation's experience was so different – we were emancipated so much earlier in life, I mean, we left home the second we graduated high school, lived in crappy apartments with our friends and called our parents once a month, if that. Where were you at 24?"

"I was in New York, dancing with the corps," Lisette replied. "Living in a crappy apartment with a friend. Where were you?"

"That was how old I was when Priya was born. The band was just taking off. We had recorded our first album and were touring to support it. It was a pretty exhilarating time."

"I remember that tour. Chris and I saw you guys in New York," Lisette said. "You wore a Freddie Mercury spandex body suit."

Shane rolled his eyes. "What an era," he said.

"I liked the cat suit," Lisette said. "It was balletic. And stretchy – no worries about split seams."

They shared a laugh at Shane's expense.

"I blame technology for extending the active parenting," Lisette said as the waiter approached to take their drink orders. Shane thought fleetingly about her comment, it was deep, but was distracted by the waiter. Lisette noticed that the waiter's hands were shaking. He definitely recognized Shane, but he was cool, sticking to business as he ran through the specials.

"Carciofi," Shane said, the Italian word for artichokes. They ordered iced teas and grilled baby artichokes. "I love that word. One thing about decades on the road – I can order a meal in any language!"

"How does that work, exactly?" Lisette asked. "I mean, do you travel all the time? Do you have a place you call home?"

"For years we traveled constantly, but now we pace ourselves," Shane explained. "For example, we tour one continent at a time, and we'll do, say, 10 shows in a leg, then a week off. European tours and beyond we try to pare it down to a total of eight or 10 shows over four or five weeks. That way the families can join us at different places, see the sights. My girls like to hook up in London, Paris, Rome, when we're there. I think their best education came from traveling with the band over their lifetimes."

"So where do you consider home?" Lisette asked.

"I'm homeless at present," Shane said, which was ironic considering he bought houses for two ex-wives and one daughter and paid rent for the other daughter's apartment. "I had a ranch in Austin that I sold this year. It seemed like a cool idea at the time, the music scene there plus horses and dogs and land, but I lack a cowboy's heart, apparently. I'm looking for a house in L.A., but until I find one I'm living in hotels pretty much. I could shack with Priya and her husband Daniel, but they need their space – they're 'nesting'. I want to respect these last months of being just the two of them. We both know what happens after the baby comes."

"Oh yes," Lisette said. "How goes the pregnancy?"

"Everything is going well four months in. I made them promise not to tell me if it's a boy or girl. I like the surprise at the end."

"I agree," Lisette said.

The waiter came with the artichokes and took their entrée orders. He was no longer shaking and asked "Mr. Stewart?" to take Shane's order. Shane got the char and Lisette ordered the kale salad, her favorite.

"You have to try it," Lisette said. "It comes with chicken, but I won't make you eat any."

They attacked the artichokes with their hands.

"What about you, Lisette," Shane asked between bites. "These artichokes are insane, by the way. With Maria going off to school, will you stay in Chicago? Is this where you are from?"

"I grew up outside Detroit," Lisette said. "Chris and I went to high school together."

"A Motown girl," Shane said.

"In every way," Lisette said. "I love big American cars and soul music."

"Who are your favorites?" Shane asked.

"Marvin Gaye and Tammi Terrell top my list. Otis Redding, Aretha and Smokey, of course, James Brown, Michael Jackson," Lisette called the roll of soul. "My favorite voice of all time is David Ruffin. Motown and the Beatles were our soundtrack growing up. Chris and I wanted to be backup singers – and marry John and Paul. Then came Zeppelin and our musical world tilted."

Shane noted that every Motown star she mentioned, with the exception of Smokey Robinson, was dead.

"What made you come back to the Midwest after New York?" he asked.

"Carl's work, mainly. Chicago's cosmopolitan enough. It's a great city if you can avoid freezing to death or getting shot. I'm glad Maria grew up here. I think it grounded her. My friends on both coasts had a lot of issues raising their kids that we managed to avoid, different pressures, different values – the 'right' kindergarten, the 'right' prep school, elite colleges. That happens here, too, but on the East Coast it's over the top. And the West Coast has its own issues. Ack. Here I am talking about the child-rearing era of my life, and that is coming to an end."

She was surprised by a sudden surge of emotion at this realization. Her face colored and her chin quivered.

"Aw," Shane said, putting down an artichoke leaf and taking her hand. His was warm and olive oily. "It's going to be okay. Maria will be fine. You will be fine."

"It's going to be so weird not seeing her every day," Lisette sniffed, internally reprimanding herself to "act right on a lunch date." "Wow," she said.

"Don't know where that came from. Sorry."

"It's an adjustment," Shane said, "letting them go."

"I guess I'm emotional with everything that's been going on," Lisette said, regaining her composure. "This convergence of changes, it's overwhelming sometimes. We've definitely decided to sell the Chicago house and either downsize or consolidate at the beach house. So many other details are up in the air, major things like whether I will keep teaching."

"And you, me, here," Shane said, putting "them" on the table. "This is pretty major for me. I've been emotional, too, giddy with antici..." pausing mid-word in the breathless manner of Dr. Frank-N-Furter in Rocky Horror... "pation."

Lisette giggled, recognizing the scene. "You, me, here is pretty exciting. I've been looking forward, too. And here we finally are and I'm talking about mommy stuff. Some first date!"

"Don't apologize for being real about the most important part of our lives," Shane said. "Just wait, in a few months I'll probably be forcing grandbaby pictures on people, like Rob!"

The entrees arrived.

"This looks wonderful," Shane said, squeezing lemon onto his fish and tasting a bite. "I'm in heaven," he reported. "This is my new favorite restaurant."

"Glad you like it," Lisette said, smiling, hoping she didn't have kale in her teeth. "Tell me about the studio. Are you all there every day?"

"We're working on a couple of tracks at the moment," Shane said. "We were all together finishing up the writing. This week was a bit more staggered, but we like to be there for everyone's bits because it helps to have all ears on deck. It's also great to step away from it for a few days."

"I know what you mean," Lisette agreed. "When I'm working on choreography I hit a wall at a certain point. When I step away and give my brain a rest, fresh ideas surface."

"They are similar processes," Shane agreed. "Music and dance, hand in glove. Ballet is amazing to me, the athleticism of it, the geometry and precision and grace. That's one of the things I find fascinating about you."

Thinking of how limber she must be lit his hazel eyes with their trademark twinkle without calculation. Lisette felt like the most important person in the world. Distracted, flattered, she realized Shane had asked her a question: "What's your favorite thing about your work at the moment?"

"Hmmm. I'd have to say my senior ballet class," Lisette said, tipping her dish to his and pushing some of her kale salad onto his plate with her knife. A chunk of chicken tumbled into the mix. They both noticed and made "ack" faces at each other.

"They are seniors in age, not ability, and I adore them. They all loved ballet as young girls but grew away from it as adults. Most of the ladies are 40s to 60s. My oldest student is 72, Evelyn. She is a very bad influence! They voted unanimously to perform at the recital!"

She didn't tell him about setting their dance to the Disgracefuls tune. Too stalker-y.

"What's your favorite thing about your work at the moment?" Lisette asked quickly, emphasizing "your." "Do you mind?" she asked, moving in for a forkful of Shane's mashed potatoes before they disappeared.

"Please do," he said. His was making fast headway with his plate. The potatoes were delish! Good restaurant choice, she internally patted herself on the back.

"Performing is the highest high, even though it doesn't always deliver the ultimate version or realization of a song. Once in a great while, it exceeds the recorded version. With live shows, the set list is so precisely timed out and we've been doing it for so long that surprises are few and far between. These past few months, I'd have to say the writing has been most satisfying – and surprising. In the end, recorded or live, it all rests on the lyrics. Without them there's no story, no message. I worship Tom Petty for his storytelling."

"For me Smokey Robinson is the ultimate song writer – the wordplay on *The Love I Saw In You Was Just a Mirage*, oh my god," Lisettte said. "But I revere Petty, too, He's the master of the cautionary tale, anthems of deliverance."

"What the fuck?" Shane thought. He couldn't recall the Miracles tune, but to show he understood and concurred about Petty he quietly broke into song, "His leather jacket had chains that would jingle"

"They both met movie stars, partied and mingled," Lisette joined in.

"Their A&R man said 'I don't hear a single'," they sang to each other, "the future was wide open."

"The business is shit," Shane said, grinning, a shred of kale between his teeth, surprised and delighted that Lisette had held her own in their little musical interlude, "but it's a living. The salad is amazing, by the way. Is that mint I taste, and peanuts? I might need one of these to go. I'll pretend it's for Autumn, but I'll probably get into it on the flight."

"I have the recipe," Lisette said. "It took me months to figure it out and work through different iterations, before I nailed it. The secret is honey!"

Shane flashed on Benjamin Franklin's "1,000 services small and great" in his appreciation of older women. "All this and she cooks!" Shane thought. Why had he wasted so many years in shallow relationships with young women who couldn't boil water? Lisette was a wonder! A full-grown woman, a femme du monde. "Anthems of deliverance!" It was killing him knowing that they only had a few short hours together. He wanted her to get on the plane to New York with him, to slip between the sheets with him tonight. The Isley Brothers replaced Petty in his head. He imagined the two of them at her little beach cottage eating kale salad at an outdoor table with birds singing and butterflies fluttering about and waves murmuring in the distance. He was grateful she couldn't read his mind. Too stalker-y.

The lunch crowd had emptied out and the light was changing on the boulevard. This time of afternoon the sun disappeared behind the tall buildings to the west. As the day waned, so had their awkwardness at being alone for the first time, just the two of them. They were no longer self-conscious. They had eased into each other. They talked about Chris and Derek, travel, politics, the favorite pets of their lives, growing up in the Midwest, architecture, and, finally, when they would see each other again.

"This was nice, right?" Shane asked. "We did all right on our own. How was our date for you, Lisette?"

"Really nice," Lisette said dreamily, lost in the way the setting sun lit up the green in his eyes and thinking about his warm hands.

"Lisette, I have to apologize once more, to your face, for bursting in on your situation in California," Shane said. "I hope there were no, uh, ramifications. Divorce is sticky enough without me butting in like I did. I was reckless."

"It was pretty surreal," Lisette said. "Did you really say that to Carl – "I think I'm in love with your wife" – or was it something I imagined in my fainting spell?"

"I said it. I've had strong feelings for you since the moment I laid eyes on you. I was feeling protective," Shane explained. "I wanted to fight him for your honor."

"It's official," Lisette said. "You are insane."

"What's next then?" Shane asked, grinning, deciding to take a chance. "If I had my way, that revolving door over there would be spinning like a fan, and we'd be racing each other to the nearest hotel, which I believe is the Four Seasons, to go missing for the weekend."

Lisette responded with a knowing smile as his bold invitation set off tingling ripples that went over and through her whole body. She shivered involuntarily. She opened her eyes (when had she shut them?) to find him looking at her expectantly. She was flushed with heat. He could see she was sorely tempted. Her blush heightened his desire, and he stifled a moan, pretending to clear his throat.

"Shane," she said, "I, uh, I love that scenario, and I would be quite prepared for that eventuality. For now, for today, can we just let this roll out?" Lisette asked. She had so many things up in the air, the divorce, the house, her semester, Maria's' high school graduation. She had to get home and let Misha out. All of these emotional chores floated in her consciousness like objects in a Chagall painting.

"Didn't George Harrison say that in 'A Hard Day's Night' – that bit about being 'quite prepared for that eventuality?'" Shane asked,

"He did," Lisette confirmed.

"Good one. I don't want to rush you, Lisette," Shane lied convincingly. They'd made a lot of ground today. He couldn't ruin it! "We have responsibilities, both of our daughters are expecting us. We are paragons of virtue at this moment in time. But please, promise to call, text, send me pictures from your day. I will do the same. And do come out to L.A. for a visit, soon, please?"

"I will work on that," Lisette promised.

He leaned over and kissed her.

"Promise," he said.

"I promise," she said.

He kissed her again, longer. His lips felt like pillows.

"Good," he said. They looked at each other dopily, smiling. Shane's phone pinged. He glanced at it.

"Car's here," he said, full of regret. "Back to the airport!"

"Drink lots of water – get up and walk in the aisle," Lisette said with alarm. They were saying goodbye! Snap out of it!

Shane burst out laughing. He wasn't flying commercial. He could do cartwheels if he wanted on the private jet.

"I will do my best to avoid deep vein thrombosis," he said. "And I will text you something far more romantic than that when I land in New York."

"You should know, I'm a prude about sexting," Lisette blurted. Where had that come from? Probably from reading the papers, as she had no first-hand experience with guys sending her pictures of their erections. It sounded awful, though.

"Good to know. Won't go there," Shane said. She was hilarious!

They left the restaurant, now buzzing with the cocktail crowd as well as the electric undercurrent of a sighting of someone famous. The hostess thought the woman might be Shane's sister, as they had the same white streak in their hair, and the woman didn't look rock 'n' roll-y. Then, from her station across the room, she saw them kiss. It was definitely not his sister.

Once out on the bustling street, they shared a final, lingering kiss goodbye, oblivious to the passersby. Shane mustered every molecule of his self-control and got into the car. Off he went to the airport while Lisette waved from the sidewalk, with the word "Wait!" caught in her conflicted heart. After the car drove off, she wobbled back to her car like a drunk. She was drunk. With relief. With desire. With antici…pation.

Chapter 36

How did it go?" Chris's voice filled the car.

On Lisette's end, rush hour traffic was bumper-to-bumper. They had nothing but time.

"It went really well, though we did not tumble immediately into the sack like a certain ho I know and her manager boyfriend," Lisette said.

"You wanted to though, right?"

"Hell yes," Lisette admitted. She recounted the part about the revolving door "spinning like a fan" and her buying a little more time. "I just want to linger a while in the anticipation phase. It's so erotic, the waiting."

"I get it," Chris said. "Sex at our age is like sport fishing. We pretty much know how it ends. It's the fight that is memorable. Then again, remember T.C. from high school? You finally bagged him and he was wearing pink girls bikini panties!"

"With white lace around the leg holes! Who could forget that?" Lisette responded. "I felt so worldly after that, like nothing could surprise me. I was 17. I remember thinking 'Why shouldn't boys wear pretty things?' He actually looked cool in them, with his tiny teacup ass."

"Wonder if his sister ever figured out where all her underpants disappeared to," Chris said. "Tell me everything. Where did you go?"

"The Boulevard. Table by the window. The Boul Mich looked like a bowl of Skittles with all the tulips."

"Oooh, our fave! I want kale salad so bad right now. What was it like to be alone for hours? Did you have to put up with any celeb stuff?"

"Not at all, but it was pretty quiet that time of day. We were both nervous at first, but we were fine once we calmed down. We had plenty to talk about, the time went by too fast."

"Did you kiss him?"

"Three times!"

"Did you blow him?"

"No, you nut!" Lisette said. "We got a table, not a booth."

They howled with laughter. Chris knew the booths were dark and deep.

"Tell me about the kiss," Chris pressed. "How did it, um, go down, so to speak?"

Lisette closed her eyes for a second, remembering. The driver behind her honked the horn.

"Asshole," Lisette mouthed in her rearview mirror.

"We'd finished our lunch and had been blabbing forever, and he said this thing about if it was up to him, the revolving door would be spinning like a fan and we'd be racing to the Four Seasons for a lost weekend. Then he asked me to come to L.A. soon, and made me promise, and he leaned over the table and kissed me. It was like 'poof,' like a soft satin pillow to the face. Quite lovely. Oh god I'm an idiot – I could be lost for the weekend at the Four Seasons right now with world's sexiest man, but I'm driving the expressway to let the damned dog out!"

"There's just no excuse for you, Lisette. You are most definitely an idiot."

"He said we were 'paragons of virtue' with daughters who were expecting us. We were very grown up about it all. Oh my god, I told him to drink water and walk the aisle to avoid blood clots!"

"Oh my god," Chris groaned. "What is the matter with you?"

"I didn't actually say 'blood clots' though," Lisette protested. "He said 'deep vein thrombosis'. And he said he would send me 'romantic' texts – but I said 'NO SEXTING'."

"You are such a fucking prude, Lisette."

"Am not! I'm just not into weird and disgusting 'Carlos Danger' scenes. How is that sexy?"

"Did you talk about the music? They are working on two scorching tracks," Chris said. "I heard them last night. Really, really good."

"We talked about logistics of touring and Motown and we sang a verse of 'Into the Great Wide Open,' but no specifics on the new material. I think he wants me to come to L.A. to hear it."

"You sang to each other?" Chris sounded incredulous.

"Yes, why? You and I sing to each other all the time."

"Did you just burst into song at a certain point in the conversation? What?"

"We were talking about how much we revere Tom Petty for his storytelling and Shane started singing the verse about Eddie's leather jacket."

"It had chains that would jingle," Chris picked up the tune. The two of them fucking loved that song. They'd seen Petty a dozen times over the years. "So when are you coming out here to party and mingle?"

"Oh, god, Chris, I have so much going on with Maria's graduation, recital, moving to the cottage," Lisette was back to her overwhelmed place.

"Is Carl coming?" Chris asked "To Maria's graduation?"

"I don't know," Lisette said slowly, emphasis on the "know." The word went up and down with a whiff of "I hadn't even thought of that" that Chris picked up on. "It took all I had to figure out what to wear to lunch."

"Time well spent. Worth it," Chris said.

"I'll text you the outfit picture. Maria said 'bombshell'!"

"Nice work. Send pic immediately when you reach the house," Chris ordered. Sometimes she still talked like she was calling the city desk for rewrite.

"Lisette, I can come out to help with the move. And if you have enough tickets, I'd love to be at Maria's graduation. Maybe after that we could take a load to the cottage and hang out for a few days."

"That would be so fantastic," Lisette said. She was overwhelmed again, now with gratitude for her caring friend who loved Maria as her own, for her steady support. Who, at their age, offers to help a friend move? Carl had left her high and dry to deal with major details. The lists were growing and the garage was filling with things they were ready to cast off. Lisette had briefly considered hiring a garage sale expert who could simply deal with it. She really should call the woman. She hadn't even called a Realtor, but knew the house would move quickly.

"But first, you need to come out here next weekend or for a couple of days during the following week, you can't torture that poor man much longer. You could do a Thursday night to Sunday – you have Fridays off from teaching."

"I'll work it out, and it will have to be soon," Lisette promised. "I have weekend rehearsals the week before recital, so that takes two weekends out.

Graduation takes out another. I'll look at flights, talk to Maria, and get back to you quickly. Anticipation is all about the end game. I get that."

She had reached her exit at last. Misha would be so happy. She and Chris said goodbye. Oh! The lights were on! Maria was home! She texted the outfit picture to Chris before getting out of the car, before she forgot.

"Hello!" she called, coming in the door.

Misha raced to the door, ears up, tail wagging, billowing clouds of fur in his wake. During their downsizing, she and Maria had unearthed more than a dozen lint rollers.

"Hi, hairball," Lisette greeted him, bending down to rub his head. Tiny hairs coated her hand.

"Mom!" Maria came out of the kitchen. "How did it go? Tell me everything!"

"I will," Lisette said, smiling up at Maria. "But first, while I think of it, is your father coming to graduation? Aunt Chris wants to come!"

"Yes, dad is coming to graduation. Alone," Maria reported. "It's okay, right?"

"Of course," Lisette assured her, "he should be there. Do you have a ticket for Chris?"

"You bet," said Maria. "That would be awesome."

"Okay, thanks. And Maria, I really admire the way you are keeping in touch with dad," Lisette said. "You are my style guru. I'll tell Chris to book her flights!"

"Thanks. Great. Now, come in here, I'm making pizza," Maria commanded. "And tell me everything about lunch."

She did not make any snarky quote marks in the air around the word lunch.

Chapter 37

Y ou're looking dapper," Autumn said, admiring her father.
"I've been courting," Shane told Autumn. "In Chicago."

"The pretty ballerina?" Autumn asked.

"The one and only," Shane said.

"You've got it bad," she observed.

They were having a late bite at a hole-in-the-wall Mediterranean joint around the corner from her place. Shane nibbled an olive thoughtfully.

"I concur," he said. "It was hard to tear myself away. But then I remembered who was waiting for me! It's great to see you, 'Auntie' Autumn."

"Oh Dad – I'm so excited about the baby. I was FaceTiming with Priya and Daniel and Priya is getting a righteous bump! I've started referring to her as 'her serene highness, Priya'," Autumn giggled. "It's so weird to think about a tiny little baby swimming around inside her."

"It's a miracle," Shane said.

"I hope it's a girl," Autumn said.

"Really," Shane replied. "Why?"

"I heard boy babies pee in your face when you change their diaper, for one thing," Autumn said. "And the girl names and clothes are better! Priya and I have a Google doc of names for boys and girls. We add to it and cross things off constantly."

"Could you share it with me?" Shane asked. "I want to be up to speed. Are you ranking the names or throwing everything at the list?"

"No, we haven't ranked them yet, we're in the collecting phase. Boy or girl, it's going to be a gorgeous baby," Autumn said. "What if it gets Priya's eyes!"

"Mixed makes the prettiest babies, I've always thought," Shane said, fondly remembering certain women from his past with lovely café au lait skin, wild hair, blue-green and amber eyes. He imagined those features packaged in a waddling toddler and couldn't help but smile.

"I like 'Inez' right now," Autumn said. "Daniel thinks it's a boy. He likes Matteo."

"Great names," Shane concurred. "Do you want to fly back with me Sunday? For a visit?"

"I can't, I have finals coming up week after next," Autumn said. "But I've been thinking about the baby and being around to help Priya – the baby will be born right when the fall semester starts. Dad, what would you think about me transferring to a school out there?"

"And have to see you all the time? That would be horrible," Shane wisecracked. Nothing would make him happier. The flight to Chicago, then the final leg to New York, had been a stretch. He was tired. "I'm actually looking for a house in L.A. right now. Should I add a bedroom for you?"

"Yes, please, Dad," Autumn said. "We can create a Stewart compound, like in 'The Godfather'."

"Or the Kennedys."

"The Kennedys?"

Shane sighed. It had been so easy to talk to Lisette. They shared so much context, their lives had intersected at different points in time. It was like Derek and Chris's game 'You Were There' when Lisette told him about the New York show in the body suit era. There was so little explaining, so much knowing.

"Here," he said, "let's take a selfie for Lisette."

They leaned in and positioned themselves. Both knew their best side. Shane took the picture. After both approved the shot, Shane texted it to Lisette with the message, 'Catching up with Autumn!'"

Lisette and Maria were standing in the guest room closet sorting decades of holiday crap when her phone pinged. Maria watched her mother's face break into a delighted smile when she looked at her phone. "Look," she said, handing it to Maria. "Let's send one back."

Lisette and Maria posed amid the clutter of wreaths and snowmen, and after both approved the shot, Lisette texted it to Shane with the message, "Sorting things out with Maria!"

Shane's phone pinged. He and Autumn looked at it on the table between them. Shane picked it up, looked at the screen, and smiled. He held it out for Autumn to see.

"Aw," she said. "Hi, Lisette and Maria!"

Shane tapped out: "Autumn says hi Lisette and Maria" and sent the message.

"Hi, Autumn!" they texted back.

"TTYL," Shane replied. He would call Lisette after he settled in at the hotel.

It was three hours earlier on the West Coast and Rob was playing with the Fire Stick.

"Rob, dinner!" Lynn called.

"Okay," he hollered back, not moving, aiming the Fire Stick at the screen.

The thing about Fentanyl is you have no appetite. It was weird. Rob was normally a hungry guy. He was spoiled rotten by a wife whose hobbies were gardening, cooking, yoga, and reading. The gardening spoke for itself and the reading made her interesting to talk to. The yoga kept her both limber and tight. But the cooking was Rob's favorite piece of home. Lynn sure could cook. Her specialties were the mixed grill, all kinds of salads, Italian, Classic American, and Soul Food. She could also channel long-lost Italian ancestors, old Nonnas in black dresses, and produce pots of fragrant sauces and stews. Her traditional Thanksgiving turkey rotated year-to-year between her mother's classic herb stuffing and a more soulful cornbread with sausage. Everyone told her she should open a restaurant.

"Rob!" Lynn called own the stairs.

Their son, his wife, and their 3-year-old had stopped by. Lynn had made spaghetti squash pie with Nonna marinara. The pie in its plate was cooling on a cutting board, ready for cutting. A salad glistened nearby. Everything was ready.

"Joel, go get your father," Lynn said, pulling a sharp serrated knife out of the drawer. She plunged it into the center of the pie and started cutting wedges. The layers of the dish – ricotta and spaghetti squash, zucchini, marinara, mozzarella – revealed themselves like striations from an archeological dig, each layer speaking its own truth.

Joel went downstairs.

"Dad, dinner," he said. "What are you doing?"

"Fire Stick," Rob said. He was rumpled and unshaven.

Joel, who had grown up with technology, saw instantly what Rob was doing wrong.

"Dad, I'll help you with that after dinner, okay?" Joel said. "Come on."

Rob switched off the remote and slowly got to his feet. He followed Joel up the stairs and into the kitchen. Lynn had prepared their plates. Everyone smiled at Rob. They ate outside at a table amid the raised beds, eating their home-grown produce while the next crop stood at attention in neat rows in the black dirt nearby. Afterward, in the flickering candlelight, Joel and his wife announced they were expecting. Lynn opened a chilled bottle of sparkling non-alcoholic cider.

Across town, Chris and Derek were cuddled up together sharing a bottle of actual wine and watching Sunset Boulevard. They were making the most of the band's three-day weekend. Derek reminded himself to call Lynn first thing in the morning to see how Rob was doing. He'd pay a visit if necessary.

Derek had phoned the Tramadol doctor to express his concern and fill him in on Rob's history of addiction. The doctor said he'd monitor refill requests and thanked him for his concern. He didn't tell Derek, out of respect for doctor/patient confidentiality, that he had also prescribed hydrocodone, with instructions for Rob to alternate between the two drugs. But Rob had been shopping around. Derek was in the dark about Rob's other doctor, who was well-known in L.A. celeb circles for his deep compassion and generosity. That doc had delivered the gold: OxyContin and Fentanyl.

Chapter 38

On Monday, Lisette's home phone rang mid-morning. She was showered but still in her robe, sitting at the kitchen table drinking coffee, Misha lying at her feet, grinning over a yellowed, scribbled Fab Two set list she had unearthed in the cleanup.

"Lisette, it's Maddie. I was just at the grocery store and, um, your picture was in the tabloids at the checkout!" Maddie said really fast. "I wanted to give you a heads-up in case you didn't know."

"That's ridiculous," Lisette said.

"No, it's definitely you," Maddie said. "With Shane Stewart at a restaurant. It looks like The Boulevard."

"What the fuck!" Lisette shrieked. The dog jumped up and ran to the door.

"Sorry, Lisette, thought you should know."

"What does it say?"

"Here, I'll read it to you. It's the picture and a caption. It says: "Disgracefuls rocker Shane Stewart has met his match! He was spotted having an intimate lunch in Chicago last week with a mystery woman. The two lovebirds even have matching hair-dos! Shane split up with his 29-year-old assistant, Tiffany Taylor, last fall. The 61-year-old singer appeared "enthralled" by his age-appropriate date, according to a witness at the restaurant."

Lisette was silent.

"Lisette?" Maddie said.

"Yes."

"You are my idol. I will bring the scandal sheet to class."

Before Lisette could protest, Maddie was gone.

"Oh my god," she said to Misha. She dialed Chris. It was 8 a.m. in L.A. Chris answered groggily.

"I'm in the goddamned tabloids – a picture of Shane and me at lunch!" she exploded.

"What?" Chris said.

"What?" said Derek's voice in the background.

"There's a picture in the tabloids of Lisette and Shane from last week," Chris said.

Derek and Chris started to giggle.

"It's not funny! It's an invasion of privacy!" Lisette stormed.

Their giggles erupted into waves, then gales of laughter.

"Are you high?" Lisette demanded.

"Oh! Oh!" they were choking with laughter.

Lisette hung up on them. And promptly burst out laughing. What else could she do?

She dialed Shane. He picked up.

"Good morning," he said. She imagined him turning over in bed and saying "Good morning." It killed her.

"Hi," she said. She had laughed off her nerves. "I had to let you know, I got a call from one of my senior students who started her day at the grocery store. We are in the tabloids! Pictures from lunch!"

"No way!" Shane said. "The hostess! I saw her hiding behind a partition taking pictures! She sold them to the scandal sheets!"

"My mother always said a lady has her picture in the paper three times: when she is born, when she gets married, and when she dies. I always thought that was bullshit, not to mention incredibly grim! But lunch? This really took me by surprise," Lisette said.

"I'm afraid it's part of the deal," Shane said, rather seriously. "Can you make your peace with it?"

"It is weird, but Chris and Derek laughed me out of." She told the story. He chuckled.

"They will track you down, Lisette. They will learn your name. Other pictures will surface."

"I made the reservation in my name," Lisette recalled. The hostess had her name and cellphone number.

"I always use 'Dr. Zurgold' for reservations," Shane said. "I'm inured to the tabloids pretty much, yet I can still work up some righteous indignation at the violation of it all. I'm finding I crave privacy now more than ever. I keep thinking of your cottage, Lisette, it sounds like heaven, the perfect hideaway. Would you give me the address so I can spy on it with Google maps? If that's not too stalker-y."

"It's Number 5 Sunset Path," she said, wishing they were hiding out there right now. "The satellite view is good for the lay of the land. I could text you some of my own pictures."

"Please do," Shane said. "Sunset Path did you say?"

"Yes. Some of the short lanes near the lakeshore are named 'path.' Isn't that the best?"

"Charming, yes," Shane said. "But the best is that I will see you in five days. Will you come to the studio? I want you to hear the new tunes. After your astute Tom Petty analysis I look forward to your feedback."

"I'd love to," said Lisette, feeling something familiar and giddy inside herself and realizing it was the girl she once was, resurfacing. "Meanwhile, I will send some pictures. And Shane, the tabloids quoted a 'witness' who said you appeared 'enthralled'."

"That part is accurate," he said. Lisette smiled broadly and hugged herself.

The seniors were atwitter – they'd passed the "magazine" around in the dressing room before entering the studio. Maddie handed it to Lisette. "Page 17," she said. They waited, watching as Lisette found the page and read the caption. Her face, though composed, turned scarlet.

They weren't kissing at least! They were in profile, in conversation. Shane's eyebrows were up and his hand was over hers. The artichokes were on the table. Lisette recognized it as the moment she had suddenly been sad about Maria leaving.

"You look pretty cute together, especially the matching hair," Evelyn said, breaking the silence.

"He copied me!" Lisette chirped, handing the rag back to Maddie.

"No, keep it for your archives," Maddie insisted. "God, Lisette, I freaked out when I saw it. I'm so impressed! I'm so jealous!"

"Way to 'trade up,'" Evelyn said, giving Lisette a squeeze around her waist. "You are my hero."

"You are my heroes," she said to the class, crossing to the piano and laying the tabloid face down. "Now, let's get to work! We have a performance in two weeks."

Lisette took the supermarket rag home with her. Maria took it in stride. No one at school had said anything, but the latest issue had hit the stands just that morning. Just the same, Lisette warned Maria to be on the lookout for any strange people lurking around the house, especially if they have cameras. Call the police. Lisette shared that Shane suspected the hostess at the restaurant, and that she'd made the reservation in her name and gave her cell phone number.

"Don't worry about it, Mom," Maria said. "There's no way they could track the mystery woman here because of our different last names."

"You are so smart, Maria," Lisette told her, feeling relieved by her logic. "Just the same, be alert."

Chapter 39

Shane was shaving, softly and distractedly singing "Love Street" between strokes of the razor. It had been looping in his head all week, since Lisette had sent pictures of the cottage in summer with everything in bloom: an exterior shot in the golden light of evening with a big yellow dog lying on the step, one of Maria and her in the kitchen washing squash flowers, and a close-up of monarchs on the butterfly bush.

"She lives on Love Street, lingers long on Love Street," he sang. "She has a house and garden, I would like to see what happens. La la la, la la la la…

He threw water on his face and patted it dry.

"I guest I like it fine, so far," he hammed to himself in the mirror before turning away and leaving the room. Another dead singer, he realized. What the fuck? He was glad he hadn't made the list. He had a lot to live for, was actually feeling excited about the future, a feeling he hadn't felt in quite a while or even named until now.

He had made a cardboard sign that said "Ms. DuPre" and planned to stand at the bottom of the escalator with the limo drivers to greet Lisette. He had agonized over whether to ask Derek and Chris to come along as a welcome party, knowing full well that he wanted only to throw Lisette over his shoulder at the airport, speed to his hotel, and tear her clothes off.

In the end he had asked Lisette if she wanted them to come along. When she said, "No, come alone," it made him sway on his feet. It had been more than six months since they first met. He had never waited that long for a woman.

Lisette could barely breathe on the plane. But four hours of torture in an underwire bra were worth it for the impact her new lingerie would doubtless have on a man who was already "enthralled." Chris referred to these moments of female cunning and male subjugation as "Brick House Situations" because they were designed to "sure enough knock a strong man to his knees." Guys were so visual. They were putty.

"Wear that first, then the teddy the second day," Chris had advised on their video fashion consultation. Maria was not part of this conversation. "And be careful! You don't want 'man down.' Well you do, that's the point, but no farther than his knees."

Lisette had her spring coat over her arm as she descended on the escalator, sharing the step with a small rolling bag. She wore sunglasses because she was officially a mystery woman. She was halfway down when Shane came into sight, holding the ridiculous sign. He, too, was wearing sunglasses. She was laughing as she stepped off the escalator and into his arms. The revolving door was spinning like a fan behind them as they raced to the car.

They made out like it was prom night all the way to the hotel. Her red lipstick transferred to his lips and he looked great in it. His hands were under her sweater.

"Ooh, I feel lace," he whispered in her ear, "I can't wait to see it."

They bolted from the car and through the hotel lobby. Shane pushed the "close door" button in the faces of other guests and mashed Lisette in the elevator like they were in an Aerosmith video. They were panting like dogs when they finally burst through the door of the room. Shane kicked it shut with his foot, threw Lisette over his shoulder, and carried her to bed.

"Show me," he said. They held each other's eyes.

She took off her sweater. He broke the eye-lock, his gaze went south, to Lisette's ballet-inappropriate D cups, which were brimming over a lace bra as delicate as a spider web.

"Oh god," he whispered, like a prayer. "Lisette, let me see the rest of you."

And suddenly everything slowed down. They were in their own time zone, their own world, and they took their time with each other because they were grownups and knew what they were doing.

"Clash of the Titans," Shane thought to himself at one point.

Lisette would not see Chris until late the next day, some 30 hours after landing in L.A.

Chris texted her once: "Will have wheelchair waiting…"

The following afternoon, they had leisurely coffee around 2, after they finally pried themselves out of bed. Their hair was a bit damp. At some point they had been in the giant jet tub, Lisette recalled with a smile. Room service dishes littered the suite.

She and Chris had once heard lore about not just being laid, but being "laid, relayed, inlaid, parleyed, soufleed, and marmalade." They could not recall the source of this quote. But Lisette now knew what it meant. She was completely and utterly satisfied at last.

Chapter 40

Shane was thinking he had indeed met his match. Lisette was a thorough-bred, strong and sure! Right from the gate she was magnificent, slowly peeling off the sweater, then the rest of her clothing piece by piece with his assistance. She was completely comfortable in her womanly body, it was her instrument and she was a virtuoso. He had experienced ringing in his ears at one point. Thankfully, it was gone when he woke up after sleeping a few hours. And what an awakening it was, with soft, luscious Lisette nes-tled into his back. He remained still, barely breathing, replaying their time together starting with her descending on the escalator. These would be tops in his memory reel for the rest of his life, he was sure of it. They would be the smile on his face when he was an old man in a rocking chair. Everything had changed now that they were lovers. They had claimed each other. He would marry her today if he could.

Lisette was stirring. He turned over and said "Good morning." Lisette smiled at the thought that his voice was not on the phone, but right beside her. She opened her eyes. "Mercy," said Miss Motown at the sight of him, pulling him close.

"Mercy sakes alive," Shane agreed. They held each other, bodies inter-twined between the sheets, and drifted into a light sleep. The memory reel played in fragments in Shane's dreams.

They were dopey as they prepared to rejoin the world outside. In the shower, Shane washed her hair. Lisette dressed privately so he wouldn't see the teddy until she was ready to reveal it. The ladies at Schwartz's Intimate Apparel, established in 1919, knew their business. If they'd seen her picture in the tabloids, they didn't let on, but they had treated her as if they were in on her secret. Genius. It was the kind of personal service a woman missed in the era of Amazon.

They were meeting Chris, Derek, and the band at the studio. It would be a little listening party at the least, a full-blown session if the spirit moved them.

"Well hello!" Chris greeted Lisette when she and Shane, holding hands like John and Yoko, walked through the door of the control room. Chris jumped up from a couch and embraced Lisette.

Lisette returned the hug but avoided eye contact. They both knew that this moment required restraint, and that at any second either or both might start freaking out about the unexpected turn their lives had taken. And if the word "wheelchair" was spoken by anyone, in any context, well forget about it. They would totally lose it. What were they now – sisters-in-law? They had to keep it together until they were alone. After all, this was the musicians' workplace. Chris was surprised to feel a stab of jealousy toward Shane. She had known Lisette for 40 years, but today she belonged to him, not Chris. It was weird, but that's the bonding power of sexual intimacy. People are claimed in different ways, and it is possible to jump rank.

"Lisette, lovely to see you," Derek said, taking her hand and kissing her cheek. He whispered in her ear, "There's a wheelchair in the closet if you need it and you know I'm an able driver."

Chris had made out the word "wheelchair," which Derek emphasized. She snorted. That set off Lisette. She erupted in laughter. No point being prim in the bawdy word of rock and roll. Welcome back, Lisette!

Shane introduced Lisette to his four bandmates. Chris and Lisette were the only women present. Wine was poured. An elegant platter of crudités appeared. Lisette realized she was famished after her exertions. She was hoping for some of that famous chicken.

"We're ready for playback," said the engineer. Shane nodded.

The control room reverberated with a frantic drumbeat, joined on the fifth measure by a heavy bass line. A guitar wailed. "Arrhythmia!" Shane's voice screamed. The rapid-fire song ripped holes in their ears as they followed the story line about a woman who sets off a man's heart super hard, told by the man suffering chest pain and shortness of breath. It was blistering! "Rob is a motherfucker!" Lisette thought, regarding Rob, sitting stoic, eyes closed, head just barely bobbing in slight, jerky movements as he listened.

It was time for a reckoning. Thumbs up or down. All thumbs went up.

"What works about it?" Shane asked the band.

"The tempo is relentless," said the drummer, complimenting his own performance. He'd never messed with drink or drugs because he was a narcissist. He was his own drug!

"You are on fire," Shane agreed amiably.

"The guitar slays," Rob said, scratching his face and stringing out "slays."

"Thank you, Rob," said the guitar player, expressing gratitude, working the Steps.

"Yeah," everyone agreed. The guitar solos elevated, tightened the song to the tension of a scream.

They debated the merits of the track for quite a while, in extreme detail, until they were spent.

"What do others think? Derek, Chris, Lisette?" Shane asked.

Derek was caught by surprise, he deferred to Chris.

"It made me want to bang my head," Chris offered.

"I agree with the band's assessment previously stated," Derek said. "I fuckin' love it!"

Everyone looked at Lisette, the most recent arrival, the "new girl," the last to weigh in.

"I like the lyrics," Lisette said. "I like the way the words describe the loss of control contrasted over the racing, but steady heartbeat of the drums. It creates a disconnect, a certain tension."

"What the fuck?" Shane thought.

The others were silent, staring at Lisette.

"Well, yeah, there's that," said Derek in his jolly British accent, jovial, offering around the crudités. He was the Hagrid of the band.

"All right," Shane said as the others nibbled on baby asparagus spears and carrot sticks. The engineer cued up the second song.

It started with slow piano, Lisette couldn't identify the chord that clutched in the throat like yearning. Some kind of minor seventh? Then the other instruments came in and Shane's voice sang, "Tip your face to the sun. Tell me I'm the only one."

It was a love song! About walking on a beach, about waves on the shore erasing words in the sand, but love enduring, coming back around as sure as the moon and the tide. It ended with an extended jam that faded.

"I hate it," said the drummer. "It's lame. It's not what we do."

"It's definitely a departure from what we've always done, but I dig it," said Rob, scratching his face again. He thought it was romantic. Lynn would love it.

"It certainly pushes the boundaries of the Disgracefuls' songbook, but it might be a huge pop hit," Derek said.

"It's a fucking wedding song," said the lead guitar player. "Why do we need – or even want – a pop hit?"

"Who were your influences?" Rob asked.

"Smokey Robinson," Shane said.

The drummer snorted. Shane wanted to smack him but refrained from delivering a lesson on the Funk Brothers. Stupid white boy, Shane thought.

After his lunch with Lisette, he had dived head first into Smokey on YouTube, conducting his own independent music study. How could he have been so unschooled on the breadth and depth of the man's genius? He needed to ask Lisette if she knew the Marvelettes' "Hunter Gets Captured by the Game," which Smokey wrote. It was perhaps the coolest song he'd ever heard. He was thinking of proposing that the band cover it. Grace Jones did.

"You must admit, Shane sang the living shit out of it," Derek said.

"It's a lighter-lifter for sure," Rob agreed.

"Who played piano?" Lisette asked.

"I did," Shane said.

In her mind, Lisette pictured the song performed live, with Shane at a gleaming black grand piano. She remembered the reflection of the roses on the shiny piano in the ballet studio. She smiled and nodded. She realized they were all looking at her, obviously an influence along with Smokey.

"It's beautiful," she said. "I love it."

She was curious what his daughters thought of it. She'd ask him later. She didn't want to talk too much as the newcomer. Shane was looking at her intently.

"My two cents worth," she shrugged.

The drummer rolled his eyes. Fucking Yoko, the drummer thought. Shane noticed. He wanted to sock him.

"Thank you. Okay, well, anything else?" Shane asked, refraining from socking.

Derek stood up.

"I want to let you all know that the song already has an offer to be optioned for a film sound track. And they haven't heard a finished version."

"How much are we talking about?" asked the drummer.

"About a million if they end up using it in the film, which will goose sales across the board," Derek said.

The drummer was suddenly interested. That meant $200,000 for each of them, minus Derek's 15 percent. Shane would earn additional royalties from the writing. On second thought, maybe it wasn't such a bad song.

They listened to it four more times, pausing at points to analyze and throw out ideas about tweaking bits here and there. Did the vocal track need harmonies? Could the bridge be a bit edgier? Boost the bass here. They decided to try a few overdubs. That turned into an hours-long project. Chris and Lisette were teenagers again, back to the basement steps and garages of their shared youth. Now here they were in a fancy recording studio in L.A. observing the same process in its ultimate iteration, the familiar breakdown, analysis, and reconstruction they found endlessly fascinating. It was their element, too. At certain points one squeezed the other's hand.

The session broke up in the wee hours. Shane invited Derek and Chris to join them for brunch at the hotel the next day and come along to the airport. Lisette was leaving! It killed him!

Shane had thought that after the day and night before, he and Lisette might not have any surprises left for each other. But when they returned to the hotel and he got a glimpse of the teddy, he realized he had underestimated them both.

Chapter 41

"What are we now, brothers-in-law?" Derek asked as he and Chris entered the suite.

"Something like that," Shane agreed, greeting Derek with a handshake and Chris with a kiss on the cheek.

He had ordered most of the breakfast menu. Lisette emerged from the bedroom, where she had finished packing her bag. They'd all take her to the airport after brunch.

"Fastest weekend ever," she said. "I'm totally discombobulated."

"I'll take that as a compliment," Shane said.

"Oh, you should," she replied, wrapping her arms around him and looking into his eyes. "Most assuredly."

She planted a light kiss on his lips.

"I am famished," she declared, spying a plate piled high with bacon and helping herself to a slice. "Derek, I thought I'd get chicken last night. I was a bit disappointed."

"Sorry," he said. "The lads are a bit weary of it, I'm afraid. Plus, I find if I keep them hungry they work harder. We got a lot done last night, wouldn't you say?"

"It seemed like it," Shane said, "but we'll have to listen with fresh ears today."

"How about Blinkie?" Derek asked, using a nickname the drummer hated. "I'm surprised you didn't clock him."

"What a tool," Shane said. "He came around fast enough when money was on the table."

"Works every time," Derek observed.

They all dug into the breakfast with gusto, but Lisette's imminent departure hung like a dark cloud over them. They compared calendars, Chris and Lisette talked about Maria's graduation and their plans afterward. Shane was quiet. The thought of saying goodbye destroyed him. The idea of crashing her dance recital in two weeks cheered him up, though. He knew it was bad form, but he continued to toy with the plan. He liked the idea of the role reversal, of being in the audience – not on the stage – to better understand Lisette's work, her art.

"We'll meet you down at the car," Derek said after breakfast. It was his way of giving Shane and Lisette a few minutes alone while moving along the airport timetable.

"This is killing me," Shane admitted once they were alone.

"That's the opposite of what I was thinking," Lisette said. "I was thinking this is keeping me fully alive. At our age, what's a few weeks?"

"No sexting?" he asked.

"No sexting!" she confirmed. "But I will keep sending YouTube videos of romantic Motown songs. I have three Arethas competing in my brain already."

"Name them," Shane said.

"'Say a Little Prayer,' 'Until You Come Back to Me' and," Lisette paused for a sly smile, 'Dr. Feelgood'."

"You are a wonder," he said. "A little white princess of Motown."

"Accident of birth," Lisette said. "Now kiss me properly. We have to go."

Shane kissed her long and well, then took the handle of her roller bag. Lisette threw her coat over her arm. It was tearing her apart to leave the scene of the crime. They mashed in the elevator again.

"Will you be sending me flowers?" she asked.

"I will be sending you a car," he said.

They were laughing when the doors opened. The ride to the airport was uneventful. The four of them talked about how unusual that was for them. They now had a collective backstory, each felt tightly connected to the others now through the shared vignettes over the past months. Chris was thinking about how it was at the airport, when she tailed Carl, that events were set in motion that led to the current scenario. Shane was thinking about consulting with Chris about whether to show up at the recital.

Lisette was thinking about talking to Chris later about the Sexual Olympics and wondering how she was going to survive weeks without Shane's touch, the taste of him. Derek was thinking about chicken, which he never would have known about if not for Chris. The four of them were world's cutest ongoing geezer double date.

"The wheelchairs are right inside the door!" Chris called after Lisette. Lisette gave her the finger before the door wooshed shut behind her.

Chapter 42

I love the idea of you showing up at the recital," Chris told Shane, mentally scrambling for a way to tactfully remind him that Maria would be at home – Chicago would not be the same adults-only scenario as last weekend. That might be a strain. Or, Chris could conspire with Maria to be away from home that night. Yes, they would work together, Chris and Maria. Meanwhile, Chris cautioned Shane not to be a distraction.

"You'll have to be totally undercover and wait until after the show to see Lisette. You can't distract her, recitals are chaos. Maria usually helps with babysitting and herding the littlest dancers, helping with lost shoes and costume crises. But I'll talk to Maria to see if maybe she could sleep over at a friend's house that night after the recital."

Knowing he might see Lisette in less than two weeks gave Shane something to look forward to. He bought a recital ticket for "Dr. Zurgold" on the conservatory website. He was writing like a fiend, and the band had shared a final version of the ballad with the filmmakers, who loved it. Quite a lot was going on. The time would pass quickly.

Lisette was preparing for dress rehearsal the coming weekend, followed by the recital the next weekend. Every group had been working on their dance for the entire semester. They were well-prepared, but Lisette was now known at the conservatory as the "mystery woman." Even though she was not identified, it was "distasteful" for her picture to have appeared in the tabloids, the director said when he called her in for a "chat."

"No one was more surprised than me," Lisette told him. He was being a tool! She had no intention of apologizing.

"It strikes me as odd, somehow, that such a publication would draw the attention of anyone from this esteemed conservatory," she said. "Does someone on staff monitor the scandal sheets?"

"Actually, my wife likes to read them in the checkout aisle," he admitted. "She came home with it and asked me 'Isn't that Lisette?'"

Lisette started to giggle.

"What is so funny?" the director asked.

"This situation," Lisette retorted. "Are you criticizing me? Am I in trouble?"

Her lusty weekend had emboldened her!

"It's 'distasteful,' Lisette," he repeated.

"There was nothing 'distasteful' about that lunch. It was quite delicious," she said, tuning up. "And if it makes you uncomfortable that one of your teachers had lunch with a famous musician who has been awarded honorary degrees from various conservatories and schools of music, then you are an ass hat. If you apologize I might consider returning in the fall. Otherwise, I'll direct the recital and be on my way, professionally."

With that she was up and headed for the door, his eyes burning holes in her short black wraparound skirt. Lisette put a little extra switch into her step as she walked out, just to torture him.

"Lisette!" he called after her. She kept walking.

"That was easy," she thought to herself.

Chris was right about Maria's willingness to be a co-conspirator. "I'm in!" Maria had responded when Chris called her to let her in on Shane's plan. "I can stay at a friend's that night after the recital," she offered without being asked.

"That was easy," Chris thought.

Maria had never seen her mother so happy. Lisette was mooning about like a teenager. Maria had never been "in love," but her mother's transformation since her weekend in L.A. gave Maria hope that one day she'd meet someone who made her all ga-ga. Lisette had told Maria about the recording session and brought her up to speed on Chris and Derek, but thankfully hadn't shared many details about Shane except to say "it was very romantic." Maria was impressed that Shane picked her up at the airport, she loved the part about the "Ms. DuPre" sign. Shane was ga-ga, too, she concluded. But she had known that since the concert in Chicago months back.

Lisette was still irate when she told Maria about her "chat" with the director. Maria was amazed that her mother, the confrontation avoider, had given it to the man.

"Did you really call him an 'ass hat?'" Maria asked.

"Yes, I did," Lisette confirmed.

"I didn't realize you knew that term," Maria said.

"I learned it in Catholic school," Lisette grinned.

"So you maybe quit your job," Maria said.

"Yep," Lisette said. "It's time for a change, Maria. I can open my own little studio in Michigan if I want to. We'll be fine."

The future was wide open.

Rehearsal weekend was long and arduous. So many details! Music, lighting, programs. All the teachers were involved, and some were divas and screamers. There were spats about how much time each was allowed to practice their groups on the stage.

"Too much behavior," Lisette thought to herself more than once. She would not miss this, she realized with surprise!

She spent the most time with her youngest students so they would be comfortable on stage. There were usually one or two who froze and cried, and never the ones she expected! After they had run through their dance numerous times, she released them to their parents. The older students were seasoned veterans who required just a couple of run-throughs for spacing. The seniors were excused from rehearsal so as not to ruin their surprise. Also, Lisette didn't want Ass Hat to hear rock music coming from the performance hall and censor their dance as "distasteful." He hadn't apologized.

When all the students were excused, the teachers ran through their dance. It was traditional for them to go last, a sort of vanity lap to show the tuition-paying parents that the staff had the stuff. It was a traditional dance as a group, within which each had a brief solo. Lisette's big moment was a rapid series of *piqué* turns across the stage. Every year they wore the same black tutus. Once again, Lisette thought, "I won't miss this!" Which led her to a sudden revelation: If this was her swan song, she should also join the seniors on stage for their dance! That would be a meaningful exit for her. She'd tell them at their last class the following week, their final rehearsal.

Chapter 43

Shane had bought a ridiculous beard at a costume shop. That was one thing about L.A., easy access to theatrical accessories. He was going to the recital in disguise: the beard, a tweed hat, an overcoat, and his reading glasses. He would not be recognized. He flew in late Friday afternoon, buying a Wall Street Journal at the airport as an additional prop. He made it to the conservatory with time to spare, presented himself as Dr. Zurgold to claim his ticket at will call, and found a seat on the main floor in the shadow of the balcony. He was a master of stealth. Chris would be proud. He hid behind the newspaper until the lights dimmed.

His heart beat faster thinking about being in the same space as Lisette. She was here, under the same roof, breathing the same air! The beard was hot and itchy.

He had been to his daughters' recitals and knew a thing or two about them: they are interminable, and they are adorable. True to form, this one started with the little ones, mindful of their attention spans. Then the usual assortment of teens with their fraught-with-meaning modern and jazz. He was so overheated from the beard and the hat that he was about to nod off when a familiar beat jolted him awake. Disgracefuls! There must have been a mix-up on the music! Shane consulted his program. "Senior Ballet." And walking on to the stage from both wings, toes first, arms rounded in first position, in perfect time to the music, came the senior ballerinas.

Shane did a double-take – was that Lisette? It was! She hadn't mentioned dancing with her favorite class! He broke a sweat. The seniors, in all shapes and sizes, were wearing not costumes, but their dance class leotards, tights, and shoes, with black wraparound skirts, a few short, like Lisette, but most to the knee. He recognized Evelyn from Lisette's stories as the spindly fourth-in-line with her gray hair skinned back in a ballet bun at the nape of her neck. Last in line but keeping time was Maddie, the tabloid whistle-blower. A smattering of applause rippled through the audience.

"Go Maddie!" called a man in front of Shane who was video recording the dance with his phone. He saw Maddie roll her eyes. With the throbbing beat of "Thunder Thighs" ringing in the rafters, the seniors delivered a balletic interpretation across a spectrum. Some were buttoned down, almost mechanical in their precision, and some, including Lisette and Maddie, were embellishing the ballet confines with little Freddie Mercury struts and back kicks, insolent head tosses. It was riveting. The audience was one giant smile. Shane drew breath for a "whoo!" but tamped it down. Don't call attention, he reminded himself.

The dancers, beaming with pride and delight, gathered and reconfigured themselves, repeated the choreography in small groups that gave everyone a moment in the limelight, then retired to the sidelines before all came together for the last bit as one. It was a visual feast for Shane to see Lisette as he had first met her, in her leotard, this time in motion. It was apparent that she was the pro.

As they struck their final pose, the audience erupted in applause. The dancers formed a line at the edge of the stage and executed an elaborate curtsey. A few people, including the man in front of Shane, rose to their feet. Shane joined the standing ovation. The dancers trained their eyes on the back of the house, waved elegantly, and departed via both sides of the stage, as they had arrived.

The lights went up. Intermission! Shane spent the time perusing the program. "How much longer?" he was wondering when he saw that the teachers had the last dance. Lisette's name was included. He would get to see her dance again!

The suspense sustained him until the last students had done their thing. Then came the finale with the teachers. The black tutus were a total turn-on. Lisette was first in line, wearing dramatic makeup. An invisible thread held her aloft, her feet did not seem to touch the ground. It was like Michael Jackson moonwalking. It was a silly little dance not unlike a band performing, parts where they all danced together, then each having their turn to riff. When Lisette spun across the stage, Shane's breath caught in his throat and tears sprang to his eyes. God she was beautiful! A black angel!

As they finished, Shane wiped his tears from the outside edges of his eyes with the heel of his hand. Then there were many bows, much applause, and dozens of roses heaped on the stage. He'd forgotten flowers – or a car! The performance hall was quickly emptying.

He easily made his way backstage in his increasingly hot and itchy disguise. It was like entering an estrogen bubble. Teenage dancers were acting all dramatic, saying heartfelt goodbyes to classmates, hating to put their coats on over their beautiful feathered and sequined costumes. Shane spotted a gray head in a far corner. Evelyn! He approached the group.

"Can you help me," he asked her. "I'm looking for Ms. DuPre."

"Madame!" Evelyn called.

"Yes," Lisette's head poked around a doorway.

Evelyne gestured to Shane, voila!

Shane approached Lisette. A dressing room was behind her, empty. He walked in and turned to her. She was still in the doorway looking perplexed. "Lisette, it's me," he said, and removed his hat. A sharp intake of air from Lisette. He was reaching for the elastic bands that held the beard in place when she slammed the door shut and turned to him, "Shane?"

He removed the beard and smiled at her. She jumped into his arms.

"That black tutu is super hot," he told her.

As the story spilled out, Lisette was shaking from the surprise. A knock on the door interrupted them.

"Lisette!"

It was Evelyn.

Lisette opened the door.

"It was so wonderful," Evelyn said. "I love it so much that you joined us in our dance."

Evelyn, sensing something amiss in the room, looked past Lisette and saw Shane. He was holding a tweed hat and a dead squirrel.

"Shane Stewart!" said Evelyn.

"Hello, Evelyn," Shane said. "Thank you for a lovely performance. You ladies brought down the house."

"Didn't we though?" Evelyn said. "Sorry to interrupt, but can I get a selfie?"

"Of course, least I can do," Shane twinkled.

"You make me weak in the knees," Evelyn said, producing her cellphone.

"I'll take it," Lisette offered.

"All right, then a selfie of the three of us," Evelyn said. "I promise I will not sell it to the tabloids!"

As Evelyn left, telling Shane she loved him on "The Late Show," she pinched Maddie on the upper arm and told her to get her ass in the dressing room, Lisette wanted to see her. "Shit, probably about Howie yelling 'Maddie' during our dance," she thought.

Maddie's jaw dropped when she entered the dressing room. "Shane Fucking Stewart," she croaked.

"Have we met?" Shane grinned.

"Um," Maddie said, staring oddly. Normally a chatterbox, she was momentarily reduced to single syllables.

"I loved your dance," Shane said. "How did you choose the music?"

"Well we had learned it to some classical music, but one day we came in and Lisette played 'Thunder Thighs' and it worked perfectly with the dance. It changed everything, and we all loved it!" Maddie explained, reclaiming her voice.

"I am deeply honored," Shane said.

"Could I?" Maddie pantomimed taking a picture.

"Of course," Shane obliged.

"Bring them all in," Lisette said. "We'll take a group shot!"

The seniors were aflutter. Lisette posed them with Shane at the center. Maddie cozied up to Shane, who threw his arm over her shoulder. Maria, who had been on the lookout for Shane, walked in just in time to take the picture.

"Hi, Shane!"

"Hi, Maria!"

Lisette insisted he put on the hat and beard for a final shot.

"Mom, I'm taking off now with Zoe," Maria said. "I'm staying at her house tonight."

Lisette had known about the sleepover all week. She sensed there had been some planning behind her back.

"Did Aunt Chris have a hand in this?" she asked.

"Yes, we co-conspired," Maria admitted. She gave Lisette a hug, then Shane.

"See ya," she said.

Lisette had started taking street clothes out of a tote.

"Wait! Don't change," Shane said. "Please."

"I can't wear these outside," she said, indicating her pointe shoes. She quickly untied the ribbons and stepped into her black New York boots, unfolding herself upward as she climbed aboard the heels.

"Wow," Shane said appreciatively.

He gently laid her coat atop her shoulders over the black tutu and they quickly exited through the stage door, deftly dodging any conversation with Ass Hat, whose voice Lisette could hear pontificating over the dressing room chatter.

"This was an epic surprise," Lisette said as she drove them home to her house.

"I had help," Shane said.

"So I hear," Lisette grinned.

Misha met them at the door, tail wagging. Shane got down on one knee and offered the dog his hand. Misha sniffed it and rolled over on his back in submission, tail thumping the floor. Shane petted him.

"Outside?" Lisette asked the dog. He sprang to his feet and shook, sending a cloud of fur billowing. Shane's sleeves were covered in dog hair.

"Dude, you have more hair than Dokken!" Shane said to Misha. "Maybe even Cinderella."

Lisette opened a drawer of a cabinet in the foyer. It contained the cache of lint rollers.

"Take your pick," she told Shane.

Misha trotted after Lisette to the kitchen door. She let him out. By the time he barked to be let in, Lisette had filled Misha's dish and poured wine. Shane had taken a stool at the kitchen island. He offered a toast: "To a splendid performance!"

After gobbling his food and a long drippy drink, Misha laid down at Shane's feet and looked up at him, white rims on the bottoms of his eyes making him look like he just asked a question and was waiting for a reply.

"He adores you!" Lisette said. "He is usually super protective of me."

"I love dogs," Shane said. "I waited for mine to die of old age before I sold the ranch." He scrolled through his phone until he found a picture of his late dogs to show her. "They were brother and sister, Jethro and Ellie Mae. They both made it to 12."

"That's a long life for big dogs," Lisette observed. "Some kind of Lab mix?"

"Yes," Shane said, Misha's head on his boot. "They were the goofiest. Until I met this guy. What is he, some kind of Shepherd mix?"

"Yes, accent on the 'mix'," Lisette said. "The vet says Misha is God's prototypical dog: 50 pounds, yellow, smart as the dickens."

Shane was looking at her strangely.

"What?" she asked.

"You should wear that every day," he said, eyeballing her tutu.

"You are the goofiest," she said. "Oh gee, I didn't ask – did you fly in to-day? Are you hungry? We have leftover pasta – with homemade meatballs."

Shane looked at the beautiful woman asking him a question, her eye-brows arched, her gray eyes rimmed black in the fashion of Amy Wine-house, her lips deep crimson, wearing a tutu and thigh-high black boots. Lisette met his gaze. She sensed another Brick House Moment. She struck a pose, shoulders on the diagonal, left hand on her hip, feet in third. Touché!

"You fucking cripple me, Lisette," he said.

"Was it the meat balls that got to you?" she asked with half a smile.

"When you were twirling across the stage never missing a beat, the light on your shoulders and arms, I had arrhythmia."

Lisette laughed. Her teeth looked like little pearls against her deep red lips. Her tongue was behind them. Shane shivered.

"Do you get dizzy? From the turns, I mean," he said.

"More than I used to," she admitted. "It's all about spotting."

"What were those kick turns at the end?"

"*Fouetté*," Lisette said. "You create momentum with your leg and lift."

"It was … impressive," Shane said.

"Thank you."

Shane needed her right then and there. He stood and lifted her up onto the countertop. She encircled his waist with her legs and his neck with her arms.

"This is a picture I'd like to have," he murmured. "You're not sewed into this thing, are you?"

"Rip it off," she said. "I'll never wear it again."

"Oh, I don't know about that," he grinned. "What if I asked really, really nicely?"

He deftly unzipped the back of the bodice and peeled it down. The tutu had its own structure built in. Lisette's breasts tumbled out. Shane buried his face in them. The crisp net of the skirt made crunching noises between them. Misha left the room.

Afterward, they had leftover spaghetti and meatballs in the kitchen, amid their DNA.

"It's always better the second time around," Lisette said.

"I'll say," Shane agreed.

"I was talking about the dinner," Lisette said.

"I wasn't," Shane said.

Chapter 44

Shane's phone rang at an ungodly early hour. Derek.

"What's up, Derek?" he answered it.

"Shane, it's Rob," Derek said. "He's in hospital!"

"What happened?" Shane demanded, springing up fully awake.

The concern in Shane's voice woke Lisette. She was disoriented. They had slept in the guest room. Lisette didn't want any lingering Carl vibes to touch them. Shane's back was toward her. She put her hand on his shoulder.

"He had some kind of seizure. He's in the ICU at Cedars," Derek explained.

"Is he conscious?" Shane asked.

"No, and he's on a ventilator," Derek said.

"Where did it happen?"

"At home last night. Lynn found him on the floor with the goddamned Fire Stick in his hand."

If it was 8 a.m. in Chicago, it was 6 in L.A. Shane figured Derek must have been up all night.

"Where are you?" Shane asked.

"Still at the hospital. Been here all night. They say he's stabilized. Shane, the paramedics gave him Narcan to bring him around. They found a bunch of pills in his pocket."

"Narcan?" Shane yelped.

"Yeah. He was on a bunch of different pain pills for the neck, and Fentanyl. He had opioid poisoning is the bottom line," Derek said.

"Oh god," Shane moaned.

"This is going to be a shitstorm when the press gets wind of it," Derek said. "We'll need to prepare a statement."

"I'll come back right away," Shane said. "We'll face them together. How's Lynn?"

"About what you'd expect, shattered," Derek said sadly.

"Okay. I'm on my way," Shane said, hanging up.

He fell back on the pillow and stared at the ceiling. He was ashen. He took a deep breath.

"Rob OD'd on opioids. He's in the ICU on a ventilator," he reported. "I'm sorry, Lisette, but I have to go."

While Shane took a quick shower, Lisette made coffee and threw some clothes on. She heard him talking on the phone to someone who was meeting him at the airport.

"The pilot is on his way," Shane reported, gratefully taking the coffee cup she offered him.

Lisette looked puzzled, then she got it.

"Ah, private plane," she said.

"Jet, actually," Shane said, with a half-smile that crinkled his sad eyes. "Derek and I will have to face the press. This will be quite the story, what with the band's history."

"Not to mention Prince, Tom Petty, and Michael Jackson," Lisette observed. "God, I hope he recovers."

She threw her arms around him in a strong embrace.

"Let's go," she said.

Shane petted Misha's dome of a head. The dog practically turned himself inside out wagging his tail. "Bye, buddy," Shane said.

They made it to the airport in record time. Shane directed her to a private terminal she had never noticed before, reminding her once again of the many things she didn't know about Shane or his life. For instance, she didn't know he had several changes of clothes hanging in a closet on the jet, hadn't thought to wonder why he had no luggage.

"I will keep you posted," Shane said as the car pulled up to the doors, turning to look Lisette square in the eyes. He cupped her face in his hands. "I'm sorry to run off. Last night was such a delight. You are a wonder. I adore you."

He kissed her goodbye. She watched him jog toward the tiny terminal building, appreciating once again his lithe body moving effortlessly through space. She entertained the thought that for the first time in her life she had woken up next to someone prettier than she. She drove home thinking about Rob. His poor wife! His poor kids! He's the one always showing pictures of his grandchildren – he had so much to live for! She could barely muster a smile when she saw the tweed hat and false beard on the back seat. This was simply too fucked up.

She dialed Chris as soon as she entered the house.

"Oh my god," Chris answered the phone.

"I just dropped Shane at the airport," Lisette said. "What's the latest?"

"He's still unconscious," Chris said. "If Lynn hadn't done CPR and the paramedics didn't have Narcan, he'd be a goner. But there is brain activity, so there is hope. If he lives, he could have brain damage, or be physically impaired. They just have to take it one step at a time."

"I feel so sad for his family," Lisette said.

"I know," Chris said. "It sucks. His son and his wife are expecting another baby. So much to live for…"

"Wait!" Chris yelped. "Tell me about the recital!"

"Oh, Chris, it was such a surprise!" Lisette said. "I didn't recognize him – I thought he was some old theory professor coming backstage afterward hoping to see naked girls. I almost shooed him out. I have pictures of Shane posing with the senior dancers, I'll text them. He was so surprised by 'Thunder Thighs' – it brought down the house, it was the hit of the show."

"Good," Chris said. "Take that, Ass Hat! And you hold on to those good thoughts during the current shitstorm."

"Jesus Christ, there's always some shit storming it feels like," Lisette said.

"One rolls out, another rolls in," Chris agreed.

"So what will Derek and Shane have to do now?" Lisette asked.

Chris switched seamlessly into reporter mode. Some habits never die.

"Well, word will get out any minute now, even though it's early and a weekend. Someone in the hospital inevitably tells someone else, and the press gets wind of it. The hospital will handle their initial questions, but not much more than to confirm he's there, and what his condition is: critical, stable, fair, good. It won't be 'good.' Then Derek and the record company will need to respond with some sort of statement. They'll work with Lynn on that, see how she wants to handle it. It might be a 'thoughts and prayers' thing or a life lesson thing, an opportunity to put a face on opioid addiction, a cautionary tale. He's still alive, at least. We should know by tonight if he's able to breathe on his own, so they might gird their loins until then before making a statement. Or he'll die, in which case we go into crisis mode: sequestering the family, autopsy results, funeral arrangements, toxicology results, lawsuits against the doctors, ripples of the story continuing over the next weeks or months. It will suck."

"Selfishly, I still want you to come for Maria's graduation," Lisette said. "But if you can't, I understand. I haven't told her about all this. She slept at Zoe's, which I believe you already know as a co-conspirator."

"I would not miss graduation for anything," Chris assured her. They talked a bit more about graduation logistics and driving a load to Michigan afterward. Then Chris rang off with "I'll keep you posted," knowing they would talk again that day.

Lisette realized with a start that she was completely free! The teaching semester was over, the recital a memory, and she had pretty much quit her job. She was one step closer to decamping to Michigan after the graduation. She should throw a graduation party, she decided. She had all week to pull it together.

Misha ran to the door.

"Hi, Mom," Maria called. "Hi, Lunkhead," she greeted Misha.

"In the kitchen," Lisette called.

"Where's Shane?" Maria asked.

"He had to go, emergency in L.A.," Lisette said. She told the story. Maria listened.

"What's going to happen to the band?" Maria asked. "Does this mean the end of the Disgracefuls?"

"Too early to say," Lisette said. "Let's just hope Rob survives, and in a way that he has good quality of life. We'll know more tonight."

Lisette asked Maria if she felt like having a graduation party.

"Mom, I'm invited to like three parties already," Maria said.

"On the day of?" Lisette asked.

"Yes," Maria said. "One in the afternoon and two that night. I'll be seeing basically the same people at three different places!"

"Sorry honey," Lisette said. "I kind of dropped the ball."

"Mother, please," Maria said. "You don't have to do it all."

"Still…" Lisette said.

"Still shmill," Maria sassed.

"When does your father get in?" Lisette asked.

"He's coming Friday. We're having dinner together," Maria said. "I think he leaves right after graduation. He knows I'll be in the social whirl."

Sitting through graduation with Carl would be weird, Lisette thought. Thank god for Chris.

"Will you have time this week to sort more stuff?" Lisette asked.

"Sure," Maria said.

Lisette had already thought beyond Maria's first year away, when she would be living in a dorm. Lisette had procured a storage space for things Maria would need when she moved into an apartment: bedroom and living room furniture, kitchen essentials. She would be well-provisioned.

Lisette would call the Realtor on Monday and get that ball rolling. She'd ask her about showing the house with or without furniture.

"I'm running out for a minute," Lisette called upstairs to Maria, letting herself out the front door. She drove to the nearby Catholic church. The doors were open. She went inside and turned into a pew near an alcove with a statue of the Blessed Mother. She sank to her knees and gave thanks for all the good things that had happened lately in her life, and for the strength she was realizing within herself to endure life's inevitable shitstorms. She lit three candles for Rob.

Chapter 45

Lynn woke with a start. She had been fast asleep in a chair. Where was she? It all came rushing back to her, the horror of discovering Rob sprawled on the floor, his lips blue, the spinning circle on the TV screen as she performed CPR and waited for the ambulance.

"Is this how it ends?" she remembered thinking. But remarkably, he was still alive. The kids had been briefly in and out earlier. She was stiff from sleeping in the chair, she had no idea what time it was. The ventilator whooshed and chirped. She watched Rob's heartbeat on the monitor above his bed. She looked at his face. She thought his eyes were fluttering. She rang for the nurse.

The nurse checked Rob's vitals, and noted the eye fluttering. It was no big deal. What she would like to see was movement in his arms and legs.

"He is in a 'light sleep' from sedation for the ventilator," she explained to Lynn. "So the eye fluttering is common. We are planning to start weaning him off the ventilator tonight for 30 minutes, and see how that goes."

"What time is it?" Lynn asked. The nurse nodded at the clock on the wall. It was 4:30. "Is it afternoon?" Lynn asked.

"Yes," the nurse said. "Doctors will be in for the extubation before 6."

The nurse handed Lynn a plastic bag with soap, a toothbrush and toothpaste.

"Thank you," Lynn said. She washed her hands and face and brushed her teeth. It made her feel a bit more human. She dragged her fingers through her hair. She returned to the chair and reached out for Rob's hand. Her head slowly drooped onto the hospital bed and she wept softly remembering the traumatic night and thinking about the terrifying future. Would he be brain damaged? Would he be in a wheelchair? How could he have gone back down the rabbit hole of addiction with them all watching out for him?

"I'm telling you one fucking thing right now, Rob," she sobbed softly. "You are not leaving the hospital without neck surgery. Yeah, you're scared. Tough shit about that, pal. You will have your neck fixed, you will do another rehab, and then and only then will I allow you to come home. You cannot keep screwing up our lives like this. We are too old for this shit. We deserve your very best, Rob. You best be bringing it."

Rob squeezed her hand.

She bolted upright and called for the nurse again. She waited for another squeeze.

"Rob, did you squeeze my hand? Can you hear me?"

Nothing. The nurse swept in.

"He squeezed my hand," Lynn said. "I swear. Just once. I was talking to him."

"The doctors are on their way up for the extubation. Be sure to tell them about it," the nurse said, repeating Rob's vitals.

Just then the doctors appeared in the hallway, with an aide pushing a cart of equipment. They were solicitous, attentive and caring to Lynn. Buzz in the hospital that day was all about the Disgracefuls' bass player in the ICU for opioid poisoning. A few TV trucks were parked outside the front entrance of the hospital for live shots. A couple dozen fans were keeping vigil on a narrow parkway across the street. They'd created one of those urban shrines with candles, flowers, pictures, album covers and other crap. They were playing Disgracefuls music on their phones. Some had brought lawn chairs to the vigil.

Lynn told the doctors right away about the hand squeeze. They glanced at each other.

"That's good," said the woman doctor.

"Right?" said Lynn.

"We'll take out the breathing tube, then observe him for 30 minutes," the male doctor said. "If he does all right breathing on his own, we'll back off on the sedation and see how he comes around. He will be under complete supervision all night. He won't remember anything. You can go home and get some sleep."

He had noticed the depth of the sadness on her careworn face. It was more than fatigue. He knew she'd been around this block before. It changes you. He suggested she step outside during the extubation.

"Is either of you a neurosurgeon?" Lynn asked.

"I am," said the woman.

"Thank goodness," Lynn said. "This whole thing started with herniated discs in his neck. He needs surgery. Could you please see what you might be able to do for him? I will sign whatever you need, I have health care power of attorney. Thank you, okay, I'm leaving. Let me know when I can come back in."

Derek was in the hallway. Lynn brought him up to speed on Rob.

"Lynn, there are TV trucks outside the hospital," Derek told her. "Earlier the hospital confirmed that Rob is here, and we – that is the record company and Shane – put out a statement also confirming that Rob is here, we're all waiting for more information, and thoughts and prayers are with you and your family."

Lynn was quiet. The door to Rob's ICU cubicle whooshed open. The neurosurgeon invited them in.

"So far, so good," said the other doctor. "We'll monitor him for 30 minutes. You can stay."

"You said he won't remember this?" Lynn asked the doctors.

"The sedative has a memory blocker," the neurosurgeon explained. She took information from Lynn about MRIs and ultrasounds, where and when, and who were the doctors. She asked about his symptoms. The doctor had seen the initial tox scan. Hearing Lynn's perspective, it became clear that Lynn hadn't known about the Fentanyl or the Oxy. They moved to the corner chairs and talked about Rob's history.

"All right!" the male doctor exclaimed. "He's breathing on his own at 30 minutes. Respiration regular, kidney function good."

He wrote on his chart.

"Do you think he heard me when he squeezed my hand?" Lynn asked.

"Anything is possible when it involves the brain," the neurosurgeon said. "A squeeze is a good sign."

Lynn was heartened. She kissed Rob goodnight and left with Derek. He had the car swing around to the back, away from the TV trucks, to pick her up at a nondescript employee entrance. They were silent as the car pulled away.

"This is a teachable moment, Derek," Lynn finally said. "With all of the rock stars who died of drugs and alcohol, if that motherfucker Rob lives I will make him convert the hearts and minds of this country by telling his story, raising awareness of opioid abuse, especially for Baby Boomers. Rob should be on the cover of People magazine, or on "60 Minutes", or that Sunday show with Jane Pauley and the brass fanfare."

All the kids and grandkids were at the house. Lynn was staggering with the fatigue of trauma compounded with lack of sleep. Derek took her arm, escorted her into the house and turned her over to her tribe.

"Please let him live," Derek prayed. He went home to Chris. She had been extremely helpful consulting on responses to the press. She had considered all scenarios, live or die, and wrote crisp responses and suggested media strategies. In Chris's estimation, the ultimate scenario was that Rob pulls through and becomes the face of the adult/elder opioid epidemic! People magazine! 60 Minutes!

Chapter 46

Rob, henceforth known as Lazarus, was sitting up in his hospital bed with his eyes open on Sunday morning.

"Well that was close," he said to Lynn as she walked into the cubicle. She burst into tears.

"Oh, Rob," she said, embracing him amid the IV lines and monitors.

"Can you move?" she said.

He wiggled his fingers and toes.

Lynn's knees buckled and she plopped down in a chair and put her face in her hands, elbows on knees.

"Dad!" the children moved in.

Many tears were shed. The doctors stopped by for a victory lap.

"Mr. Hamill, the reason you are alive is this woman right here," the neurosurgeon told him. "If she hadn't performed CPR, you would be severely brain damaged or dead. We're moving you to the neurology wing, and we're going to fix your neck. I think we can get you some significant relief and improve your mobility."

Rob looked at Lynn with a mix of junkie defensiveness and sheer terror. She'd seen it before. She was not intimidated by it. She knew both came from a place of weakness. She was beyond that.

"Non-negotiable Rob," she said. "Your pain relief plan didn't work out so well. You have to address the physical problem, not simply treat the symptoms. And while you recover from your neck surgery, you will do rehab, both physical therapy and drug rehab. You can't come home until you take those steps."

"The fucking Steps," Rob said bitterly.

"Your other option is to find yourself another life," Lynn said calmly. "I can't live through this again. I'm too fucking old for this shit."

Oh how Rob longed for the comfort of his opioids! He despised the thought of returning to drug rehab, the séance circle of group therapy, listening to a bunch of losers tell their sad tales. He was a rock star!

"I found your stash, the Fentanyl and Oxy," Lynn said. She had torn up the house. "The party's over."

Shit!

The kids started talking then, words of encouragement, reminders of how important he was in their lives, to the grandkids. Rob recognized the format of intervention. He'd been through it before, so had they. The mention of the grandchildren started to break down Rob's resistance.

"Dad, we know you're afraid of surgery, but how can that be scarier than dying?" his daughter said at one point. As if logic played any part in irrational fear.

Lynn asked everyone to give her a few minutes alone with Rob. She told him about her plan to turn this near-death into an example for other families, to be not only transparent but public about it to shine awareness on the opioid crisis. It was a hard lesson, apparently, for their Baby Boomer peers, who were deeply attached to their comforts and hated any kind of personal pain.

"We'll talk about it more after rehab," she said. "But I really think we can save some lives, Rob. And I'm committed to it. I plan to start working on it today, in fact."

The doctors came back in, announcing they were moving Rob to the neurology wing for further observation prior to surgery. Lynn kissed Rob goodbye, told him to get some rest, and said she'd see him later in the day. She had asked Derek and Chris to meet her to craft a statement for the press.

Derek called a press conference for 4 p.m. outside the hospital. He, Lynn, and Shane stood up in front of the cameras.

"Thank you for being here," Derek said. "Lynn, Rob's wife, would like to share a statement. Afterward, we'll take a few questions."

Lynn stepped to the mic with a prepared statement:

"We are extremely relieved to report that Rob is conscious and talking after a very close call Friday night. Rob had injured discs in his neck and was prescribed a number of pain medications by a number of doctors. I found him unresponsive on the floor at home Friday night and performed CPR until the ambulance arrived. Paramedics administered Narcan, which interrupted the overdose. If not for those timely interventions, we would be planning Rob's funeral.

"As you know, Rob and his bandmates have battled addiction before. They have been sober for 20 years. But the opioid epidemic in this country continues to grow – and to kill – with no regard for gender or age. The Centers for Disease Control report that deaths from drug overdoses tripled between 1999 and 2016. In 2016, more than 63,000 people died from drug overdoses. More than 42,000 of these deaths involved prescription or illicit opioids.

"We continue to grieve the losses of Prince, Tom Petty, so many others, all of whom would still be with us today if not for similar prescription drugs. Rob would be on that sad roll call if his timeline had been off by mere minutes.

"We are overjoyed that Rob pulled through. But we can't forget the millions of people out there who are struggling with pain and addiction right now. Please, families and friends, understand that prescriptions from the doctor can be just as deadly as shooting heroin into your veins. We all need to be vigilant and informed. Help is available. Our family thanks you for your support."

"What drugs was Rob taking?" a reporter instantly barked.

"He had prescriptions for OxyContin, hydrocodone, Tramadol, and Fentanyl patches," Lynn answered.

"Were all of those drugs in his system?" the same reporter asked.

"Yes. All of the above," Lynn said.

"What was his condition when you found him?" another reporter called out.

"He was unresponsive and his lips were blue," Lynn said. She choked on a sob. The cameras fired in burst mode, capturing her emotion. Derek took hold of her upper arms and gently moved her to the side.

"With Rob's history, how did he get all those drugs?" the reporter followed up. "Why wasn't he being closely monitored?"

"Let me take this," Lynn said, moving back to the mic. "Rob was under a doctor's care, we were monitoring him at home and at work. But addiction is insidious. Addicts are sneaky. It's often very difficult to know exactly what's going on."

"Shane! What will happen with the Disgracefuls' summer tour?" another reporter shouted.

Shane stepped up to the mic.

"We're working that out. The important thing is that Rob gets well. We'll be waiting for him."

"Shane, how would you describe Rob's role in the band?" a hippy chick reporter asked in Valley Girl speak.

"Rob is our foundation. His sound is instantly recognizable. He is indispensible in the recording process, he has an excellent ear," Shane elaborated. "We depend on Rob in more ways than we even realize."

"Could this be the end of the Disgracefuls?" a British journalist asked.

"Absolutely not," Derek broke in. "In fact, the band has been in the studio working on new material for the past month."

"When will we get a taste?" asked the Brit.

"Soon, very soon," Derek said, mastering the art of saying nothing at all. "Thank you, everybody," Derek ended the press conference.

Within hours, the record company's publicity wheel had heard from an editor at People magazine, offering the cover in exchange for an exclusive interview with Rob and Lynn ("Back from the Brink – Disgracefuls' Rob Hamill Crusades Against Opioid Abuse") as well as various assignment editors from the networks and reporters from the music press who had covered the band for decades and were on a first-name basis.

"Told ya," Chris said.

Chapter 47

Friday night, Lisette picked Chris up at the airport. On the ride back to Lisette's, Chris delivered a blow-by-blow recap of the past week from her insider perspective. Lisette had daily updates from Shane, of course, but it was interesting to hear Chris, a skilled storyteller, tell the tale from beginning to end.

Rob's neck surgery the day before had gone well. His body had been to hell and back. Still, they had him up and walking and booted him into physical therapy right away. It seemed cruel. (Lynn gloated – back atcha, Rob!) Everyone was relieved that Rob would be under close supervision with the pain relief meds as he recovered. It was exhausting hovering about an addict: constant searches of favorite hiding places, counting the pills every four hours, turning the pockets inside-out. And still, look what happened! Lynn brought in an old acoustic guitar no one cared about to give Rob something to play around with. Derek cautioned her not to bring Rob's bass – artifacts from the band tended to go missing. Fans swipe stuff, which is ridiculous.

The upside for Lisette and Shane was this: The band would be on hiatus until Rob completed rehab! To Lisette, it meant that Shane could join her in Michigan! He was excited to, as he said, "hide out" with her there.

But first graduation. And Carl.

Carl had sent several tentative and conciliatory emails to Lisette expressing regret, offering apologies, promising to be on his best behavior at graduation.

"Can we at least be kind to each other for Maria's sake?" he said.

"Well duh," Lisette thought when she saw that one. No need to be melodramatic. They would be among friends, they'd circulate separately. They would be paragons of virtue.

"Hello, Lizzy," he greeted her at their seats. "Hi, Chris."

"Hi, Carl," Lisette said. So her last words to Carl wouldn't be "fuck off" after all.

She had been thinking about all the years leading up to Maria's graduation, the days after days, years after years, that brought them to this proud moment. Of course they could behave themselves for a few hours. Lisette's sudden new romance, still in its blooming phase, sure took the sting out of any hurt feelings. Shane had sent Maria a congratulatory note with a gift card to burn on her European trip.

"Lisette!" Maddie called, approaching with Howie in tow. Their nephew was in the graduating class with Maria. The two women hugged.

"Can you believe our video went viral?" Maddie asked. "We have over a million views!"

Lisette looked at her blankly.

"The video of the senior ballerinas! The recital!" Maddie explained. "Howie posted it to YouTube!"

"Oh my goodness!" Lisette exclaimed.

"You haven't seen it?" Maddie said, disbelieving. Did Lisette live under a rock? Then again, she realized, Lisette was having a torrid affair with a rock star. She had other things on her plate at the moment.

"Hi, Carl, nice to see you," Maddie said in a perfunctory aside. "Lisette, call me after you see the video! We'll debrief! Enjoy the graduation."

"Did you know about this?" Maria asked Chris.

"I heard a little something," Chris said with a smile.

"You've seen it?" Lisette asked.

"I am one of many," Chris said. "It is quite brilliant. Don't be surprised if you get a call from the chat shows."

Chris had gotten wind of it through Derek, who had been alerted to a possible copyright infringement of "Thunder Thighs." Luckily, Shane had written the song. Permission granted! The senior ballerinas were well on their way to being folk heroes. Take that, Ass Hat!

Chris called it up on her phone and handed it to Lisette, who watched with a furrowed brow that slowly relaxed into a broad smile, interspersed with giggles. Her head was bobbing.

"This is so great!" she said. "How did Howie do that?"

"I'll give you a tutorial when we're at the beach," Chris said. "It's simple. Misha could do it."

The day was warm for late May, with abundant sunshine that warmed the outdoor crowd under a deep blue sky. The music started and the graduates marched in and took their seats. Maria spotted them and gave a thumbs-up. Lisette would see her only in brief snatches for pictures and in between graduation parties when she popped in at the house for a wardrobe change. Little by little, Lisette could feel herself releasing Maria. She had not been having so many fearful thoughts, she realized. In some ways, it was the calm after the shitstorm. What they'd been through had not been pleasant, but it had ultimately deposited all three of them in a better place. Maria seemed happy and carefree, excited about the future. Carl would go home to Edie, the love of his life, without encumbrances. He had decided to retire! Lisette would do whatever she liked whenever she liked as she took baby steps into her newly independent life.

But how independent was she, really? She worried about going straight from a long-term marriage into an intense romantic relationship. What if Shane wanted to marry her? Did she want to marry again? What would be the point at their ages? She was in love with him, she was sure of that, and that was more than enough for now. Shane was totally respecting her request to "let it roll out." He would join her the next week and stay while Maria was in Europe. They'd figure it out as they went along.

If independence was new to Lisette, dependence was new to Shane. The intensity of his feelings frightened him – he wanted to be with her all the time! But he cautioned himself about being too needy. He would never be a barnacle!

That said, they were practically panting until they could be together again. In preparation, Lisette and Chris planned a visit to the lingerie shop after graduation to do a little shopping.

Lisette had been tearful watching Maria walk across the stage. Chris squeezed her hand. Lisette had looked over, Chris was weepy, too. She squeezed her back. It was a happy kind of weepy for they had come such a long way together. The best part was that they had more adventures to look forward to, whatever they might be.

"Brick House #1 calling Brick House #2," Chris yodeled across the dressing room at Schwartz's.

Both women opened the doors of their facing dressing rooms to weigh in on the selections.

"Va va voom," Lisette said, endorsing Chris's selection.

Their sales lady materialized silently, a gray apparition – Schwartz's clerks were older women. Lisette appreciated their professional understanding about the shifting sands of middle age and their know-how for relocating drooping body parts. (Lisette had boycotted Victoria's Secret ever since a 20-something saleswoman directed her to the rack of "comfortable" bras. How rude!)

"Very nice," the saleswoman said, admiring them both. Turning to Chris, she said, "We also have that in champagne. Let me bring it to you."

"Derek is the next 'man down,'" Lisette predicted.

Lisette treated herself to a couple of silk nighties and a kimono-like summer robe. She and Shane would not be on a schedule, so loungewear was her primary mission today. Her sleepwear at the cottage was oversized t-shirts and an ancient flannel robe. Oh, no no no no. Not this time. She let Chris talk her into trying on a thong, and the sight of it sent them into gales of laughter.

"Thong long gone," Lisette concluded. "The lace boy shorts are good on you, though."

"Oh yeah," Chris agreed, admiring herself in the three-way mirror.

The salesladies wrapped their exquisite little purchases in tissue paper. Chris and Lisette headed home to let the dog out, stopping at the expensive deli for take-out.

"Hot pastrami and hot lingerie," Chris proclaimed. "It doesn't get much better than this."

Chapter 48

The rental truck was stuffed! Chris hopped into the driver's seat. Maria blinked in the bright light of day. She'd had a glorious afternoon and night of parties. She kissed a girl! It was awesome!

"I'm riding shotgun with Chris!" she announced. She needed to talk to Chris about the girl kiss. And her father's imminent remarriage to Edie. "Misha, you ride with Mom."

Lisette locked the front door behind her. Misha bounded into the back seat of the SportWagen. They were off!

The tollway traffic thinned as they headed south, then east. The billboards and cell phone towers faded into the distance. The road ahead was framed by trees and sky. It was a stunning day. They exited the highway onto a two-lane road that would take them north along the lakeshore.

Lisette's phone rang.

"Shane, we're almost there!" she said, describing their location. She recapped the graduation, including Maddie's surprise about the video.

"You knew about it!" Lisette said.

"You didn't?" Shane said.

"No!" Lisette said.

"Well congratulations on your first platinum hit! Over a million views!" he said. "That's awesome. Derek said the video seems to have spiked downloads of 'Thunder Thighs.' I have a feeling that women all over the world are learning the dance. It might become a fixture, like those line dances at weddings."

"I'm nearly there," Lisette announced, "turning into Sunset Path now! Oh Shane, I wish you were here!"

"Enjoy a few days with Maria and Chris," he said. "Next week and the week after are ours alone."

"You're giving me arrhythmia," Lisette said truthfully.

"I will cure that soon enough," Shane promised. "Dr. Feelgood signing off."

The cottage looked forlorn in late spring, the grill and porch furniture covered in tarps. Lisette couldn't wait to get a rake into her hands and get the garden going.

Maria ran to unlock the front door. Misha leapt from the car and raced around like he was insane, smelling the warming earth and the creatures that had visited over the winter.

The women also raced around like they were insane, throwing open the windows, unloading groceries, lighting the burners of the stove, flushing toilets and running water to make sure everything worked.

"To the beach!" Lisette commanded.

They left the house and walked to the end of the sandy lane, Misha padding behind then, then over a slight dune. The lakefront spread out below them, impressive as an ocean.

"What a day!" Chris said.

The gulls cried above and the lake, calm today, rippled at the shoreline like whispering lace. The women walked the beach for an hour, picking up stones and beach glass and reacquainting themselves with the landscape, which re-sculpted itself every winter under huge ice shelves.

It was all so dear and familiar to them that they were giddy. Once back at the house, they opened bottles of beer and tackled the moving. As "new" stuff came in, old stuff went out. Furniture was moved to accommodate the new items. They hung clean sheets outside over the porch rails to take the fresh air before making up the beds. Late in the afternoon, Chris drove the refilled truck to Habitat for Humanity. When she returned, Lisette was working her magic in the kitchen while Maria giggled to someone on the phone. Chris paused in the doorway to take it all in.

"Salmon on the grill," Lisette called out, even though no one had asked.

"Yum," Chris replied.

And so the pattern continued for two days. The women readied the house for summer with gusto, knowing that Maria and Lisette would be digging in at the cottage when Maria returned from Europe. (And Shane would be there in the meantime!) A "to-do" list was started and posted on the refrigerator. They walked for miles in the mornings and spent afternoon hours on the beach reading and talking. They toasted Chris's family tradition of hard drinking with bottles of wine because that is what you do at the beach, where every day feels like vacation. Chris would rejoin them in late July or August to freeze her ass off in Lake Michigan, maybe go along for college drop-off if the timing was right. They were sad to leave, but all agreed it was a perfect getaway. They drove back to Chicago in the same configuration. Whatever Maria and Chris were talking about, Lisette was grateful that Maria had Chris's counsel. Having Chris as a sounding board had served Lisette well over the years.

The night before, Lisette had shared with Chris her concerns about being alone with Shane 24/7 day after day for such a long time – two weeks.

"What if we get on each other's nerves? What if he doesn't read? What if he has weird political views? What if he sits around watching sports on TV?" Lisette worried, constructing a conceptual framework of doom. "I mean look what happened with Carl. I thought I knew him and he turned out to be a weird stranger! Oh god, what if I fart?"

"Each of those horrors is a negotiating point – set your terms up front," Chris advised. "And don't worry about farting. Guys find it endlessly hilarious. Or take a Maalox."

Chris left for L.A. the next morning and the ensuing days were spent organizing for Maria's big trip. She had a Eurail pass and an itinerary that would have her connecting with various friends along the way. While Lisette's "roll call of doom" regarding Maria, had not completely silenced, it had significantly abated. Maria's assertiveness in the Carl drama, followed by graduation, had left Lisette with a feeling that her work was done, that she had graduated, too. Lisette took Maria to the airport and sent her off with genuine joy, telling her to "have a blast." It was a surprising turnabout. Maybe her worries about Shane were a temporary substitute.

Lisette returned to a quiet, empty house.

"Just me and you tonight, buddy," she said to Misha. He wagged his tail and made a whiny sound deep in his throat. "But guess who's coming to visit – your friend Shane!"

Misha barked and turned in a circle.

"You are a smart boy," Lisette said, letting him outside.

Lisette packed several huge bags for the beach. Two whole weeks! She continued to fret about the fact that she and Shane had mostly been together in a protective bubble of hotel rooms and group situations with familiars.

But she'd taken a lesson from their lunch date: They would fly under the radar during their "hideout." She shopped for provisions that would sustain and deliciously delight them for days on end without having to leave the cottage for the market in town, where everybody knew everybody – and their business. It was like Mayberry.

She went to bed early. She'd pick up Shane at a private airport not far from the cottage late the next day. She was so heart-pounding excited she did not find her sleep until the wee hours.

Chapter 49

Back in the car the next day with world's sheddingest dog, Lisette was ebullient. She loved her life! It was a miracle! Maria sent a picture from Abbey Road that morning of herself, barefoot, striding across the crosswalk. She always loved Paul best. For Lisette it was John. Meanwhile, Lisette had a really cool boyfriend who she loved and who loved her! They would be together in just a few hours, encamping for two weeks of shenanigans. PS: Her boyfriend was a famous rock star! He was 61. She was 57. Her destiny had been fulfilled at long last, apparently. But fulfilled nonetheless.

Once she pulled in at Number 5 Sunset Path, she unpacked and readied the cottage. She Furminated Misha, like that would make a difference. She walked over the dune and surveyed the lake. Righteous waves today. They'd hear them breaking from the cottage. It was her favorite soundtrack.

She brushed her teeth and called Misha. They drove to the tiny airport, which was more like a landing strip amid farmers' fields. They were cleared to park on the tarmac. The jet came in smooth and whining like the dog. She put Misha on his leash and they waited outside the car as the jet taxied.

She watched Shane descend the steps with the most intense sexual longing she had ever felt. God. He. Was. Beautiful. He moved down the stairs with liquid grace, a brown leather bag slung over his shoulder. She realized she was trembling.

Shane spotted her straightaway and experienced the most intense longing he had ever felt. God. She. Was. Beautiful. He wanted to jump straight to the bottom of the stairs and run to her.

"Lisette! Misha!" he said as he approached, putting his hand out. The dog turned himself inside out wagging his tail. Shane dropped to a knee and patted his head. That out of the way, he threw himself onto Lisette, mashing her against the car and devouring her. She was out of her mind with desire.

"We gotta go," she said in his ear, over the jet whine. "Do you have other baggage?"

"They'll bring it around," Shane said.

Lisette wondered, in quick succession: Who were "they"? Why couldn't "they" just put the stuff in her car and be done with it? Ah who the fuck cares, she thought to herself, relinquishing control and opening the back door for the dog. Shane jumped into the passenger seat, waited for her to fasten her seat belt, then planted a scorching kiss on her lips.

"Drive!" he commanded, pointing into the golden evening light toward the lake.

Lisette peeled out on the tarmac, mashing Misha into the back seat from the rapid acceleration. They drove swiftly, barely speaking, across the five miles of back roads from the speck of an airport to the cottage. Misha put his head out the open window, creating a furnado. Shane grabbed Lisettte's right hand and held it tight, using his right hand as a dog hair shield.

The sunset was warming up as they arrived. The cottage looked far more inviting than when she had pulled up the week before with Chris and Maria. Flowers that had been under the leaves were showing themselves: poppies, purple phlox, lilacs, irises. The car moved silently over the sandy lane. The birds were singing their evening songs. The light was golden. The shadows were long.

"Here we are," Lisette said, pulling up.

"It's perfect," Shane said.

They got out of the car and Misha bounded away. Shane reached out for her hand and led her toward the sunset.

"I'm having intense déjà vu," he said as they walked to the end of the lane and up the gentle incline of the dune. "Wow," he said when they got to the top.

The sun was a deep orange ball balanced above the broad expanse of the horizon. It had ignited a fire on the surface of the lake. Thin clouds spread out across the horizon, edged in fiery orange, with cool purple at the far reaches. The sky seemed endless.

Shane turned to Lisette. He put his hand behind her neck and gently, slowly, pulled her to him, face to face.

"I have never been happier to be right here, right now," he told her, pulling her even closer. She could feel his burning desire.

"Shane," she started, then kissed him instead of words, which were utterly extraneous in that moment.

They sat on the sand and watched the sun set. Lisette felt so complete. She put her head on Shane's shoulder and tried not to cry. Her heart was so full! They lingered and watched the afterglow spread across the sky, reflected in the water. Then they stood up, brushed the sand off them, and went home. The best was yet to come.

They made do just fine with Lisette's queen-size bed and her ancient boom box and CD collection. Like many vacation places, the cottage was a repository for obsolete technology. But it was fun listening to albums all the way through again, Shane thought. The Temptations were on heavy rotation. The lovers woke up late and knocked around the place. Shane's things had been delivered the day after his arrival, and his guitar case looked right at home in the small living room, next to Lisette's high school Cortez. He also had a small electronic keyboard, a suitcase, and a case of wine. The man who delivered the items gaped with surprise when Shane emerged from the bedroom with thanks and a tip.

"Uh oh," Lisette thought. "Mayberry."

The lake was freezing but the beach was splendid. As they walked over the rise of the dune with beach chairs and a cooler, Shane stopped suddenly and looked around.

"Stay right here," he told Lisette. He ran back towards the cottage, pulling out his phone, turned, and snapped a picture.

Rejoining her, he explained that he had a recurring feeling of déjà vu every time they had walked to the beach.

"I think I've finally figured it out."

He did not elaborate, but once they settled in on the beach he texted Autumn: "Can you please text a pic of the landscape we bought at the art show in Chelsea?" He'd "show, not tell" Lisette about the uncanny resemblance of the picture to Lisette's hideaway.

The days melted into one other as Shane and Lisette settled into a comfortable routine. After breakfast on the porch, they'd walk the beach. Shane would spend a couple of hours writing while Lisette worked outdoors or went into town. She was working in the garden one morning while Shane, in surfer shorts, was sweeping fallen buds and sand off the porch. He was singing "Love Street," she realized, smiling. She joined in when he reached the bridge: "She has wisdom and knows what to do. She has me and she has you."

Shane leaned over the porch, his forearms on the railing, to deliver his best Jim Morrison impersonation for the talking part: "I see you live on Love Street. There's the store where the creatures meet. I wonder what they do in there, summer Sunday and a year…"

"I guess I like it fine, so far," Lisette finished the song.

"You are a rock-a-rina," Shane said.

"Honestly, how do we remember this stuff?" Lisette wondered aloud. "I can't remember my PIN half the time, but I can remember lyrics with the dust of ages on them!"

"It's how your brain is wired," Shane said. "Music is a powerful mnemonic – a memory device. I saw this piece on a magazine show about a man with Alzheimer's who was so affected he lived in a nursing home. Couldn't even dress himself. But his daughter would take him out every Sunday to sing with his old barbershop quartet and he never failed – he remembered all the words and parts. It was amazing."

Shane's phone pinged. He picked it up and saw Autumn had texted a picture of the landscape from the art show.

"Lisette, look at this," he said, descending the stairs to her and holding out the phone.

She studied it for quite a while, glancing between the path to the beach and the image on the phone.

"That is uncanny," she said. "It's as if the artist set up an easel right here. Where did it come from?"

"I bought it for Autumn at a gallery in New York, the same day we ran into each other at the bookstore last fall," he explained. "Something about it captivated us."

He paused before speaking, not wanting to sound insane.

"Maybe it was destiny calling," he said, grinning at her, noticing how the sun had brought out freckles across the bridge of her nose. She looked up at him, spread her arms, and borrowed a line from Marvin and Tammi.

"Like sweet morning dew, I took one look at you, and it was plain to see you were my destiny," Lisette sang.

He took her hand and led her into the cottage for some mid-day love.

Chapter 50

The first week had been languid to the point of decadence. Everyone who needed to know where they were knew, and left them completely alone except for the occasional text. Rob's recovery was going well. His pain level was 3-4, a vast improvement, and that gave him the will to step away from the opioids. He was on 800 mg. ibuprofen, nothing else. According to Derek, the doctors said his condition and pain level would continue to improve with physical therapy. Maria posted daily on Instagram and they tracked her progress through France. She had found some DuPre cousins on Facebook and planned a day trip to their town. Shane downloaded Instagram to Lisette's phone and taught her how to access the app, follow people, and post. She was amazed!

The second week they were more purposeful. Lisette did her barre work on the porch each day, continuing the habit of her lifetime. Shane watched her through the window, pretending to write, justifying his voyeurism as inspiration for the process. Lisette led Shane through some simple yoga, which devolved into hysterical laughter because kale salad the night before had left them gassy, and their yoga positions expelled a veritable windstorm of flatulence. They unearthed tennis racquets and an unopened can of balls and walked over to the public court to volley a couple of times. They dragged bikes out of the cobwebby shed and took a leisurely trail ride, swapping stories about growing up in the Midwest.

They were feeling so comfortable, so anonymous, they decided to go into town together to poke around and pick up a few groceries. Shane tucked his hair into a baseball cap and put on sunglasses. Lisette noticed a few people staring quizzically at Shane, but no one approached for a selfie. The market was busy. Lisette was grateful most of her neighbors were week-enders this early in the season. At the checkout, the boy at the cash register was staring at them.

"Aren't you…"

"Here it comes," Lisette thought, bracing herself. "We've been outed."

"Aren't you the lady from the 'Thunder Thighs' video?" the boy at the register finished his question. Shane snorted behind Lisette. Lisette busted out an actual guffaw.

"Can I get your autograph for my mom?" the boy asked. "She loves that video! She and her friends are learning the dance. It's hilarious."

"I'd be delighted," Lisette giggled. He tore a piece of paper off the receipt roll and handed it to Lisette with a pen. She wrote "Keep Dancing!" and signed it "Lisette Zurgold."

"That was close," Shane said outside, looking at Lisette over his sunglasses. "We really have gotten away from it all, my love. When we get back to civilization we will be mercilessly chased. Someone's going to connect the dots if they haven't already. Maddie's probably giving interviews."

"There are probably 50 messages from her on the home phone," Lisette speculated, grateful Maddie didn't have her cell number. "Chris says some TV show in New York wants us to perform the dance. As if they'd fly all 12 of us there. Ha!"

Shane studied her. She really didn't get it, the money that flies around in the entertainment industry, the profound influence of social media, the food chain of publicity. He loved her innocence but knew it would soon be tarnished. The future was already in motion: Because Lisette used "Thunder Thighs" for the dance, and then the video went viral, Shane was reaping unexpected royalties from the resurrection of a hit he wrote more than 30 years ago. And once it got out that one of the ladies in the video was his age-appropriate girlfriend, she'd suddenly be famous. Views of the video would triple. The single would re-appear on the charts. They'd be hounded. There was no way around it. Knowing what was to come, he doubled down on enjoying their hideout, willing himself to be fully present in the dwindling moments of now. He couldn't remember the last time he felt so relaxed. He was well rested and sun kissed, and he had been disciplined with his work every day, with a time limit. He had drafts of two more songs to bring back to the band.

But as precious as the present might be, they really did need to talk about the future. First to prepare Lisette for the wave of publicity that was waiting outside their temporary bubble. It would be a cruel bitch slap! Second, he hated asking her to leave her paradise, but he truly wanted her help picking out a house in L.A. And he wanted her to meet Priya and Daniel. The third and overarching issue was how they were going to manage to continue seeing each other. This retreat had set a high bar for both of them, ignited a need for physical presence neither had anticipated and that both were keenly aware of. They had passed the point where phone calls and texting and emailing could sustain them. They needed physical presence, ongoing conversation that flows from close proximity. How and when could they merge their lives? And what about the tour?

Shane sighed. He knew that the two of them would forever look back on these days as their age of innocence. He worried whether reality – celebrity, the travel, the lifestyle – would upend her. At the same time, he could not underestimate Lisette. After all, he'd fallen for her because she was a full-grown woman, certain of who she was. Just the same, it worried him. Was it fair to Lisette?

"Lisette," Shane wondered out loud as the sun dropped into the water that evening, "how will we ever get back to reality?"

"This is reality," she replied, "though I have to pinch myself numerous times during the day to make sure I'm not dreaming."

"Being here makes me realize how much I miss having a place to call home. Or maybe I just never knew what home was until you. You've spoiled me, woman. Now home can only be where you are."

"You really like me that much?" she asked, snuggling closer. "Am I the center of your universe?"

"Dead center. True center. As the Temptations put it, 'you're my everything,'" Shane whispered in her ear. "Will you come to L.A. and help me pick out a house?"

"Ah, Eddie Kendricks," Lisette complimented. "A house, seriously?"

"Yes, seriously," he said. "Just a quick turnaround if you can manage it. I'll send the '40' to fetch you."

"Who's that?" Lisette asked.

"The Learjet," Shane explained. "I could talk to the Realtor and narrow down the search. After we cull the herd, would you be willing to come out for a couple of days and help a brother out?"

"We can do that online – narrow the search," Lisette said. "There will be pictures inside and out. I've been snooping on real estate for years, I'm practically a pro!"

Lisette flashed suddenly on her earlier doubts about what a woman of a certain age was supposed to do with her lifetime of amassed talents, her fears that life might never again present her with opportunities to use her knowledge and skills. Those same fears were part of what kept her married to Carl. Yeah, she knew how to buy a damn house. Her skills were transferrable!

"I know this summer is a special time for you and Maria," Shane said. "You could bring her along, you know. And maybe Autumn can come, too. She now wants to live in L.A. to be close to Priya and the baby. She's transferring schools and I'm looking for a place with a guest house for her."

Jesus H. Christ. So many changes, so many decisions were on the table! Lisette was sort of freaking out. She had her own stuff going on, but she had back-burnered everything for the hideout, foolishly not thinking beyond her dedicated time with Shane. And Maria would be back in four days! She started to feel overwhelmed. She needed professional help – a consultation!

"Shane," she wondered out loud, "how would you feel about inviting Chris and Derek out to visit for a couple of days? You could all go back to L.A. together."

"Sure!" Shane agreed. "Love it! That would be fun!"

Lisette dialed Chris and handed her phone to Shane.

"I'm going to the country, baby do you want to go?" Shane sang to Chris over the phone.

"If you can't make it baby, your sister Lucille said she want to go," Chris warbled. She loved a shuffle.

"And I sure will take her," Shane finished it off. They left it to her to round up Derek. Shane arranged for the "40" to fetch them early the next morning. He and Lisette would pick them up over yonder at the rural airstrip. Yee ha! Company's coming!

Chapter 51

Shane was gone when Lisette woke up. So was the car. So was the dog. There was a note on the table: "Gone to town. Won't be long. Dog is my co-pilot." Then a lopsided heart with an "S" in the middle. Lisette smiled. Her freak-out the night before was still on her mind. She poured coffee and sat on the porch in her kimono.

She teased apart the source of her anxiety. It was mostly about Shane inviting her into his life in a bigger way sooner than she had anticipated. Pick out a house? Really? What comes after that, pick up and move to L.A.? She had only spent a few scant weeks as a "single" woman. Was it wise to jump into a new commitment? What about her own plans? Oh, right, she didn't have any really, beyond whiling away the summer and seeing Maria off to college in August. Then what? She didn't have a job. She was selling the Chicago house. Would she and Misha hole up at the cottage for a long, lonely, fur-covered winter? What kind of a plan was that? The whole "blended family" thing seemed far too aspirational.

Lisette tried to imagine what Chris would advise, like those "What Would Jesus Do?"' bracelets. It is truly a treasure to have a friend so wise, so known, so dear, that you can have imaginary conversations with her. Knowing Chris, she would make a list of talking points:

Live part-time in L.A. We will have a blast!

Stay part-time at the cottage to visit with Maria whenever!

The timing is perfect. Really.

What about the dog? (He can fly on the "40" and be bi-coastal Misha.)

What about the tour? (Cross that bridge…)

Is she merely insinuating herself into Shane's world? What about her world? (Sometimes it is just time for a new life. You gotta try new things, take new paths, explore possibilities. That is what it means to live fully, with courage. Be grateful, not suspicious, when people invite you into their lives.)

This is not subjugation. This is an opportunity to grow and have new experiences.

At our age, "too sudden" is bullshit. Everything should be sudden – we did not live this long to be cautious! We should live boldly!

What if it doesn't last? What if it falls apart badly?

Self-analyzing and constructing the list in her head, hearing Chris's voice in her imagination, calmed Lisette. She flashed back on the craziness of the past months. She had lived in such a rigid lane for decades, her life prescribed by the responsibilities of motherhood and marriage and work. She had honored those positions in strict poses, like ballet, staying within the lines and straining for perfection. Until it all exploded.

Yet the dust had settled surprisingly quickly, and here she was, in her favorite place, which would always be here. And no matter what happened, she would always remember working in the garden and hearing Shane's voice and guitar floating through the window, and a thousand other moments, both epic and small, they had shared so far. It was a grand affair. There were other favorite places out in the big world she had yet to discover. All she had to do was be open and brave. If it falls apart badly, well, she survived that once...

The black Jetta SportWagen rolled up the lane, the sandy path silencing its approach. Shane emerged with groceries and a Walmart bag, standing back as Misha leapt to the ground.

"Thought I'd stock in a few provisions for our company," he announced, walking toward her and taking in her sleep-rumpled condition in the morning light. He found it extremely sexy and intimate, completely unpretentious. "Love that woman better than any woman I ever seen," floated through his head, a leftover lyric from the day before. He handed her the Walmart bag as he passed and took the groceries into the house. She grinned imagining the absurdity of Shane navigating Walmart. "Attention Shoppers: Rock Star in Aisle 5!" She reached into the bag.

He bought them planners – old school 12-month calendar books! One black, one turquoise.

Shane re-emerged and sat down on the top step.

"What are these for?" Lisette asked.

"For us!" Shane answered. "I was up in the night worrying about how we're going to work this out. I know it's complicated, Lisette, but we can do it. I thought these would give us a start at least."

Lisette wanted to weep with relief. Her eyes filled. He was worried, too!

"Can I have turquoise?" she asked in a shaky voice.

"Of course," he replied.

"I was worried, too," Lisette confessed. "About insinuating myself into your life."

"What does that even mean?" he asked. "I love you, Lisette. I want us to figure out how we can be together. Build a life together. Not your life or my life, but a new shared life, you and me. We won't be together every minute, as we've been these past days. But we can figure it out, as you once said, just let it roll out. These will help us be intentional about it."

Lisette joined him on the step and wrapped her arms around his neck.

"Thank you," she said, kissing his cheek. "I needed exactly this."

"Open your planner to June," he said, handing her a yellow plastic mechanical pencil from a box of 12 that were also in the Walmart bag. "These are the best pencils ever manufactured, always sharp. I write in pencil because it anticipates that things change and you can erase."

They started by finding their place in time on the June monthly calendar, recording the dates of the "hideout." Then both jotted in the square for that day: "Chris and Derek arrive!" and "Back to L.A." in the box for the day after tomorrow. Next, they filled in Maria's return. They flipped ahead to August, marking Maria's move to Ann Arbor and, soon after, the due date for Priya and Daniel's baby.

"It's silly, but this makes me feel more in control," Lisette said. "Look at July – wide open!"

"Nothing but time," Shane said, thinking to himself that Rob might be out of rehab by then, they might go back into the studio, and that would be a good moving month if they found a house quickly. He'd have to talk to Derek about the tour, whether they'd try to honor some dates – depending on Rob's recovery, of course. Then he thought about Lisette's July, which was equally important and attractive. He had loved every minute here – how could he deny her the brief summer months!

"Maybe I can come back for a bit in July, if that's all right," he said. "The lake might actually be swimmable..."

"The days are so long then, yes, do come," Lisette said dreamily. "Say, when do Chris and Derek get in?"

"Around 3," Shane said. "What would you like to do until then?"

"Let's straighten up and get their room ready. I'll cut some flowers, and we can do some food prep. We'll walk the beach when they get here," Lisette said. "But first put on some Marvin Gaye and tell me all about Walmart!"

Shane put on Marvin Gaye, intercepted Lisette at the linen closet, and danced her into the bedroom. They had hit a little glitch and successfully recalibrated. At such seams are relationships knitted together.

Chapter 52

"Hi!" Chris shouted over the whine of the jet, hugging Lisette before jumping into the back seat of the car.

Shane met Derek at the foot of the stairs. Derek handed Shane his briefcase and each took a rolling suitcase. Derek was looking exceptionally pleased with himself.

"You are looking at the most recent inductees to the Mile High Club," Derek confided gleefully to Shane. "The '40' is the best investment the band ever made, if I do say so myself."

Derek had picked it up used for just under $2 million and the band claimed it as a business expense. It was everyone's favorite toy.

"Welcome and congratulations, my man," Shane congratulated him, patting him on the back.

"How are things here in the heartland?" Derek asked. Not that he needed to ask. Shane looked great – fit, tan, and rested. Derek was suddenly aware of his whiteness. His English skin never browned up in California, merely weathered like an old barn.

"We won't have to take part in any beachy activities, right?" Derek asked. "No surfing or contraptions with sails, water skiing or other potentially dangerous or embarrassing situations…"

"Not this time," Shane assured him. "Lake Michigan is so cold your balls would be in your ears! But we will walk the beach. You'll love it."

"Will I have to take my shoes off?" Derek asked. "None of that barefoot stuff for me. I'm an Englishman!"

"Only if you want to," Shane said.

"All right then," Derek said. "Hi, Lisette!"

"Hi, Derek, welcome to Michigan! Are you ready to rock?"

"Ah, Michigan, home of Motown, Bob Seger, Ted Nugent, and George Clinton," Derek said, communicating agreement on the rocking aspects.

"Don't forget Kid Rock," Chris chimed in.

"Fuck that wanker!" Derek retorted.

"And Eminem," Lisette added.

"Him, too!" Derek bellowed.

They were off and running.

"This is absolutely charming," Derek said as they turned in at Sunset Path. "Lisette, I had no idea."

They quickly settled in at the cottage before setting off on the traditional welcome walk of the beach.

"Good Lord!" Derek exclaimed as they cleared the swell of the dune. "I thought you said it was a lake! This is a bloody ocean!"

"Unsalted!" Chris proclaimed.

"Shark free!" Lisette added.

"Gitche Gumee!" Shane added.

"That's actually Lake Superior, Longfellow's 'shining big-sea-water,'" Chris corrected him. "See Derek, Lake Michigan is only the third largest Great Lake! Together they account for 20 percent of the planet's fresh water."

"No wonder you Yanks rule the world," Derek observed. "Hoarding all the water."

The three Midwesterners were puffing up with American pride. They challenged each other to name the five lakes from largest to smallest as they walked the shoreline with glasses of wine. Lisette carried a beach blanket. Shane carried an extra bottle. They paused their walk to spread the blanket and sit with their feet in the sand. (Except for Derek, who had changed into sneakers and kept them fully laced.)

"Should we tell them?" Chris asked Derek after Shane refilled their glasses.

Lisette and Shane, eyebrows up, looked at Chris and Derek, then at each other, then back at Chris and Derek.

"Well?" Shane said.

Derek cleared his throat.

"Chris and I have decided to be married," Derek announced. "I asked for her hand and she, incredible as it seems, accepted my proposal."

"It's true!" Chris said, beaming.

"This is great news!" Shane enthused.

"Oh! Oh!" Lisette sputtered, completely surprised. "I'm so happy for you!"

"A toast to the happy couple," Shane said. They clinked their glasses in celebration and exchanged warm embraces in all the possible combinations.

Derek told the story of getting his nerve up the night before last and popping the question at the restaurant where they had their first date. His network of contacts at the restaurant, in on the secret, had the Taittinger chilled and waiting.

"Derek had just ordered – what else – the chicken, of course. Then he went down on one knee. I said 'Did you lose something?' And he looked up at me and said, 'No, actually, I've found something I want to keep forever.' It was so romantic!"

Eight eyes sparkled with happy tears. Shane was thinking what a great lyric 'found something' would be.

"When? Where? Have you set a date?" Lisette asked.

"We're thinking late September," Chris said.

"Oh my little bride-to-be!" Lisette cooed, hugging her friend once more.

"We should change tonight's dinner menu from steak to chicken in their honor," Shane said.

"Mixed grill?" Lisette said.

"Perfect," Shane agreed.

Chris and Derek were observing them. Shane and Lisette had a little life going on here, they noticed. They were perfectly at ease, in synch – with each other and their surroundings. Derek was thinking how interesting life had been since last fall.

"I have another toast," Derek announced. "Lisette, if you hadn't stepped in with your needle and thread, none of us would be here. As fate would have it, you did. I propose a toast to Lisette, emergency seamstress, for leading us to this moment!"

"To Lisette!" The other three raised their glasses and toasted her.

"The happy company of friends is truly one of life's greatest gifts," Lisette responded, toasting them in return. Shane was captivated by her elegance in the moment, the wind catching her hair, the graceful arm as she raised her glass. What a woman!

The shadows lengthened and the bottle of wine was drained, so they moseyed back to the cottage for a raucous celebration that would continue late into the night, featuring a Motown cavalcade. Chris and Lisette demonstrated their elaborately choreographed dance moves to "Your Precious Love."

"I see why you love it here," Derek said as the sun disappeared into the water. They'd paused between courses for the ceremonial sunset.

"All this – and recreational marijuana!" Chris agreed. "It's almost too good to be true!"

After dinner, they celebrated the passage of Proposition 1 with a bud of delicious Indica, then watched the Beatles' "HELP!" Derek, the non-smoker, fell asleep first. Chris pranked him by removing his shoes and socks. Lisette and Shane talked her out of filling them with sand. By the time the Beatles were in the Bahamas, all were fast asleep. Shane started awake as the credits rolled, roused Lisette, who in turn roused Chris, who took Derek by the hand and all stumbled to bed.

Chapter 53

The next day, the four of them perused online real estate listings in L.A., creating a short list of five properties that met the major specifications, two being a view of water and a guest house. Lisette loved the Spanish influence in the architecture as she studied hundreds of pictures. It seemed so exotic, palm trees and tropicals – citrus trees! She was intrigued.

She and Chris went to the beach while the men talked about the new songs and tour scenarios. Lisette was bursting to tell Chris about her "moment of doubt and pain" and making the list of talking points. Chris needed to inform Lisette about the shitstorm brewing over the viral video.

"You know you are a few days from a major shitstorm over that video," Chris started right in as soon as they settled in their beach chairs. "The senior ballerinas have been invited on 'The Chat.' They took a vote in favor, but they are waiting for you before proceeding."

"What is 'The Chat?'" Lisette asked.

"It's a chick talk show, daytime TV," Chris answered. "But if you go on, they'll want to talk to you as the teacher – and Shane's love interest."

"No way!" Lisette said.

"Lisette, you represent the hope of every woman in America over 50 of ever again having a mad love affair! You are a mystery woman and a folk hero. A couple of the ladies have been talking to the producers. They know everything and they are salivating. The only thing they don't know is where you are."

"Christ on a cracker," Lisette moaned.

"Wait, there's more. The senior ballerinas, who are quite the tour de force, let me tell you, want to start a foundation to either bring ballet to seniors where they live or fund Alzheimer's research! They are emerging as celebs in their own right! Evelyn in particular wants the world to know that with the right lubricant, Viagra, and ballet, women can have great sex for the rest of their lives."

"Holy shit!" Lisette said. "And I'm supposed to be the face of that?"

"No, that's all Evelyn," Chris explained. "You are the hope of love."

"I am not going on a daytime talk show to talk about my relationship with Shane," Lisette declared. "Not gonna happen."

"It might be as vague as acknowledging that you are involved and telling the story of how you met," Chris said. "It's a great story, Lisette. Five minutes. If you tell it on your own terms, it will blow over quicker and fade out."

"And if I don't?" Lisette asked.

"You'll be hounded," Chris said. "You could decline all requests – and they'll come, from Colbert, from Kimmel and Farrell, from "20/20." This isn't about the Disgracefuls any more, Lisette. This is apart from that. This is about you. And if you go on 'The Chat,' the network has pledged to donate $50,000 to Alzheimer's research."

"So if I don't do it, the pledge is withdrawn?" Lisette was outraged. "That's blackmail!"

"It's a powerful incentive, Lisette," Chris chided her. "The tabloids are already on to you. Elvis has left the building, word is out. Your private life is temporarily on hold while we work out a media strategy."

Lisette was what Chris labeled "a reluctant witness." But she had sweet-talked more than a few into going on the record in her career. She just never thought it would be her best friend. But she was determined to make it as painless as possible for Lisette, knowing about the speculation already humming on social media. If the pretty ballerina with the white streak in her dark hair could answer a few burning questions, the beast might be fed for now.

"All right, I'll think about it and meet with the senior dancers when I get back," Lisette said. "I do appreciate your perspective, as always, Chris. I had a moment yesterday that caused me to conjure you to talk me back from the ledge."

Lisette recounted the talking points she had created for her struggle with herself. Chris was impressed.

"I totally understand your freakout. I've been having the same conversation in my own head about marrying Derek – we've only known each other for five months! It seems so impulsive! But I agree that worrying about this being 'too sudden' is bullshit and choose to live boldly. Why not marry Derek? He's smart and funny and we have a blast together. I love him and he adores me. What more could a crone like me ask for?"

"A wedding dress that shows off your dowager's hump?" Lisette offered.

"I do not have a goddamned dowager's hump!" Chris objected. Later, back at the cottage, she checked in the mirror just to be sure. She might have sprouted one without realizing it.

"Phew," she said later, studying her back from all angles in the bathroom mirror with a second hand-held mirror.

"This just in – I do not have a dowager's hump," she announced as she emerged from her examination.

"Thank heavens for that!" Derek said.

"What is it?" Shane asked, looking up from his guitar.

"A hunchback!" Chris informed him. "Like old ladies get."

"You girls worry about the darndest things," he said, returning to his work.

Later, taking a final beach stroll as a storm moved in off the lake, Lisette confessed to Chris that she doubted she would ever marry again.

"I am thrilled for you and Derek, don't get me wrong. But for me, marriage was about raising children, a sort of structure that supported the family unit," Lisette explained.

"And look how that worked out," Chris said pointedly. "For Derek and me, it's about committing to each other – not to the children we will never have because we are too old. It's about the comfort and joy we bring to each other, the two of us. It is a proclamation, wildly aspirational, Lisette. It is hopeful. I want that crazy man to be in my life for the rest of my days. And I choose to be fearless, to proclaim love, to commit to being there no matter what, to embrace the fullness of life together, with no concern whatsoever about how much time we have left."

Lisette grabbed Chris in a tight embrace and rocked her back and forth, telling her she loved her and wanted her to be happy with Derek forever.

"Careful, my hump," Chris said through tears.

Later, the four camped on the dune in beach chairs and watched the dramatic thunderstorm roll in from the west. They could see the rain falling far out in the lake, and lightning amid the roiling thunderheads. The storm gathered speed, or perhaps they were hypnotized by it, and they were pelted by fat plopping raindrops in the final steps of their race back to the house. Thunder crashed, then rolled and rolled in gradually diminishing echoes over the expanse of the lake.

"Nice resonance," Shane said, listening acutely as he toweled off.

Shane and Lisette had made a vow not to be maudlin about their last night at the cottage. As it turned out, that would be impossible with such jolly company. Shane promised to come back the following month. They took out their planners and put their heads together to mark possible dates for that and, in between, for Lisette to come west to weigh in on the house hunt.

Over dinner, Chris referred in passing to the cottage as "ye ol' stabbin' cabin" and they all laughed so hard Derek nearly aspirated his food. The two of them brought Shane up to speed on the latest developments in the senior ballet viral video.

"I've done 'The Chat,'" he said. "The ladies were super nice! Do whatever you feel comfortable with, Lisette. I trust you. That's a lot of money on the table for a good cause. Hard to say no when they incentivize like that. Bastards know just how to get you."

Later, in bed, Shane started to feel the real world seeping in. Back to L.A., the studio, perhaps making up a few tour dates if Rob was up for it. The house hunt. It all churned in his mind. But then he remembered "stabbin' cabin" and went off on another laughing jag.

"What?" Lisette, awakened, asked. He said the words and she got the giggles.

The hideout had been just what Shane had needed for a very long time. He would miss Lisette horribly, and this quiet life tucked behind a dune. Leaving pained him already. But he would be back, and they would figure this out.

Chapter 54

Maria came home with hair the color of fruit punch and a tattoo on her back shoulder of a bird on a wire, full of stories of her travels. Lisette had missed her but had plenty of her own excitement to fill the void. They were in the process of releasing each other to the next stages of their lives. Maria was on board to accompany Lisette on the house-scouting trip in a few weeks.

"Are you kidding, a private jet?" she'd responded. "I'm totally on board."

Lisette's voice mail was full of messages from Maddie. The show would be taped the following week. They would fly the dancers in the day before, put them up at a luxe hotel, and comp them on tickets to a Broadway show. The class had voted: the network's donation would go to Alzheimer's research.

"Do it, Mom, you'll be great," Maria said. "I'll work with you on talking points!"

Shane, a talk show veteran, also coached her. His most important advice: listen well, talk directly to the people, ignore the camera, be yourself. Unknown to Lisette, he told the producer that if they treated her nicely, maybe the two of them would agree to come on together at a future date to talk about finding love late in life. He knew a thing or two about wheeling and dealing in the media food chain.

Lisette packed her suitcase yet again. The senior dancers were in high spirits as they set off for New York. Their hotel floor turned into a sorority house with room parties up and down the hall. When they returned from dinner and "Hamilton," the revelry continued into the wee hours.

Thank heavens they didn't need to be at the studio at the crack of dawn. Despite the travel and the late night, the ladies were perky and pumped in the morning. The producer explained that the dancers would perform, then Evelyn, Maddie, and Lisette would be interviewed. The dancers took their positions on opposite sides of a small stage. "Smile!" Lisette cued them, miming a smile with her hands drawing apart at the edges of her mouth. She'd worn the red lipstick and everyone had been "freshened" for TV by a bank of makeup artists. They looked great!

They could hear one of the hosts introduce them.

"The video of their dance has more than a million views, and no wonder! These senior dancers' enthusiasm for ballet – and life – have inspired people the world over. They are here with us today to perform their dance to the Disgracefuls' hit, now back on the charts after 30 years, 'Thunder Thighs'!"

The music started. The dancers stepped out on the beat. They gave themselves to the dance and nailed it as never before, full of exuberance at their newfound celebrity and the full flower of womanhood. They represented.

As the applause died down, Lisette, Evelyn, and Maddie were ushered to the big table, seated, and mic-ed. The hosts made welcoming small talk – "you were fantastic, so nice to meet you, thanks for coming on," then swung into the real thing.

"How did you ladies come up with this idea?" Host #1 asked. Chatty Maddie jumped right in, explaining that the dancers had learned it to different music, but when set to the Disgracefuls song, it had "a new kind of swag!"

She shimmied her shoulders and smiled at the audience. They applauded wildly.

Host #2 turned to face Lisette and lobbed a softball. (The three alternated asking questions during interviews. It was the format.)

"Lisette DuPre, you are their ballet teacher," she said. "How did this class start?"

"Well, it was an accumulation of so many women telling me how they loved ballet as girls and young women, and how they missed it. So two years ago I started a class for older adults. These dancers are amazing, as you just saw." She had reached her three-sentence limit and stopped, as Chris advised.

Host #3 wound up for a hardball.

"Lisette, you are romantically linked to Shane Stewart of the Disgracefuls," she said, looking sideways into a monitor. Lisette followed her gaze. On the screen was the picture and caption from the tabloids!

"Here are the two of you in Chicago last February. At that time, you were described as a 'mystery woman' and 'age appropriate.' What were the circumstances?"

"We had lunch?" Lisette smiled and arched her eyebrow. She looked like an aristocrat.

"Shane is a friend of the show," Host #3 gushed, batting her eyelashes, "he's been on with us before. He gave you permission to use the song, AND he is matching our network's $50,000 pledge to Alzheimer's research by contributing all earnings from the resurgence of 'Thunder Thighs' to the same worthy cause!"

The audience went wild. Host #3 looked at Lisette expectantly, meaningfully, hoping Lisette would spill the beans about the relationship. But instead, Lisette did what Chris had taught her: pivot!

"Everyone knows someone affected by Alzheimer's Disease," Lisette said, casting her gaze across the audience and seeing heads nod in acknowledgment. "Sadly, there have been no significant research breakthroughs in 15 years. As Baby Boomers age, the need will overwhelm the health care system, so it's up to us to support research leading to a cure."

"Lisette, back to Shane Stewart," Host #3 persisted. "How did you two meet?"

The senior ballerinas at the table giggled.

"She sewed up his pants when he had a wardrobe emergency at a concert!" Maddie answered for Lisette. "She always carries a sewing kit!"

"It's quite a charming story," Evelyn interjected. "He sent her flowers for 'saving the day.' Terribly romantic. We've all met him – what a charmer! He is a stone fox!"

Evelyn struck a pose, crossing her wrists and dipping her head, looking up, like Princess Diana. It was theatric and balletic. The audience howled and stomped.

"I agree!" chirped Host #3.

"Shane was so generous to let us use the song," Maddie cut in. "He even came to our dance recital in a disguise."

Another cutaway to the monitor. Maddie had provided the group picture at the recital with Shane in the ridiculous hat and beard.

Lisette looked between Maddie and Evelyn with an expression that was both serene and amused. She was thinking to herself that they didn't know the half of it, a fraction, a neutron of the romance quotient of this epic affair. She and Shane were up there with Liz and Dick in Puerto Vallarta. Clash of the Titans! Her face did not give her away. She held her secrets close. What if Maria was watching!

Lisette braced for another question, but the director signaled for a break – they wanted to get Evelyn talking about lubricants, boner pills, and ballet.

"Well the ballet part is sure catching on," Host #2 said after Evelyn shared her sex secrets. "Line dancing clubs across America are learning your dance from the video."

"My husband Howie posted it!" Maddie announced. "He's a fucking genius! I love you, Howie," She blew a kiss to Howie at the camera. The audience roared. Later they bleeped out "fucking."

As the applause quieted, Lisette said in a quiet voice (she had learned the power of a quiet voice as a teacher – the room silences to hear the maestra), "Imagine if each of the million people who watched the video gave a dollar to Alzheimer's research. Now that would really be something."

Applause...and out.

"Thank you so much!" the hosts gushed to the dancers. "You were amazing!"

Host #3 leaned toward Lisette and whispered in her ear.

"You're a lucky woman. I only had him for one night."

Lisette was aghast but didn't let on. The nerve!

Back out in the light of day, wearing TV makeup and leotards, the 12 women looked like they were auditioning for a Boost commercial. Thankfully, a van was waiting to take them back to the hotel for a change of clothes and then the airport. They were spent. For all except Lisette, it was the most exciting thing that had ever happened to them.

Chapter 55

In the weeks that followed, Shane and Lisette were like a pair of nesting cardinals – so purposeful! Lisette put the Chicago house on the market and her Realtor had scheduled back-to-back open houses that weekend. The finality of unloading it whetted Lisette's appetite to walk through the properties in L.A.

Misha was at the Pet Palace and Maria and Lisette were winging westward in the '40.'

"Mom, I thought backstage was the ultimate thrill. But this is insane!"

Maria, her hair now restored to its natural color after the fruit punch faded to a sad Pepto Bismol, took unfettered advantage of the on-board snacks and drinks and being "free to walk about the cabin." She reconfigured the seats into beds. She has excellent spatial intelligence, Lisette observed. Lisette worried about how easy it would be for Maria to slip into a Kardashian lifestyle in L.A. Half of her peers already subscribed, and it troubled Lisette.

It was now mid-July. Shane and the band were writing and recording, Rob was back! Shane had rejoined them for a few days over the Fourth of July holiday. The fireworks over the lake were spectacular. The water was a miraculous 74 degrees! The fireworks back at the cottage continued to amaze them both. He proclaimed himself her sex slave. Shane had made it clear that Lisette would have the final word on his next address.

"Your happiness is my only desire," he said, handing the ultimate decision to her. This guy! He worships me! Take that, Host #3!

They would see two houses today, and a third tomorrow, with time to re-view, if necessary. It was all scheduled. Autumn would join them. Priya was on bed rest due to early contractions. The doctors said every day they could delay the birth would benefit the baby, which currently measured at just over five pounds, according to the ultrasound. The due date was a month away.

Lisette and Maria greeted Shane and Autumn at the car. Maria was relieved her hair was no longer hideous. When they met in New York at Thanksgiving, they were wearing hats and coats and boots. In July in L.A., they were sporting beach attire. Shane, smiling broadly, stepped out of the car to greet them. He hugged Maria first and she tumbled into the car, saying hello to Autumn. Next he grasped Lisette in a tight hug and planted a scorcher on her lips.

"Here we go," he said, looking into her eyes. "We're really doing this, my love woman."

"I simply adore you," she said, feeling like Morticia Addams with her absolute love control over this besotted man. "Hello, my baby."

Oh, how prescient those words would be!

They were wrapping up the tour of the second house, which everyone liked better than the first, when Shane's cell phone rang.

"What's up, Priya?" he answered.

"The birth spasm has begun," Priya said in a Conehead voice, from the story she had heard on her birthday forever.

"Holy fuck!" Shane exploded.

"What is it?" asked Lisette.

"Priya! She's in labor!" Shane said.

"Oh my god!" said Autumn. "Dad!"

"Shhh," Shane said, his index finger on his lovely lips.

"Okay, okay," he said in a calm, soothing voice to Priya. "We'll meet you there, keep breathing. Is Daniel there? Hand him the phone."

"Daniel, keep it together, man, whatever she wants, you do. We will meet you there. It's going to be all right, man," Shane said.

They dove comically into the car like clowns at the circus and roared off to the hospital. They piled out again at the Emergency Room entrance and the four of them swept into the hospital. Shane had the driver take the Realtor home.

"Priya Louis? She's having a baby," Shane said at the reception desk. He pronounced "Louis" "Loo-EE," and the name came out as one lilting word, "PriyalooEE."

The clerk looked at her computer screen.

"She's been admitted to maternity," she said. "Ninth floor."

She wrote ID tags for the four of them, handed them out and pointed to the elevator. A short woman with blonde hair, wearing a sun dress and gladiator sandals, came up fast behind them, flustered, and demanded to anyone within earshot "PriyalooEE?"

"Jill!" Shane greeted his first ex-wife.

"Oh my god!" Jill said, collapsing on Shane.

The clerk made a fifth visitor's pass as Shane introduced Jill to Lisette and Maria. Jill hugged Autumn and made worried clucking noises.

They took the elevator to 9.

"The baby is over five pounds, so that's good," Shane said on the interminable ride.

"Oh!" cried Jill. "That's so tiny!" Priya had been over eight pounds. Jill was a small woman. Maybe this is better, she thought. Passing a five-pound object through your va-jay-jay was infinitely preferable to an eight-pounder.

The door opened at last on 9. The five of them swept as one to the nursing station.

"Priya Louis?" Shane asked.

The nurse checked her computer.

"She is in the labor room," the nurse said. "I can let her husband know you are here. Please take a seat."

She indicated a waiting room of plastic chairs and a flat-screen TV tuned to the Hallmark Channel.

Lisette, Maria, and Autumn obediently sat. Lisette did her breathing. Shane paced. Jill hovered in the hallway. It was both nerve-wracking and terribly exciting!

"Daniel!" Jill cried.

"Hi," Daniel said, hugging his mother-in-law. "She's doing really well! The baby is definitely coming. I'm going back in."

"Good man," Shane said, patting his shoulder and sending Daniel back into the lion's den.

Fifteen minutes later, Daniel poked his head out into the hallway and called "Jill!"

Jill raced to the room. The door closed behind her.

Not a minute later, they heard the cry of a newborn infant. The baby might be small, but it had the lungs of its grandfather. It struck a perfect A.

Matteo Shane Louis surprised the statisticians by weighing six pounds even. He had a full head of curly hair and a love of the breast. He latched right on, still sticky from his birth.

Priya cooed to him. Daniel cooed to Priya. Jill wept and blew her nose. Shane approached the new mother.

"Congratulations, mama," he said.

Priya handed him the baby. Daniel beamed. He'd already held the baby – hell, he caught him on the way out of his wife!

"Hello, little man," the new grandfather greeted his progeny.

The baby made little snorting and fretting sounds and punched his tiny fists. He looked his grandfather in the eyes.

"He is perfect," Shane said, handing the baby to Jill, who took her turn, then handed him to Autumn, who handed him to Lisette, Maria leaning in to examine him.

"Hi, Matteo," Lisette said. Overwhelmed at holding an infant in her arms for the first time in many years, Lisette fell back on her own years of experience.

"Heaven must have sent you from above," she sang, so softly it was barely discernible, to the baby.

"Heaven must have sent your precious love," Shane joined in. Maria and Autumn were mortified and impressed in equal measures.

Lisette handed the baby off to Daniel and with "Congratulations" ringing in the air, left with Maria. Shane and Autumn stayed another minute. Jill stayed.

Shane, Lisette and their two daughters went out for a celebratory dinner. A six-pounder who loved the breast was truly heaven-sent, cause for celebration. It was a best-case scenario.

Lisette and Shane called Chris and Derek from the car with the news. Derek spread the word to the band. All were amused at the thought of Shane as a grandfather.

Shane proposed a toast at dinner: "To Matteo Louis, welcome to the family!"

Lisette let Maria drink wine. She'd been to Europe, she deserved wine.

"To the new granddad!" Autumn toasted.

"To the new auntie!" Shane toasted her back.

The next day, three was a charm. The third house captivated them all as soon as they walked through the wide Mission doors. Autumn and Maria spent most of their time in the guest house by the pool, speculating on décor.

A tree with lemons the size of softballs hugged a corner of the patio off the kitchen. Lisette picked three and stashed them in her big black bag. Other citrus trees – grapefruit, Clementines, tangerines, and oranges – dotted the property. It was fenced and gated for Misha.

Chapter 56

Derek cleared his throat as he clinked a spoon against his Champagne flute. The room quieted and the guests looked up expectantly as waiters circulated with trays of Champagne and sparkling cider. Chris had done the party planning herself. Everything was exquisite. The flowers were over the top. She wore an ivory knee-length dress with three-quarter sleeves and a plunging back (no dowager's hump!), fabulous shoes, and a glittery comb in her curly hair. Maria and Autumn were flower girls. Shane was best man, and Lisette was best woman. Lisette found Shane devastating in his top hat and morning coat and entertained impure thoughts of peeling it off of him.

"Thank you all for being here as Chris and I celebrate our marriage," Derek said. Chris's bright eyes were shining as she looked at her new husband. So was her sparkling Tiffany wedding band with fiery round diamonds all the way around that together totaled over 3 carats.

"Every time I look at it I feel like my retinas are detaching," she told Lisette the night before.

Two acoustic guitars were tuned and waiting for the bride's surprise toast to her new husband, the Fab Two's slow, breathy version of "I Want to Hold Your Hand." Lisette was aflutter, even though they'd played it like 10,000 times. But first the groom spoke.

"A mere year ago, this scenario was so far off the radar screen as to be unimaginable," Derek said. "I was a middle-aged, lifelong bachelor who considered himself very fortunate indeed to manage one of the greatest bands in the history of rock."

The drummer shouted "Yeah!" and applauded. Others joined in.

"A wardrobe malfunction in Chicago – a simple matter of 'sol, a needle pulling thread' – proved to be a magical turning point in all of our lives. In the past year, collectively, we've experienced divorce, near-death, rebirth, and birth. And now we have a wedding. We have hit all of life's major milestones in just a few short months."

Matteo squawked in acknowledgment.

"I agree, Matteo!" Derek said. Everyone laughed.

"Seriously though," Derek continued, "I am so very amazed and humbled that this lovely woman consented to enter into holy matrimony with the likes of me, and I pledge today to cherish her for all my days. To think that over the decades before we met, we had – more than once – been in the same places at the same times, continues to blow my mind. Better late than never, right, Chris?"

He turned and faced his bride and held his glass high.

"To us!" he said.

The guests erupted into applause, whistles, shouts, stomping of feet. It sounded like a concert was about to begin.

Acknowledgments

I am deeply grateful to my pre-readers: Jeff Bailey, Marcia Broadway, Jeff and Bernadette Gernand, Cristi Kempf, Tracy Laughlin, Dave Leonard, Lorrie Lynch, Bethany Mezzadra, Maureen O'Donnell, Raquel Rios, Janet Rosen, Cathy Scheckel and Ellen Skerrett. Without your encouragement, I wouldn't have had the nerve.

Special thanks to Ms. Kempf for her copy editing and to Marj Charlier for her assist with layout, design and technology that brought *Long Live Rock* over the finish line.

About the Author

Leslie Baldacci was a newspaperwoman for 25 years, including 17 years at the Chicago Sun-Times, where she was a reporter, editor, columnist, and member of the editorial board. She hosted "The Leslie Show" on WLS talk radio in the '90s. She left the media to become a Chicago Public Schools teacher.

She is the author of Inside Mrs. B's Classroom: Courage, Hope, and Learning on Chicago's South Side.

Long Live Rock is her first novel.

Visit www.lesliebaldacci.com.

CPSIA information can be obtained
at www.ICGtesting.com
Printed in the USA
LVHW111707141220
674152LV00028B/417